Death
By
Platinum

GARY R. LOWELL

Cover Design by B. Lee Helton

Full Moon Publishing, LLC
Glade Spring, VA
Fullmoonplublishingllc.com

ISBN-13: 978-1-946232-90-8

OTHER WORKS BY GARY R. LOWELL

Burnt Corn & Other Creepy Stories
(Chapter 18 originally published in Burnt Corn & Other Creepy Stories)

Dreams of Professor Canine

Four Candles of Opogodó

Lazarus the Goat

Prisoner of Zarembo

Rocina Leitão

Slate and Crows

CONTENTS

CHAPTER 1

No Head, No Hands, and No Luck

Dense fog had rolled off the ocean during the early morning hours and immersed the waterfront district of the great city in a pall of grey nothingness. Yokosuka police inspector Kazuo Komatsu awakened at 6:45 a.m. with a premonition that this day would be a bad one and was staring meditatively at the ceiling above his bed when the telephone began ringing insistently at exactly 7 a.m. It was a homicide and an ugly one. The corpse of a Caucasian gentleman had been found in an alley near the waterfront and his head and hands were missing.

Mrs. Komatsu kissed the inspector and handed him a thermos filled with a liter of hot tea as he went out the door to his car, his necktie draped over one shoulder. The drive to the crime scene took 25 minutes, during which, the fog began lifting and the inspector managed to drink two cups of tea and knot his tie. He regretted not having time to shave and brush his teeth. A young police detective by the name of Akihiko Ogawa met him at the alley entrance which was already choked with police vehicles, uniformed officers, crime scene technicians and an ambulance to transport the corpse to the police morgue.

"I am sorry to call you at home so early Inspector, but we have a most unusual homicide and I was certain you would wish to inspect the scene before the body was removed" said the younger policeman apologetically.

"Yes, Detective Ogawa, there is nothing quite like a beheading before breakfast" replied the 17-year veteran chief of the homicide squad sardonically. "Where are we in terms of the investigation?"

"Victim is Caucasian, 55 to 65 years old, found at far end of this alley a few minutes before 6 a.m. by a young boy chasing his cat. We have searched the entire length of the alley, including most of the trash cans, but have been unable to find the victim's head or hands. It appears that he was dismembered and the missing appendages as well as the weapon were carried off by the killer. There are no identification papers on the body so it will not be easy to determine who our victim is in his present state. We have not quite completed the search of the garbage containers, but those that have been inspected, are marked with a spot of red paint."

Komatsu looked down the alley, a distance of approximately 250 meters, to see a string of at least two hundred garbage receptacles with, perhaps, thirty policemen in white jumpsuits sifting through them. "If they find anything unusual, please inform me, detective. Now, let us examine the corpse." They walked in silence, their footsteps echoing eerily off the wet pavement, nodding solemnly along their way to the crime-scene crewmen engaged in their unenviable tasks.

The corpse, or what remained of it at least, was wet from condensation of the morning fog but was otherwise in the state in which it had been found at the extreme limit of the dead-end alley. Inspector Komatsu walked around the body in a semi-circle four times viewing it at every angle from a distance of 10 feet before he approached it. The body was positioned on its ventral side with the severed neck aimed towards the alley entrance. "What do you make of the elongate blood stain on the back of the man's coat, Ogawa?" asked the Inspector peremptorily.

"The killer wiped his blade off on the victim after he finished his work. This stain geometry indicates quite a long blade, probably a Katana; only a Katana makes such a clean cut through the neck of a human being. Of course, we all know that murder by samurai sword is almost unique to Japan. We also know that our killer is tidy and meticulous. With all this blood on the pavement one would think we could find some footprints of our suspect but there are none, Inspector" answered the young detective.

"Yes, Ogawa, we certainly have a meticulous murderer and probably the sword is a family heirloom which narrows our search to about half the families in Japan. Also, I see that our killer is right-handed but this is not very helpful either. Notice the slight smudges of dirt above each wrist, Ogawa, where the killer placed his foot to facilitate removal of the hands. Make sure the forensic team examines those marks minutely."

"Pardon me, Inspector, but how did you determine the killer is right-handed?" inquired the young detective respectfully.

"Because the head flew off towards our left, that is to say the right side of the victim assuming he was facing the killer. This is clearly indicated by blood spatter on the handle-side of the garbage can lid that he employed defensively when the killer cornered him at this end of alley. The flight path of the spinning head is shown by the crudely helical pattern of cast off blood drops. One may conclude that the head came to rest over there where we see a significant pool of blood with a disrupted central area. Our murderer surely thinks of himself as a samurai warrior and possesses excellent agility and eyesight and therefore is probably a young man with martial arts training. All of these traits are required to approach and retrieve the head from that pool without disturbing the spray pattern or leaving a footprint. Perhaps, the sword was used to impale and retrieve the head." Detective Ogawa grimaced in revulsion as this ugly thought sank in. Ogawa was young and already a good detective for his years of experience. But he was always awed by the unholy union of acute observation and stony deductive logic that his boss brought to a crime scene.

At this moment, a white-suited technician approached the detectives with a transparent evidence bag containing a heavy-duty cotton sack with sock-like geometry sealed with copper wire wrapping. "Excuse me sir, but we have found something quite unusual in one of the garbage receptacles about midway down the alley. It has not been touched by any of us."

Inspector Komatsu examined the new evidence without removing it from the plastic bag. Squeezing the item revealed that it contained particulate material, extremely heavy for its volume, and this implied that it contained a granular metallic substance. This sack and its method of sealing suggested a miner's ore sample to the inspector's practiced eye. He asked the technician who was standing nearby "Have you measured the distance from the container where you found this item to the body?"

"Yes, Inspector. The distance is 119.6 meters and the can is marked by green paint."

"Thank you. This is a most unusual thing to find in a Yokosuka trash can. I have a strong inclination to view this as the motive for this murder" murmured the senior policeman to no one in particular. "We must ask our lab men to determine what it is. If it is gold or silver, or something of that sort, then I must inform Inspector Kuno at National Police headquarters in Tokyo."

CHAPTER 2

Doc Martin

What can you do with a name like Purple Ulysses Martin? As a youth, he considered the alternatives, P. U. Martin, U. P. Martin, P. Uly Martin, but they all had negative consequences in the hands of teenage cretins. It was true that everyone, including Martin himself, liked purple martin birds, *Progne subis,* but they liked them in their back yards devouring mosquitoes, not as a name for a male child. The younger Doc Martin hated the name "skeeter-eater" and other equally rude appellations derived from his unusual name throughout his school days. He understood how his father, an ornithologist, and his mother, an artist, both with peculiar senses of humor, could select this avian name, but he did not like it. The senior Doc Martin, actually Oscar McKinley Martin, obviously could not have been overly fond his own name as he went by 'Jack' all of his life. The elder Doc Martin, a native Texan, spent his career, from Ph.D. days at the University of Texas, till his death a year ago, teaching biology and ornithology at the small college in Llano, Texas. During this time, he published three books and many articles in journals devoted to Texas birds.

His wife, Melba Kate, mother of the younger Doc Martin, was an artist of the Georgia O'Keefe School in west Texas and had passed away two years before his dad.

The younger Doc Martin was also a Ph.D., but in his case, the degree was in geology from New Mexico Tech. He had recently retired from a full-time, tenured professorship at an eastern university to take over the family ranch following his father's death. Doc Martin, the younger, was a bachelor and had made a good of deal money working as a precious metals consultant for mineral industry during his 25-year academic career. Now, as a full-time consultant, he could afford to teach one course a semester, gratis, at the local college. His academic salary, plus $1000 a semester, went into a scholarship fund in Jack Martin's name.

There were oddities about the Martin ranch deriving from the eccentric nature of Jack Martin. The first would be noticed when you turned off the highway onto the half-mile dirt lane leading to the ranch house. Most Texas ranches have an arched entrance sign identifying the owner with a clever brand symbol and a word translation such as a pointy star underscored by a concave curve and the name "Rocking Spur". The Martin ranch had the usual arched entrance sign but it told you the name of the ranch was "ranch" and in lower case at that. Another peculiarity was, upon arrival at the ranch house, instead of your car being attacked by a large, fierce mongrel dog, it was attacked by a large, fierce Boer goat. The latter individual, General Longstreet by name, was trained as a guard dog by the elder Martin and to fetch the morning paper from the highway. Jack Martin did not like dogs because they were unfriendly towards birds.

You would also notice, from your car, a row of elaborate birdcages, 36 walk-in units that formerly contained Jack's collection of rare birds. They were empty now, all but the one occupied by General Longstreet, but their well-built protective sun-wind screens and automated water and feed systems mutely testified to the importance of these birds to their owner.

All the ranches along this part of the road had panoramic views of Enchanted Rock, a gigantic 1.1-billion-year old dome of pink granite that attracted visitors throughout the year. On rare occasions this mountain, actually a granite exfoliation dome, made audible groans which locals naturally ascribed to supernatural causes. Martin knew these eerie sounds resulted from erosion-induced stress relief, but he still enjoyed them as much as his neighbors. He certainly appreciated Enchanted Rock more now as a professional geologist than he ever did as a kid growing up in its shadow.

On this particular morning, Doc loaded his pickup with copper and lead ore specimens from famous mines around the world for a 3-hour lecture and laboratory in mineralogy. The class met twice a week from 2:00 till 5:00 pm at the college in Llano 20 miles north of the ranch. Today, his lecture would be on the distinguishing traits of the numerous copper and lead minerals, their metal contents and formulae, and their occurrence in nature. The museum quality specimens he was packing were eye-candy for the students.

After class, Martin re-packed his specimens and headed across town for his usual week night haunt, the Grey Parrot Bar and Grill. He smiled at Rhoda behind the bar and walked down to his usual seat at the end. From this position, he could see into the kitchen and greet Nestor Gallegos, the cook, with *"Como vai, Senhor Nestor?"* Nestor spoke Spanish perfectly but not Portuguese. This was the point.

Nestor always answered Martin in French which was not one of Doc's languages. *"Très bien, monsieur l'docteur, et vous?"* This ritual was repeated every week night evening when Martin came in for his dinner. Nestor and Doc were friends in high school and, in fact, had played on the same varsity football teams for three seasons. These were remembered as good years for the Fighting Yellow Jackets by Llano old timers.

Llano itself, pronounced in the Anglo way, definitely not the Spanish way, is a rather small, yet typical, central Texas town with a population of about 3200 souls and an elevation of 1030 feet above sea level. It perches on the banks of the Llano River which drains eastward through picturesque rapids of red granite and is considered scenic enough in this hot and dry climate. Beyond this river, the major claim to fame of the city is that it is the deer hunting capitol of Texas and, by extension, the world. Then there is the Red Top Jail, located at the intersection of Oatman and Haynie streets, famous for its tower with a fourth-floor-gallows.

However, they don't hang folks there these days and the attractive 19th century building is being preserved by local history enthusiasts.

Beyond these simple things, the list of attractions dwindles considerably. But if you need more, you might consider collecting a sample of a unique rhyolite dike rock known as "llanite" with colorful blue quartz at a site about nine miles north of town on Highway 16. Doc did this when he was 16 years old and it may have influenced him to become a geologist. During his high school years, Doc also collected specimens of iron ore at Iron Mountain which lies 16 miles northwest of Llano. This ore resided patiently in a mason jar in his bedroom for five years while he learned enough geology to determine that the material was actually a mixture of magnetite, hematite and goethite. This deposit at Iron Mountain was sufficiently rich to trigger a modest "boom period" from 1886 to1893 during which Llano styled itself "The Pittsburg of the West". The mineral assessment by local worthies was overly optimistic, of course, and now the only vestiges of these boom years are streets in north Llano named after steel towns such as Birmingham, Pittsburg and Bessemer.

Nestor Gallegos had a reputation as a Mexican bad-ass, drinker, and fighter in high school but was also known as a good man with saddle horses and a deer rifle. Doc, on the other hand, was Nestor's polar opposite in most ways, an Anglo and good college prep student from a well to do, educated, landowning family. So, it came as a surprise to folks in Llano that these two boys got along. But that is one of the things about high school football; it is a true democracy when the pads go on.

After graduation, Nestor went into the army and Martin left for university. Sergeant Gallegos served 30 years as an army cook all over the world and Purple Martin earned a Ph.D. and became a university professor. Nestor's current position as cook at the Grey Parrot plus his army retirement provided for his simple needs and allowed him to live in his hometown after a lifetime of foreign postings. He loved his job at the Parrot and he loved working for Rhoda.

Unbidden, Rhoda poured Doc a glass of red wine and sat down on the stool next to him. "How did class go today, Doc; did they learn how to find a gold mine?" she inquired with a wide smile.

"No gold today, Rhoda, I could only teach them how to find world class copper deposits. What does Nestor have for dinner tonight?"

"He made one of your favorites, red beans and rice."

Rhoda Jefferies, formerly Rhoda Lomquist, was the owner of the Grey Parrot, a widow going on three years, and a home town gal. She was also a former cheerleader at the local high school and, more importantly, a former girlfriend of Dr. Purple Martin during their high school days.

For her age, Rhoda was still a very attractive woman, in high school she had been a major knockout. Her dark brown, medium-length hair showed no trace of grey but perhaps this was not a purely natural effect. Her teeth were perfect and very white and she had a beautiful smile which she presented to her customers. However, it was chiefly her grey eyes that you noticed. They were like high voltage X-ray beams that bored through you; they could read your heart. At least, that was what Doc Martin thought.

Rhoda and Doc were good friends and frequent sex partners. The sex began in high school when they were both sixteen and resumed the first night Martin entered the Grey Parrot. Rhoda had not seen him since the tearful day he left for university some 30 years before. The local paper occasionally had short articles covering Martin's major publications, foreign travels, and rare visits to Llano and she tried to follow his career. This had become much easier in the last few years because Google kept very close track of Dr. P. Martin, precious metals consultant and professor; it even carried a few photos of fairly recent vintage. So, Rhoda recognized him before he sat down at her bar. That was a year ago, and she had heard about his father's death so it was not that much of a surprise.

"Howdy stranger" she had said and gave him the smile and the X-ray treatment at maximum voltage. "What brings the famous geologist back to our dusty little town?"

"You probably heard my dad died. I had to come back to make the arrangements and settle his affairs. Also, I have to decide what to do with the ranch."

"I was so sorry to hear the news about Jack. You know everybody around here loved that man, especially at the college. Why he even helped me pass the biology course."

"Now Rhoda, dad told me you were an excellent student and he gave you an A."

"He did, but it was due to his great teaching and encouragement."

"Thanks Rhoda. This ranch business is driving me crazy. I'd like to talk it over with you. You're a business woman here in Llano and you know everybody for miles around. Can you get off at a decent hour and come out to the ranch and talk with me?"

That was how it started, or perhaps we should say, resumed. It ended with sex, naturally, and the major decisions to retire from his academic position, become a Llano-based consultant, and manage the 640-acre ranch at the foot of Enchanted Rock where he was born and raised.

CHAPTER 3

Punta Jaqué to Truk Lagoon, August, 1943

At 2:42 a.m. local time, Lieutenant Commander Meiji Tagami of the Imperial Japanese Navy brought the submarine I-25 to periscope depth 1000 meters off Punta Jaqué, Panama. This obscure Pacific port, located at latitude 7°31'09" N, longitude 78°11'43" W, lies only a few miles north of the border separating Panama and Colombia. Tagami waited for the signal, 10 seconds of blinking yellow light, followed by 10 seconds of solid green, followed by 10 seconds of blinking yellow again. The signal came at exactly at 3:00 a.m., as arranged, and he ordered the submarine to surface and gave the answering signal. The dock was dimly back-lighted by the few lights of the village but this was sufficient for the commander to observe a flurry of activity involving men and mules on the village dock through his binoculars. Men were off-loading the mules and carrying items onto a small unlighted fishing vessel.

I-25, based at Kwajalein in the Marshall Islands during WWII, is well-known to naval historians. Its surface displacement of 2,600 tons, length of 108 meters, and beam of 9.3 meters meant it was big as submarines go. Its range of 25,928 kilometers, surface speed of 43.5 km/hour, and submerged speed of 15 km/hour meant that it was fast as well. More importantly, it had six torpedo tubes forward and could launch a seaplane by catapult from its deck.

Meiji Tagami and his crew of 94 officers and enlisted men departed Yokosuka, Japan on 21 November 1941 to play their role in the Pearl Harbor attack two weeks later. After December 7th, the I-25 and eight other Imperial Navy submarines sailed eastwards to patrol the waters off the west coast of the United States.

The submarine I-25 was assigned to patrol off the mouth of the Colombia River and initiated the only aerial bombing attack on the continental United States during the war years. Warrant Flying Officer Nobuo Fujita, piloting a two-seater recon float plane was catapulted from the deck of I-25 on September 9, 1942 and dropped four 168-pound bombs with the intent of starting forest fires near Brookings, Oregon. This incident is recorded as the Lookout Air Raid and Bombardment of Fort Stevens. Now, nearly nine months later, the captain and crew, still basking in the glory of their victory at Pearl Harbor, hovered off the small dock of Punta Jaqué, Panama.

Commander Tagami watched intently as the fishing boat moved cautiously alongside his submarine. One of his officers kept a machine gun trained on this vessel, its name covered by canvas, its crew masked. Each of the five grim-looking men aboard the fishing craft carried a pistol and machete on their belts.

Tagami thought they looked like pirates but in fact they were ordinary Colombian platinum smugglers, a common war time profession in this part of the world.

The captain was aware that the element platinum was first discovered in the mid-sixteenth century by the Spanish along the San Juan River in west-central Colombia, a jungle wilderness that later became known as the *Intendencia del Chocó*. He also knew that Russia, South Africa, Canada and the US were the only producers of platinum besides Colombia and they were not inclined to permit Axis Powers, Japan especially, to purchase this strategic metal required for spark plugs, ignition points, and magnetos in aircraft engines.

The damnable "preclusive purchasing policy" instigated by the US to purchase the entire platinum output of the Chocó district forced Japan and Germany to extreme measures. His country, and the Third Reich, had not only to acquire the platinum they needed at inflated prices and establish a network of fascist agents in Colombia, but also sustain the cost of corrupting already-corrupt public officials. These intrepid fascist agents ventured into the jungle with boats and mule trains and traded coffee, rice, beans, sugar, alcohol, and tobacco to the independent native miners for what they called *arena negra*, or black sand. Naturally these agents also contrived ingenious methods, as in the present case, to smuggle this platinum ore out of Colombia and into fascist hands.

The masked ruffians on the deck below him might even be such agents, or perhaps they were enterprising miners, but this seemed unlikely. It was Commander Tagami's guess that they were simple muleteers hired to transport smuggled goods, but whoever they were, and wherever they were from, it was quite certain they were aware that these crates contained illegal Chocó platinum.

A boom was raised from the fishing boat and a pallet of five rather small wooden boxes swung over to the narrow deck of the I-25. At 45 kilograms or 99.2 pounds per box they were extraordinarily heavy for their size and two crewmen were required to transport each container to the main hatch where they disappeared below deck. A second pallet of five crates was brought over to the deck of I-25 and taken below.

Commander Meiji Tagami had done the calculations himself, 450 kilograms of black sand was the mass equivalent of 978.3 Spanish *libras*. This panned concentrate from Chocó would assay about 85 weight percent platinum and 1.5 percent iridium and was sold to the Imperial Navy at $1.00 US per *libra*, ten times the rate the Chocó miners usually received. It all worked out to about $2.61 US per kilogram of refined platinum metal, a price so trivial that Tagami felt like a thief, which in fact he was in the eyes of Colombia's National Bank, the sole legal buyer of Chocó platinum. The captain was, however, immensely amused by the fact that each of the parties involved in this criminal transaction thought they were screwing the others.

One of the masked smugglers came to the rail of the fishing boat and looked up at the captain with his hand extended in a meaningful way. Commander Tagami retrieved a canvas bag containing 31 troy ounces of gold coins worth a little over $1000 US and heaved it down onto the deck of the smaller boat near the smuggler. It landed with a metallic thud. The smuggler picked up the bag, gave it a knowing heft, and without opening it, gave the international thumbs-up sign. Both vessels began to make way. The entire operation was completed in twelve minutes and not a single word of Spanish or Japanese had been spoken. Tagami gave the submerge order and told his executive officer to set course 285° for Truk Lagoon.

The Chuuk Island Group, centered on 7°20' N, 151°45' E, might appear to some persons as an insignificant speck on a map of the Pacific Ocean. These 16 eroded basaltic islands, with a total land area of only 49.1 square miles, feature volcanic peaks rising as high as 1422 feet above sea level. Rain forest prevails throughout these islands at the higher elevations while mangrove swamps dominate their shorelines. The largest islands in the group are Weno, formerly known as Moen, Tonoas, Tol, Uman and Udot. Each individual island is bounded by a fringing coral reef and the entire group lies within a very large barrier reef which is the major attraction for present-day tourists and was certainly the attraction for the former Imperial Navy of Japan.

Today the Chuuk Islands comprise one of the four member states of the Federated States of Micronesia with a population of 48,000, but to naval historians and WWII Pacific veterans the place will always be known as Truk Lagoon or Truk Atoll, the so-called "Japanese Gibraltar of the Pacific". This island group is one of thousands of mostly low coral islands comprising the Caroline Archipelago, but this particular atoll complex is unique in that it developed an amazing, almost circular, protective barrier reef 45 miles in diameter that encloses 882 square miles of one of the best natural harbors in the world.

War has played a preeminent role in the history of Truk Atoll. Magellan first claimed the Caroline Islands in 1521 as part of the Spanish East Indies and subsequently the Spanish ruled the archipelago until 1899 when they were forced to sell them to Germany after the Spanish-American War. Germany governed until 1914 when the islands were invaded by the Japanese at the outbreak of WWI. After the war, they were officially awarded to Japan in 1920 as a League of Nations Mandate. In 1945, Japan ultimately lost them in the same manner that Germany did. The 607 islands of this group, including the Chuuk Islands, became part of the Trust Territory of Pacific islands (TTPI) that remained under US authority from 1947 until May 10, 1979 when the constitutional government of the Federated States of Micronesia was declared. Full independent status of this sovereign nation was eventually achieved on November 3, 1986.

During World War II, Truk Lagoon served as the forward anchorage and supply depot for the Imperial Fleet, the most formidable Japanese naval stronghold in the Pacific. Controlled by the Japanese since 1914, the Imperial Civil Engineering and Naval Construction Departments had decades to build roads, trenches, coastal defenses, and bunkers beneath the 127 square kilometers of land area of the 11 major islands of the Truk group. Under the able command of Admiral Masashi Kobayashi, these facilities included five airstrips, a seaplane base, a torpedo boat station, submarine repair shops, communications center, fuel bunkers and radar stations in addition to the ideal anchorage for hundreds of heavy war ships. Protecting these facilities were innumerable large coastal artillery and anti-aircraft guns, mortar emplacements and machine-gun pill boxes. The lagoon itself sheltered the Imperial Navy's giant battleships, aircraft carriers, cruisers, destroyers, tankers, cargo ships, tugboats, gunboats, mine sweeps, landing crafts and submarines. It was, in the view of the Emperor and the Imperial Admiralty, fully equivalent to Pearl Harbor.

Captain Tagami guided the I-25 into a slip in the Truk submarine yard at 10:16 a.m. on 16 August 1943. The 14,240-kilometer voyage from Punta Jaqué, Panama required 16 days at an average speed 40 km/hour. Most of this voyage across the vast expanse of the Pacific was on the surface but travel time and distance were increased by the necessity of submerging to divert around the US naval air station on Palmyra Atoll. US naval pilots patrolled as far as 350 miles from Palmyra in search of just such Japanese submarines as the I-25.

A dock crew and six armed guards were waiting as I-25 moored and lost no time in unloading the 10 boxes of black sand from Punta Jaqué and placing them on a flatbed truck. The load was covered securely with canvas and taken from the dock area under guard. Tagami watched the truck disappear thinking that these boxes would see his homeland long before he would, that is, if he ever did. The submarine captain, like all Japanese naval officers, understood the significance and the profound implications of the loss of the four aircraft carriers *Akagi, Kaga, Soryu* and *Hiryu* at the Battle of Midway in June of 1942. His reverie was, however, interrupted by two Imperial Navy policemen who handed him sealed orders for his next mission. The submarine I-25 was refueled, took on stores, and was ready to go to sea in less than six hours' time.

The I-25 met her tragic fate off the New Hebrides Islands only nine days later. She was sunk with all hands by the destroyer USS Patterson on 25 August 1943. Six months later on 29 January 1944, American forces began their attack on the Marshall Islands. Upon capture, the Marshall Islands served as the springboard for US attacks against Truk Atoll that began on February 17, 1944. In this action, known as Operation Hailstone, the Japanese lost 60 naval vessels, 275 airplanes, and virtually all the infrastructure built up on Truk since 1914. Today, Truk Lagoon, or more properly Chuuk Lagoon, is famously known as the largest ship graveyard in the world and as such is a Mecca for scuba-diving tourists. It is also an official and solemn Japanese war grave.

CHAPTER 4

Party at Doc's

The coffee grinder turned itself on at 6 a.m. Sunday morning; it was Doc Martin's alarm clock and he began every day in the same way at the same time. Obviously, he was one of those damned morning people. By the time he was dressed the coffee was ready so he moved out to the front porch with his cup. The night birds were silent now and the morning birds were on the job at 6:15. Orange horizontal beams of sunlight illuminated the dome of Enchanted Rock as Doc watched a road runner in his lane; it had caught a lizard. General Longstreet was returning with the paper and Martin sat down to enjoy his coffee and scan the headlines in the Llano News-Deer Capital of Texas. He perused the paper and drank coffee for about an hour and then went to the kitchen where he made toast, ate his garlic clove, and had some cereal with cold goat's milk.

After breakfast, he went to lab/art studio and resumed work on the Alaskan samples. They were of interest as they recorded granite skarn mineralization in Caribou Valley of east-central Alaska. The rocks were mainly an assemblage of the minerals vesuvianite, diopside, scapolite and grossularite garnet cut by secondary veinlets of colorless fluorite and scheelite, the latter important as a tungsten ore. He was familiar with this type of mineralization and had even worked part of a summer in this same Caribou Valley back in the early 80's. The present samples were from a recent exploration drilling program conducted by Bushwalker Exploration. He took some photos of microscopic images, made some notes, and looked at his watch; it was nearly noon and time to get ready for the Martin Sunday afternoon barbeque. It was a tradition his father began and one which Purple Martin continued on those Sundays when he was not away from the ranch on a job. He got up, turned off the microscope, put his notes in order and weighted the stack with an elegant specimen of melanite garnet crystals and headed for his truck.

At the market in Llano, Martin bought a dozen chicken thighs, six smoked spicy sausages, a pound of medium-sized shrimp, and six limes. He gassed up the truck at the quickie mart, bought four bags of ice, loaded the ice and food in a large cooler he kept in the bed of the truck and headed south on Highway 16 back to the ranch.

Social gatherings at the Martin ranch were always held in the outdoor courtyard connected to the living room by double French doors. The rectangular floor was granite and measured 20 by 40 feet, the surrounding four-foot-high walls were of the same granite. An exterior entrance to the courtyard was reached from the drive way along a path of granite stones. His dad had done all of the masonry work. It was a lot of granite for sure; pink Texas granite, of course, from a small abandoned quarry in the extreme northwest corner of the Martin property; it was the same granite that formed the magnificent dome of Enchanted Rock.

As a teenager, Martin had lifted every piece of this rock onto a flatbed trailer in their quarry, pulled it a mile behind a tractor, and stacked each piece of rock where his dad directed. The work required two entire summers for father and son but the result was spectacular and both were proud of the results. Christ, that must have been 35 years ago, maybe even 40, thought Doc as he busied himself starting a charcoal fire in the barrel-style grill-smoker unit.

Two hand-made picnic-style tables for guests occupied the center of the courtyard and another narrow rectangular table stood in the corner near the grill. Above this table, called the "prep table", was a panel of electrical outlets for appliances such as Nesco cookers, electric skillets and the like. The remaining feature was a circular fire pit, four feet in diameter, with a raised ledge of granite, of course; the pit interior was lined with fire brick and filled with sand. This structure could accommodate four Dutch ovens at once, or a kick-ass log fire as occasion required.

The final feature, and perhaps the most important, was not made of granite; it was a galvanized steel livestock water tank with a 100-gallon capacity to accommodate party beverages. Doc put his ice in the tank, loaded it with Lone Star and Shiner Bock beer, four bottles of Dão Valley red and four of bottles of vinho verde from Vale de Raposa. Both wines were imported from Portugal.

Probably more than his guests would drink but you could never tell about such things. Two dozen bottles of assorted soda pop completed stock tank offerings.

Martin saw a cloud of dust in the lane and this was the signal to bring out the chicken, oil, garlic and onions and begin his paella. It was Dona Modesta and her family but General Longstreet made a show of charging out to the family car. He knew the family, of course, and settled down immediately. Naturally, none of the members of this family had a fear of goats. Dona Modesta patted the General on the head as did the children João and Maria; the husband Felice did not. Felice was not one to treat goats as pets.

After the requisite *abraços*, or traditional European greeting embrace, between each of the family members and Martin, Dona Modesta took her salad into the kitchen, placed it in the fridge, and returned to lay her table cloth on one of the picnic tables. She then set the table with Melba Martin's china and silver. Doc and Felice opened a beer and exchanged farm talk as Martin got the paella in motion by browning the chicken and sausages. He enjoyed cooking in front of guests.

Born in São Pedro das Águias, Portugal, Felice Gomez da Silva came to the states with his parents at age 12. He was a conservative, hardworking rancher with a degree in livestock management from Texas A & M and very good with his hands, particularly with wood work. Of course, in Texas culture this meant he was an "aggie" and had shit on his boots even when they were spotless. His ranch shared a section line with the Martin property and on it he raised about 200 registered Boer goats for the meat and breeding stock markets and about 50 Nubian goats that he milked twice each day.   Jack Martin had insisted that Felice graze his goats on the adjoining Martin land and the younger Doc Martin continued this arrangement, so in effect, Felice ran his operation on the combined two sections which equated to 1280 acres.   Neither of the Doc Martins had an interest in raising livestock.

Another cloud of dust in the lane announced the arrival of Nestor pulling a horse trailer behind his pickup followed by Rhoda in her red Volkswagen beetle.   General Longstreet greeted them in the usual way and was rewarded with a pat from Nestor and a carrot from Rhoda.   The General loved Rhoda and she spoiled him with treats whenever she came to the Martin ranch.   The usual crowd was complete and everyone served themselves with drinks and watched Martin make the paella sauce, and pour in the rice and chicken stock.   As the paella bubbled away in its special pan, Martin opened a bottle of red and a bottle of white wine.

As usual the conversation began with questions about the area where these wine grapes were grown.   What were the people, climate, and terrain like?   Martin and Modesta fielded most such questions with Felice contributing less since he left Portugal at a relatively young age.   Usually the conversation drifted next to what was happening on the Gomez da Silva farm, then to what Nestor was doing in the way of training saddle horses, and from there to how business was going at the Grey Parrot.   At about this point the meal, paella on this particular Sunday, was ready and four, perhaps even five bottles of wine had been consumed and conversation became predictably less predictable.

General Longstreet was not a direct participant in these proceedings but he felt it was his duty to watch over these humans as the evening went on and they became more exuberant. He played with the Gomez da Silva children during the twilight hour. On this night, it was soccer. The General did not care much for soccer because João was forever kicking the ball out of the play area causing the General to spend most of his time chasing the errant ball. Maria, on the other hand, played the ball to the General and although he could not kick the ball, he could use his horns to make the return play. Maria was nice, João was an ass. The game ended when it became too dark to see and the children returned to the adult area.

General Longstreet retreated a considerable distance from the party whenever the participants reached the point of all talking at once. He made periodic patrols around the parked cars and on occasions got the opportunity to route a possum, raccoon, or some other creature of the night. No such luck on this night.

After the dishes were cleared, Rhoda pulled a fine bottle of well-aged port wine from her bag to general applause. As Martin pulled the cork there was a discussion of the upper Douro River district in Portugal which is known for port wine culture. For a change, Felice was a lively contributor because his home village, São Pedro das Águias, lies in the heart of this district. Martin contributed some geological facts relevant to soils considered best for port grape culture and Nestor offered a recipe for what he insisted was a spectacular port wine sauce for pork loin or turkey. As the port fest drew to an end, Martin mentioned that an agent from the U. S. Treasury would be calling on him the next day. Rhoda cracked "Did they find your secret Swiss bank account?"

"I don't think so" said Martin with a grin. "It seems as if he wants to talk about platinum deposits. At any rate, he is going to meet me for dinner at the Parrot tomorrow after class. I'm going to bring him here for our talk so I can show off my platinum specimens and have the literature and microscopes at hand if they are needed."

"I hope you don't get arrested, Doc" Rhoda retorted with a gleam in those X-ray generating eyes. This look was a signal that she would be staying for the night. It was also the signal for the guests to leave, first Nestor, then the Gomez da Silva family but only after another full round of *abraços*. Altogether, a typical Sunday afternoon and evening at the Martin ranch.

Doc and Rhoda enjoyed washing the dishes together in the old-fashioned way even though Doc had a relatively new dishwashing unit. It was a kind of foreplay that reminded them of their high school years when nobody in central Texas had a dishwashing machine. After dishes, they straightened up the kitchen and courtyard area and often split a bottle of wine, if any remained. On this night, there was a bottle of crackling cold vinho verde in the stock tank. Doc opened it and poured two glasses.

They sat on his granite wall holding hands and watched tiny pinpoints of light snaking up the path to the summit of Enchanted Rock; each pinpoint recorded a flash light in the hand of an adventurous night-climber. Most would not reach the apex until well after midnight, but from the summit, these energetic hikers would be rewarded with a spectacular view of every light for 50 miles in all directions. If the climbers remained on the summit until dawn they would see the equally spectacular view of the massive pink granite mountain and its surroundings bathed in the red glow of the rising Texas sun.

CHAPTER 5

Special Agent Simmons

Special agent Monty Simmons flew from Washington D.C. to Dallas, Texas and rented a car at the airport, arriving in the small town of Llano at 4:15 p.m., Monday afternoon. He had no trouble finding the Grey Parrot Bar and Grill. But he definitely felt conspicuous in his grey suit, tie and Florsheim wing-tips. Jeans, T-shirts and scuffed working cowboy boots were the ticket here. He asked the lady behind the bar if she knew Dr. P. Martin, the geologist. Rhoda smiled professionally and said "He will be walking in that door about a quarter past five. Then he will sit at the far end of the bar. He has a trimmed full beard, mostly grey."

"A regular I suppose?" asked the agent. "Perhaps I should introduce myself. I am special agent Monty Simmons, U.S. Treasury."

"I'm Rhoda Jeffries, the owner here. We have been expecting you. I hope you aren't here to arrest Doc. You're not, are you?"

"Oh no, it's nothing like that, really. I need to talk with Dr. Martin about his technical knowledge in the area of metal deposits.

I hope I can interest him in being a consultant for a case I am investigating. Could you bring me a beer, Miss Jeffries?"

"Just Rhoda, please. This is Texas, Monty and we are very informal and friendly people unless we get a burr under our blanket." Special agent Simmons pondered this western aphorism but could not work it out. Instead he took a big gulp of the beer Rhoda set before him and studied her as she moved off to another customer. Not bad, not bad at all, he was thinking. His assessment of Rhoda's attributes was interrupted by the entrance of Doc Martin who walked straight toward him and extended his hand.

"Hi, I'm Martin, and you have to be the guy from Treasury."

"That's right. I am special agent Monty Simmons, U.S. Treasury." Simmons shook hands with Martin and fished out his identification and badge. Martin took the trouble to examine both.

"Ok, Monty. I hope you don't mind if I skip the special agent title. You can call me Doc or Martin as you prefer. I'm here for dinner and you are invited to join me. I know the cook here and he is a good one." At this point, Martin and Nestor had their usual Portuguese-French exchange. Martin noted the puzzled look on special agent Simmons' face and said "Don't worry about it, Monty. We have been buddies since high school." Then he shouted into the kitchen "What's on the menu, Nestor?"

"Fried horse shit with Dijon mustard sauce for you, your friend can have smoked brisket or baby-back ribs in my special barbeque sauce with mashed potatoes and cole slaw" Nestor shouted back from the steaming kitchen.

"Nestor likes you, Monty" said Doc with a broad smile.

"He does!" chimed in Rhoda.

"Well I would rather the cook like me than the rest of this crowd" laughed Simmons.   It was a good beginning for the Treasury agent.

Monty Simmons was a soft-spoken, balding, smallish man, perhaps five feet seven inches tall and 150 pounds. He was clean shaven and spoke with a noticeable down-east accent in which a very slight sibilance could be detected. The man appeared to be in his mid-forties and in good physical shape for his age. According to Rhoda, he was a dyed-in-the-blue Yankee but Doc Martin was far more tolerant of Yankees than most of the residents of Llano.

Simmons had been a Treasury enforcement agent for 21 years, mostly in the Office of Foreign Assets Control within the Bureau of Financial Crimes Enforcement Network. He was a money cop essentially and for the last 10 years had been working investigations dealing with international fraud and theft, sanctions, bullion transactions, and smuggling of precious metals.   His education, a B.S. in economics from the University of Maine-Orono and various law enforcement courses for federal agents, did not prepare him for an interview with Dr. P. Martin, a hot-shot precious metals geologist.   Preparing for this encounter, he examined a couple of text books dealing with ore deposits but they seemed to be mostly about chemistry and were filled with equations and words he could not find in his Webster. He would have to strictly control the course of the interview if he wanted to get useful information from this geologist. Chemistry was definitely not his field.

They had eaten their meal at the bar and had two glasses of wine. Monty, being an easterner, had never had Texas style barbeque. It was fantastic he thought but a little on the spicy side. After some small talk with Rhoda and Nestor, who had come out from the kitchen to be praised for his ribs, brisket and sauce, Martin suggested they head out for the ranch. "You can follow me Monty, it will be about 15 miles south on Highway 16 and another 5 miles or so on county road 965. We'll have privacy there and you can stay the night in the guest bedroom. I will feed you in the morning if you can get up at 6 a.m."

On arrival at the ranch, special agent Monty Simmons was treated to an unusually intense display by General Longstreet when he tried to get out of his rental car. The General pawed the ground throwing dirt in the air and lowered his impressive horns in a threatening way. Evidently, he did not appreciate federal agents on the Martin property. Doc had to say "Knock the shit off, Longstreet. He is a friend. Go back to bed."

Safely inside the ranch house Treasury Agent Simmons said, "What the hell was that about?"

"He thinks he is a dog and king shit around here and he likes to scare strangers. He is really harmless as long as people respect our property."

"Did you call him Longstreet, the name of the Confederate civil war general?"

"Yeah" laughed Doc, "after the civil war general. My dad gave him the name because he has been a belligerent bastard from the time he was born and because Longstreet was dad's favorite figure in the war. This is Texas, you know Monty. Now, do you want a drink or anything before we get down to your business?"

"Let's plan on a drink after we talk. I don't have any idea how long it will take and I don't want to be sloshed before we begin."

"Ok, step this way into my lab where I keep my stuff. I have a feeling we will be looking at some of my specimens." They moved into the lab where Martin arranged two chairs on opposite sides of the microscope table and turned on the powerful desk lamp. Doc leaned back in his chair and gave his guest the professional look. "Ok Monty, suppose you tell me what brings you to way out here to Llano, Texas."

Monty Simmons returned Doc's direct gaze, cleared his throat and began. "First of all, I am not a science guy so I need you to keep the science vocabulary to a minimum and explain things when I ask you. I am a law enforcement guy and the investigations I deal with involve international criminal conspiracies and precious metals. About two months ago, my office was contacted by the Bureau of Criminal Investigations in Japan asking if we could provide information on the source of material referred to as 'black sand' that turned up at a violent crime scene. Our chemists analyzed the stuff and tell me that it is a concentrate of platinum group metals. That is how Treasury got interested. One of the metallurgists in the U. S. Mint group told me that the ratios of individual platinum group elements can be like a finger print or DNA in the hands of an expert such as you. That's why I'm here. Am I making any sense, Doc?"

"Your metallurgist is right in a way. Platinum deposits usually have distinctive chemical signatures so, in theory, a good analysis could be associated with a particular source locality. However, it all depends on whether the sample is actually representative of the source deposit or whether it has been manipulated in some way to disguise its origin. The smaller the sample, the less likely it will be representative. You called the sample 'black sand' and this indicates to me that it is placer material and they are more variable than samples from lode deposits"

Agent Simmons mulled this statement over for a few moments and then said "I understand a placer ore is mined from steam sediments and a lode ore is mined from bed rock. That's right isn't it?"

"Yes, it is, Monty. The ratios of minerals containing the metals are more or less constant in a lode sample but not in placers because of grain size, density, abrasion resistance and solubility variations among the minerals entrained in the stream's bed load. Paystreaks in platinum placers are usually short and drop off rapidly in value with distance from their source rock. Placer samples always vary with downstream distance due to settling, abrasion, and individual tributary contributions. You see Monty, mining platinum placers is very much like placer mining for gold.

In fact, many placers contain both types of metal although they usually have different source rocks. In the case of gold, you end up with a gold-silver alloy called electrum in the concentrate. The electrum is then sent from the mine site to a refinery where the gold and silver are separated from each other; this is a relatively simple process.

The situation with platinum ores is a lot more complicated because two different platinum-alloy minerals are usually involved. One alloy is platinum-iron with small amounts of the other platinum group elements; we call that ferro platinum. The other alloy has iridium-osmium dominant with low platinum content; we call this one osmiridium. Both alloys are themselves variable in composition and may or may not be intergrown with each other as composite grains entrained in the stream sediment. Once you have the concentrate, the six PGE's then have to be separated from the other elements that are present like iron, copper and gold. Then these six PGE's have to be separated from each other. This is a very complex chemical process and requires real metallurgical expertise. Are you with me at this point Monty?"

"I think I could use that drink now, Doc" said Monty with a wry smile.

"Well it just so happens I have a nice red wine, two glasses, and a cork screw here in this cabinet." Agent Simmons remained silent as Martin poured the wine. They looked across the table at each other and took their first sip.

"So, Doc, are you saying it can't be done? We can't determine the point of origin of a placer sample?"

"I did not say that. I said it can be difficult, it can even be impossible if the bad guys mix material from several different localities or add adulterants to a natural sample, or modify its chemical form in a laboratory. There are a thousand and one tricks devised by smugglers and con men to disguise the provenance and grades of ore samples. I like the challenge of your problem and am willing to help. But it occurs to me that the source approach poses more difficulties than the law enforcement approach. Why don't you just beat the information you need out of whoever had possession of the sample in the first place?" Martin refilled the glasses.

"First of all, neither Japanese National Police nor US federal agents beat information out of suspects, Dr. Martin. Secondly, the suspect in question has suffered the indignity of having his head and hands removed via samurai sword before he could be interviewed. Japanese police have been unable to identify this gentleman, so all we know at this point, is that he is Caucasian, probably American and about 60 years of age."

"That's certainly awkward, isn't it" Martin managed to say. "The evil doers really mean business if they cut off heads. Evidently a ton of money is involved in this mess. With the current prices on PGE's it doesn't take a lot of ore to be worth a fortune."

"You keep mentioning PGE's, what is that?" asked the agent.

"Sorry, that is an acronym for platinum group elements which include platinum, iridium, osmium, palladium, rhodium, and ruthenium. Since that is a mouthful, the acronym is pretty useful. You work for the government so you ought to be familiar with acronyms."

"Yeah, we have a pant-full just in my own working group. The problem is that we have reason to suspect a big-league criminal conspiracy and our headless guy leaves us with no other place to start. If we knew where the stuff came from we might be able to trace it from its point of origin to Japan. There is a shit-pot-full of paper work involved in moving platinum from mine to refinery to retail outlet and that might be enough. By the way, I should have started by asking if there is any possibility of the platinum originating in Japan. Could it? Jap cops said no and told me such metals must be imported to Japan."

"That's right. Japan has never had a producing platinum deposit so it has to be imported from one of the few countries that are platinum exporters. That means your source must be Alaska, Canada, Russia, South Africa, or Colombia. A small amount of platinum ore was mined in Finland during World War II but it all went straight to Germany, of course" answered Martin. "Now suppose you show me some of this material Monty."

Agent Simmons reached into his brief case and produced a small glass vial containing about 50 uniformly rounded, black grains about 3 millimeters in diameter. "This is it. Doesn't look like it would be worth losing your head over, does it?"

"Well appearances can be deceiving, can't they Monty?" Doc Martin spilled out a few grains on a white sheet of paper and began examining them with forceps and a teasing needle under the bright light of the table lamp. He ran a pencil magnet over the grains and they were attracted to it. Next, he laid one of the grains on the microscope stage and switched on its bright vertical illumination system. Holding the grain with forceps with his left hand and scratching the grain with the needle in his right as he looked through the optics of the microscope; then he applied a mortar pestle to the grain with considerable force. The grain flattened out dramatically. With the forceps, Martin dragged the flattened grain across an unglazed white porcelain plate and then applied a drop of concentrated nitric acid to it. Simmons watched with fascination thinking this was real science. In reality, it was simply a cursory examination of physical properties that any mineralogist would make with an unknown mineral brought to him for identification. The acid had an unpleasant odor and Doc wiped it up with a tissue.

"Ok Monty, here is what I have for you. These are small stream-worn grains of so-called native platinum; what could be called small nuggets. The metallic mineral here is ferro platinum alloy which means that it is not pure platinum; it is a natural mixture of PGE's, mainly platinum, with iron. The iron causes the attraction to the magnet you saw. The mineral has a metallic luster and whitish-grey color and streak which your headless guy tried to disguise by coating the grains in graphite flakes, probably to deceive customs. You can see the black stuff came right off onto my fingers. This metal is quite dense, malleable, and inert to nitric acid; it has a hardness of about 4 on the Moh's scale. In addition, it lacks cleavage and the crystal faces, although rounded and deformed, indicate that it is an isometric mineral. Nothing but a platinum-rich alloy fills the bill my boy. This is what the miners call *native platinum*. Now I know you have questions at this point but hold them until we have looked at a good placer nugget and an example of lode platinum from my collection."

Doc went to a shelf and returned with a wooden tray. "Check this one out, Monty. It's from a Russian placer and exhibits all the properties that we see in the small grains of your sample except for the carbon coating" and passed him a heavy, stream-worn cubic nugget with crystal faces about 1 inch square. "The combination of metallic luster, color and high density are almost diagnostic by themselves. Add the other properties I mentioned and there is no doubt. Stream platinum is very rare of course Monty but it is easily identified; I like to say it stands out like a diamond in a goat's ass."

Martin picked another specimen from the tray and said "Ok Monty, now take a look at this rock. It is brown, dense and rather ugly, I suppose, but in fact it is the most famous rock on earth. It is a sample of the Merensky Reef that I collected in the underground Rustenburg Platinum Mine in South Africa a few years back. It is a coarse-grained, layered igneous rock composed of pyroxene, chromite and plagioclase and small amounts of platinum group metals, copper, nickel, and gold. The ore metals might form as much as one percent by volume but they are quite tiny grains dispersed throughout the rock. On the sawed and polished surface of this specimen you can just barely see the small, bright, reflecting grains of these metallic phases. The platinum minerals, ferro platinum and other rarer species, are too minute to see except through a microscope. This rock is definitely not spectacular in appearance, Monty, yet it hosts about 85 % of the world's PGE supply. This is a damned good example of what is meant by lode platinum. Now Monty let's have those questions."

"I'd like a little more wine please and a moment to collect my thoughts before I launch into the questions." In fact, Mr. Simmons was slightly dazed and evidently the special agent had never seriously contemplated a goat's ass with or without a diamond. Doc left the room and returned with another bottle. While he was opening it, Monty asked "What does the term 'black sand' mean in terms of placer deposits?"

"Just what it says, when the heavy minerals in stream sediment are concentrated by removing the light-colored, low density minerals, say by hand panning or dredging, that concentrate is likely to be sand-size and black because of the abundance of magnetite, ilmenite, chromite and other dark phases which are the common heavy minerals. Even the platinum is usually dark grey so the overall impression is a black color. The only things in black sand that won't be dark in color are gold which will be bright metallic yellow, ferro platinum and osmiridium which are silvery-looking metals, and pyrite which shows up as dull, pale yellow grains. This is the case with virtually all heavy mineral concentrates from stream sediments. Gold, scheelite, tin, platinum or diamond placers will all be black sands at an early stage of concentration. It's a useful miner's term, nothing more."

"Ok Doc, if you can tell so much from a single grain why can't you tell where it comes from right now?"

"Because all platinum alloys, wherever they come from, have these same physical properties except for density and magnetism which vary according to the iron content. We can't determine the platinum: iron ratio, or relative amounts of the six PGE's to each other by just looking at the material. We need a good chemical analysis and to get that we need a sample that mirrors the traits of its source deposit. Get it?"

"I'm beginning to get it" replied agent Simmons staring down at the Russian nugget in his hand. "I think you are telling me the sample I brought here is shit, therefore the chemical analysis of it is shit and I'm going to have to go to Japan, aren't you, Doc?"

"Now you are getting it Monty. Let's have one more glass of wine while I tell you why your sample is shit in a way that you can use to convince your bosses that Japan will be necessary if you are to pursue this case from the point-of-origin view". Doc got up and went to a corner of the room returning with a quart Mason jar full of marbles. He placed the jar in front of agent Simmons and asked, "Is this jar full Monty?"

"This is a trick professor-type question, isn't it, Doc?"

"Yes, but it is going to be important if you want to find out why the dude in Japan lost his head."

"Ok, the jar is full. No more marbles can be placed in it. Are you satisfied?"

"Very good, now watch what I am going to do." Martin left the table again and returned with a bag of sand and poured a large portion of it into the jar. By tapping the jar, the sand grains were forced to trickle into the open spaces between the marbles. "You see Monty the jar now represents the sample we need, marbles plus sand. The sample you brought was just the marbles. Someone has screened it or handpicked the larger grains for some reason. The missing small grains are likely to include minerals other than platinum-iron alloy so their absence alters the chemical signature and this could make it impossible for us to determine the source area no matter how good your chemical analysis is. I would have to guess that the original material was taken from a dredge concentrate but they always exhibit a very large range in grain size. In the present case, I can't even be sure of this because your sample has been tampered with, which is to say, it is shit".

"Just so I understand this Doc, you are saying I have to go to Japan and somehow find a sample of this stuff with a range of grain sizes like sand to marbles and bring it back for analysis, right?"

"You have the makings of a geologist, Monty, but there is one more thing. The sample you bring back has got to be as large as possible, 1 kilogram or more, even 10 kilograms would not be too large for our purposes. When you find it, call me, I will advise you how to bag it or box it up so we retain the full spectrum of grain sizes present. This is important Monty, if I am to help you."

The men looked across the table at each other sipping their glasses of wine; each taking the measure of the other. Finally, agent Simmons said "There is another point to clear up, Doc and that would be the fee for your services. I have been cleared to offer you $500 per eight-hour day plus any expenses related to the case as long as you provide receipts. That is pretty standard for consulting fees for government agencies."

"Well, Monty, I have news for you. My rate is $1000 a day plus expenses…that is if I were going to charge anything. I will work on your problem as hard and as well as I can for free because it's my duty as a patriotic citizen. But, and mark this, my friend, I don't want a bunch of federal agents descending on Llano, or my ranch, and if I give you an expense invoice for something I think our little project requires I don't want any bullshit about receipts in triplicate and getting three bids from approved vendors."

Simmons smiled "Have you have worked for the feds before Doc?"

"Ok, it sounds like we understand each other. By the way, I'm pretty sure you are going to have to visit all the mints and refineries in Japan that deal with PGE's and talk with their head metallurgists. We need to know if any of them have analyzed test samples or shipments of placer ore from an unknown, or unusual, source in the last few years. You'll need someone with a

44

background in metallurgy who speaks Japanese fluently. Perhaps I can come up with a name. I'm tired now, so let's go to bed. We can discuss anything you think of in the morning. I'll show you to your room."

"Fine Doc, but you have to walk me out to the car to get my overnight bag. I don't want to fight with General Longstreet after I've been drinking."

CHAPTER 6

Truk Lagoon: 1944

The famed Nippon Dental University in Tokyo was founded in 1907. It is the oldest and most prestigious dental school in Japan and lays claim as the largest institution of its kind in the world today. In December of 1941, Aoki Fugimora graduated from Nippon Dental with honors and immediately entered the Imperial Navy at the rank of *Kaig Daii* or lieutenant. His first duty station was the forward naval base on Truk Atoll where he, along with 39 other newly graduated dentists, was assigned to work on seamen's teeth. The dental facilities, like everything on Truk, were housed in underground bunkers. Here, there were 20 chairs devoted to general dentistry for seamen and the new dentists worked these chairs in eight hour shifts around the clock with enlisted assistants and X-ray technicians. This training period, under the watchful eyes of senior dentists, lasted six months and during this time the young dentists were expected to become skillful in all of the dental arts: filling cavities, dental surgery, crowns, bridge work, and dentures as well as one of the specialties offered in the state-of-the-art dental laboratory that supported this massive dental program. If, after six months, they were approved by a committee of their supervisors they either went on sea duty or were transferred to a different wing of the underground facility to devote their skills to officer's teeth.

Dr. Aoki Fugimora was an excellent student and an excellent dentist and, accordingly, was transferred to the officer's wing on 1 June 1942. Life was very good in this facility since one worked without supervision and only the dayshift, 8:00 a.m. to12:00 noon and 2:00 p.m. to 6:00 p.m. This schedule left time to do one's laundry, write letters home, read, drink at the Officers Club and, of course, visit the infamous "comfort women" whenever the need arose. But there were plenty of bad teeth to fix with something like 40,000 men and officers living on the many ships anchored in the lagoon.

The ebullient mood prevailing on Truk changed overnight to somber with the tragic news of events at Midway Island during June 4-7, 1942. The devastating loss of four fleet aircraft carriers and a heavy cruiser meant that nearly everyone in the Imperial Naval dental service on Truk lost friends or family members. Some, and this would include Dr. Aoki Fugimora, began to harbor forbidden doubts about the invincibility of the Imperial Navy, the divinity of the Emperor, and the future of Japan.

On 16 August 1943, an unusual event occurred in the dental lab while Aoki was casting gold crowns. Six armed guards from the Imperial Navy Police, the *tokeitai*, delivered 10 unmarked small but sturdily-built wooden boxes to the dental lab with an order from Admiral Kobayashi himself to store them for later shipment to Japan. They were to be secured in the vault carved into coral rock at the rear of the lab where dental gold was kept. Lieutenant Fugimora was the senior officer on duty in the lab on this particular morning and had to supervise a reorganization of the vault to accommodate these mysterious boxes. He asked the ranking police guard what the boxes contained but received a shrug in answer and a copy of the admiral's orders for the lab files. The stoic guards remained until he locked the door of the vault. Dr. Fugimora was certainly curious but returned to his crowns; one definitely does not question orders of an admiral in the Imperial Navy.

Several months passed after this incident during which life on Truk followed the normal routine. There were no unusual events to disturb the equanimity of the Imperial Navy dentists. But, by the beginning of 1944, the war news was worsening almost daily. The Marshall Islands were threatened and the Japanese Gibraltar of the Pacific no longer seemed an invulnerable tropical paradise. On 10 February 1944, all major ships including carriers, battleships and heavy cruisers were relocated, without explanation, from Truk to Palau. This was definitely not a good sign in the opinion of the Imperial dentists who thought they knew the explanation for this action. There was an insidious and pervasive feeling that payback for Pearl Harbor was impending.

On 17 February 1944, simultaneous U.S. attacks on Truk Atoll and Eniwetok Atoll in the Marshall Islands brought the war up close and personal to all Japanese forces, even to the dentists. During two days of bombing, an overwhelming U.S. naval attack force destroyed virtually everything on the surface of Truk Island and in its lagoon; ships, planes, air fields, docking facilities, virtually everything. In all, the U.S. Navy destroyed 270 planes and sank 5 light cruisers, 4 destroyers, 32 merchant ships, and 8 smaller war ships. All of the exit passages through the wondrous barrier reef to the open sea had been blocked by American submarines and this meant that Japanese ships were trapped in the lagoon and as vulnerable as fish in a barrel. The toll was heavy without doubt, but if Admiral Kobayashi had not moved the major ships, the war would have been over for Japan at this point. In fact, the war was over for the tens of thousands serving in the Truk Islands but the Warriors of the Rising Sun did not yet realize this.

Bloated bodies floated in the lagoon and littered the beaches. The devastation on Truk meant that the large Japanese garrison on nearby Eniwetok had no hope of reinforcement and support from Truk; Eniwetok was invaded by U.S. ground forces on 18 February, 1944. The Japanese Navy later sent about 100 of their remaining aircraft from Rabaul to Truk. These aircraft were soon destroyed in U.S. bombing attacks by carrier forces on 29-30 April 1944 but Truk was not invaded; instead, it was by-passed and completely isolated from all sources of supply as U.S. forces continued their advance towards Japan. Other Pacific strongholds such as Guam, Saipan, Palau, Iwo Jima and Okinawa were invaded and their large, determined garrisons annihilated.

Cut off from all possible sources of supply, the forces on Truk slowly starved. Law and order eventually broke down as discipline in the Imperial Naval Police evaporated and life for everyone evolved to a primordial struggle in which each man was concerned only with the desperate search for food to fill his belly. There would be no escape for the thousands of stranded Japanese or the native population of Truk until the Americans finally came at end of war. By then most would be dead.

In the dental compound, there was panic, or perhaps it would be more accurate to call it controlled apprehension, at least at first. Practically no one was hurt in the bombing raids but they were afraid, afraid of the hungry thousands prowling the small island in search of food. All appointments were cancelled immediately, of course; then they locked the barred gates at the entrance of their underground compound and erected a stone and mortar barrier behind these gates. Thus entombed, the dentists lived off food stocked in the well-supplied dental commissary until it gave out.

Dr. Aoki Fugimora, lieutenant in the Imperial Navy was hungry, he was frightened, and he clearly saw that the dental officers were losing control over their enlisted assistants and technicians as commissary supplies dwindled. He made the decision that the Emperor must be content without him giving up his life and began making nightly raids on the commissary, tea, rice, dried vegetables, dried fish, and salt; a little at first, but cartful's later as he became bolder. These were dishonorable actions, of course, but the bushido code did not run very strongly or deeply in his family; perhaps the Fugimora clan was overly westernized.

The dentist stockpiled his goods in the dental lab to which he had keys and constructed a barricade to prevent anyone else with a key from entering. The lab was equipped with metallurgical ovens, gas burners, and various types of hotplates that operated off compressed gas cylinders and electrical generators housed somewhere beneath the lab. The water supply in the lab was adequate for his needs but the dentist thought it might be cut off from its source by prowlers on the surface. He filled numerous 10-liter plastic containers, that formerly held ethyl alcohol, with water from the taps and stored them in the supply room with his stolen food; he also took the liberty of storing one 10-liter container of ethyl alcohol with this bottled water supply. He moved his clothes, books, and personal items, including the samurai sword handed down to the eldest son in the Fugimora family for 400 years, into the lab.

These surreptitious preparations occupied the lieutenant for several weeks but he could not be sure exactly. It was impossible to keep track of time while living in underground isolation. He was now residing in the lab full time with the outer lights on; he cooked on hotplates and slept in the store room which could be closed off from the oppressive white glare of the lights. He had no communication at all with his fellow dentists.

One night, at least he thought it was night, he was reading in the main lab, out of sight from the small window in the entrance door, when his thoughts wandered to the mysterious boxes stored in the vault. He went to the toolbox, extracted a hammer and pry bar, and went to the vault, unlocked it with a special key and stood staring at the neatly stacked boxes for what seemed like many minutes. The lieutenant recalled the admiral's orders but thought it unlikely that these crates would be going to Japan anytime soon. It was not even likely that the admiral was still in residence on Truk Island at this point in the war.

Aoki Fugimora smiled as he pried the lid off one of the boxes. It contained 10 relatively small sock-like white canvas bags measuring five centimeters in diameter and about 15 centimeters in length; they were sealed with wire wrapping. He pulled one the small bags out of the container and was amazed at its weight. He placed it on a scale; it registered 4.5 kilograms. Next, he took the bag to the nearest work bench where he adjusted the lamp to illuminate the bag and untwisted the wire seal. Inside he saw what appeared to be rounded, dark-grey metallic pellets and grains ranging from a few millimeters in size down to minute specks.

Dr. Fugimora spilled a few of these grains out on the table under bright illumination. He had seen small one-ounce troy ingots of refined platinum plenty of times but this material looked quite different. It was a dirty white color with considerably less brilliance than the ingots. By smashing one of the grains under his hammer, he found that it flattened easily; it was quite malleable. Next, the dentist placed the flattened grain under a microscope; the newly exposed surface was white with a slight grey tinge.

Aoki had worked with refined platinum and knew that it had a density of 21.4 grams per cubic centimeter. He measured the volume of the flattened specimen by sinking it in a volumetric flask containing exactly 100 milliliters of water. The volume increase produced by the sinking metallic pellet was 3.1 milliliters. Then he dried it with compressed air and placed it in an analytical balance and determined its weight to be 63.5 grams. A quick calculation led to a density of 20.5 grams per cubic centimeter; less than pure platinum for sure but that would be the result of impurities of lighter elements like iron.

Dr. Aoki Fugimora was no mineralogist, but he was enough of a chemist to know that he was sitting on approximately 450 kilograms of high-grade native platinum ore. He was rich, exceptionally rich, even astronomically rich. His hands were trembling with emotion. He needed a drink to steady his nerves and went to the 10-liter container of ethyl alcohol in the storeroom and filled a beaker with 50 milliliters; it burned like fire going down but allowed him to regain his composure. He needed to think, he needed to figure out how he was going to get his new treasure off this coral hellhole called Truk.

After some hours of concentrated thought and several more trips to the 10-liter container, a plan began to emerge in the mind of the euphoric dentist. He sat down and began to compile a list of logical inductive statements. 1) Japan would lose the war. 2) He could not get off this festering carbuncle of an island before the

Americans came. 3) He would be a prisoner of war along with the many thousands marooned on the island but, eventually, they would all be repatriated to Japan. 4) The size and mass of his platinum horde would require transport to Japan by ship at a later date. 5) The Americans, when they came, would search the bunkers thoroughly so the platinum must be hidden with extreme skill. 6) The gold ingots in the secure dental vault were small enough in size and total weight that they could be smuggled past the Americans and travel with him back to Japan; they would have to be cleverly hidden or disguised, of course, but they would make him quite wealthy while he waited to recover his platinum. 7) The Americans could appear in his lab at any time and would probably loot the entire hoard if they found it, thus a plan for hiding his fantastic new wealth must be developed immediately.

The Americans would no doubt capture the engineering plans showing the layout of all of the Imperial Navy's underground operations including those of the dental facility and this meant construction of a new vault large enough for the boxes that would not appear on those plans. He would need laborers, tools for excavating in coral, mortar, plaster and white paint to match the existing paint of the passages and rooms. Except for the laborers, he thought the other items could be found in the mechanical-janitorial room located at the hub of the various dental wings.

As his plan evolved, Aoki realized that to get his laborers he would have to leave the dental complex and take his chances up on the surface with the marauding bands of hungry prowlers. Two laborers sounded like what he would need, he could bribe them with food, but if there were two men they would be tempted to overpower him and take everything for themselves. No, that would not work. He would have to do the job with a single man and this man would have to be killed. With this question settled, the next concerned the location of the new vault; should it be an extension of the present vault which surely appeared in the engineering plans or should it be and entirely new structure? It must be the latter of course. Looters will surely come to the old vault hoping to find the dental gold.

Dr. Fugimora shaved, showered beneath the overhead chemical emergency shower, brushed his dress naval uniform and made himself presentable as an officer of the Imperial Navy. He wore his sword, a Katana that had been in the Fugimora family since the 15th century. As he stepped into the lighted hall, a wave of fear approaching nausea passed through him and he began to sweat. He had not been out of the lab in days, perhaps weeks, and did not know whether it was day or night. With his cart in front he pushed it down the empty, silent corridor towards the hub of the dental complex. His cart wheels seemed to create an immense echo up and down the hallway which seemed to shriek out his presence and unworthy intentions. The hub, where all of the corridors converged, was also empty and as silent as death beneath the unrelieved white glare of the institutional lights. Where were his brother dentists?

He found the entrance to the mechanical-janitorial room but

the door stood ajar, its lock already forced. The lieutenant peered cautiously inside, everything was in disorder, clearly it had been ransacked by people looking for food, but the tools he wanted were still there. He loaded his cart with two sizes of sledge hammers, a pickaxe, several smaller hammers, various stone chisels, two sacks each of dry mortar and plaster, a trowel, a stick of blue chalk, and a mortarboard. It took some searching but he finally found a large bucket of white paint, a heavy-duty paint brush, a push-broom, and paint thinner. The cart was full as he emerged from the mechanical-janitorial room. Fugimora looked carefully in all directions; he saw nothing and he heard nothing but his own labored breathing and pounding heart.

Safely behind the locked door of the dental lab again, Dr. Fugimora changed out of his uniform into his customary dirty sleeveless undershirt and shorts. He used a small hammer to tap on the rear wall a few meters away from the existing vault chamber hoping to find hollow zones in the natural coral reef rock. The original excavation had left uneven reef rock at this end of the chamber which was crudely filled in with plaster and painted. Wherever he detected a dull sound he marked this area with blue carpenter's chalk. Next, he began working on one of these spots with a large chisel and hammer. The plaster spalled off easily exposing the reef rock which in turn fractured and fell out in small chunks. He would require much larger pieces in order to build a false wall to close off his new vault.

The dentist carefully marked the position of the original wall on the floor and ceiling with chalk and calculated how much additional volume would be required to accommodate the 10 boxes. These calculations indicated that the existing wall must be moved back about 2 meters horizontally into the reef to accommodate the 10 by 10 by 31.5 centimeter boxes as well as the new wall. It would take effort, but the rock was relatively soft and large voids might be encountered which would mean less rock to remove.

At this point in his considerations, the dentist realized that the proposed new vault area had neither lighting nor a source of electrical power and began searching the lab for a long power cord. He found one long enough to reach from a power supply on a work bench to the vault wall. It was an easy matter to take apart a lamp, remove the bulb and socket, wire it up to the cord and suspend the system to the ceiling with a coat hanger. It worked perfectly.

The lieutenant grabbed one of the sledge hammers and began frantically flailing away at the reef rock. After 15 minutes, he could not hold onto the hammer or lift his trembling arms and he had removed only about two centimeters of pulverized rock from a zone about the size of a coconut. It was obvious to Dr. Fugimora that he needed help, help from a man experienced in this kind of work. Fortunately for him, the Imperial Navy had imported hundreds, maybe even thousands, of Korean laborers for this exact job. He would find one tonight.

After a modest meal and a few hours of sleep, Aoki showered again and donned his dress uniform for the second time since the bombing. Sheathed sword in hand, he crept silently toward the outer gate of the dental complex. He saw no one until he reached the commissary. This room was in chaos, overturned tables and chairs, parts of uniforms and hundreds of empty food tins were scattered about. Two high ranking dental officers, a captain and a commander, sat at opposite ends of one of the tables smoking and drinking tea in their regulation white gloves. Lieutenant Fugimora approached them and saluted. Neither man took notice of him, or each other, for that matter; both continued to stare hypnotically at the wall in front of him. The lieutenant left them to their reveries and made his way to the outer gate. The masonry wall had been breached from the inside as had the barred gate. It appeared that all of the dental officers, save the two tea drinkers, had joined the surface prowlers in their desperate quest for food.

Dr. Fugimora emerged onto the street leading past the dental complex. He was glad to see it was night time but the road was virtually unrecognizable due to the wreckage of planes, vehicles, even parts of ships. There were parts of bodies too, horribly scorched black flesh picked over by surly gangs of insanely shrieking seagulls.

The dentist walked toward the officer's club, giving wide berth to the scrambling swarms of gulls. He held his sword in a position permitting an instant draw but he saw no prowlers and, of course, none of the comfort women. He briefly wondered what had become of these accommodating ladies. Dr. Fugimora was unaware that these Korean women had all been cruelly shot to avoid embarrassment to the Emperor when American troops finally landed. When he reached the club, he saw an unshaven man in dirty civilian clothes sitting on the entrance stairs. This man watched as the officer approached and presented him with a token, half-bow from his sitting position. Officers in the Imperial Navy are simply not greeted by lower class civilians in this manner and Fugimora spoke sharply to him "You will stand when you are in the presence of an officer. What is your name? Why do you block the entrance to the officer's club?"

The man reluctantly and slowly got to his feet and bowed properly this time. "I am 3-1-27 most honorable one."

From his broken Japanese, Fugimora knew the man was a Korean laborer and said, "Why do you give me a number instead of your name, you worthless foreign dog?"

"The honorable lieutenant must know that no dogs, or even cats, foreign or domestic, remain on Truk and that we must give labor number when addressed by naval officers."

Ignoring the gross impertinence of this man, Fugimora asked "3-1-27, are you capable of masonry work in exchange for food?"

"Yes, honorable one. I am strong and do anything for food. I am trained as mason here on Truk and educated as civil engineer in Korea."

"Very well then, worthless turd-eater, come with me and you shall have food in your belly." With this Lieutenant Fugimora spun on his heel marched off toward the dental complex with the imperial strut adopted by Japanese naval officers in the presence of the lower classes.

For his part, 3-1-27 considered himself fortunate indeed to meet this arrogant, shit-eating, ass-hole of an officer with a stash of food; he would follow, but he was very good with a knife, a shovel or a mason's hammer. Marching across the silent, eerie, war-torn landscape in moonlight toward the dental complex, these two figures brought to mind the famous Knight of the Rueful Countenance and his loquacious squire in quest of adventures along the rural byways of La Mancha.

Safely behind the locked and barricaded door of the lab again, Dr. Fugimora changed back into his dirty shorts and shirt while water boiled for tea, rice and fish. 3-1-27 nearly swooned from the smell of the food but could not discover where the supply was located because the dentist has taken the precaution to blind-fold him. Fugimora set a cup of tea, a bowl of boiled rice and fish and chop sticks in front of the Korean and told him to eat. The man was so hungry that he swallowed the rice-fish mixture in a single greedy scorching gulp. This scene was repeated two more times before Fugimora brought it to a halt and told the worker he must fill up with tea. After six cups of tea the Korean was still hungry but visibly calmed by the hot meal. He reached to remove his blindfold but his hand encountered the cold steel of a Katana blade. Knowing the feel of such a blade, he lowered the hand slowly. 3-1-27 understood he was a prisoner of a dog-fucking Japanese shit-head officer but at this moment he did not care. This shit-head had food.

The dentist instructed the Korean to move to the rear of the lab guiding him by taps on the shoulder with the long, curved cold blade. When he was secured in the vault behind a locked barred door, Fugimora told him to remove the blind fold and rest for a few hours.

The work began with Fugimora explaining his plan for moving the rear wall back by two meters into the coral bedrock and using the removed material to reseal the chamber at the initial position. 3-1-27 understood immediately and began with the carpenter's chalk marking out a grid system of 20 centimeter squares. He then took a hand mallet and a large chisel and began chipping out the central block in this grid system. With the same tools, he then removed adjacent blocks, more or less intact, through the newly-created opening with relatively little work.

Fugimora could clearly see that this man was experienced and skilled in coral masonry. He stacked each block as it was liberated at the starting position where the new wall was to be erected. In four hot sweaty hours of labor the wall had been moved back 30 centimeters. Dr. Fugimora could now estimate the time it would take to complete the new vault. Three four-hour work shifts per 24 hours should yield one meter of displacement so the work could be completed in two days. 3-1-27 was allowed an hour of rest, a bowl of boiled rice and fish, and as much tea as he wanted after each shift. Fugimora watched his worker intently, the gleaming Katana blade always close at hand.

At the end of two days, the new vault extended a little more than the required two meters and it was time to place the boxes in the vault. During the periods when 3-1-27 was sleeping behind the barred vault door, the dentist returned to the mechanical-janitorial room and secured two sets of double-reeved blocks, rope tackle, steel hooks that could be screwed into coral rock, and a heavy four-wheel dolly. He needed these items so his worker could move the boxes which weighed a little more than 45 kilograms each to their new home unassisted.

Fugimora directed 3-1-27 to install one of the hooks in the ceiling rock above the stacked boxes and another in the ceiling rock at the back of the newly excavated vault. He attached the pairs of blocks and demonstrated their operation for the Korean laborer. Using a rope harness, the first box was loaded onto the dolly and rolled to its new position and lifted off the dolly with the second pair of blocks under the watchful eye and sword of the navel dentist.

When all of the platinum crates had been transferred in this manner, the dentist called a halt to the work and informed 3-1-27 that it was now time for a celebration. He had made a special meal of rice, vegetables, fish, tea, Korean kimchi and a liter of pure alcohol. The Japanese officer opened this ceremony with a solemn toast to the Emperor and both men emptied their cups. This was followed by equally solemn toasts to the Imperial Navy, Admiral Kobayashi, and finally Nippon Dental College. Fugimora placed the food on the dolly, and leaving the remaining three quarters of a liter of alcohol behind as if by accident, he locked the gate saying he must have sleep.

The dentist intentionally left the vault light on and took up a position where he could watch his man eat and drink. 3-1-27 leaned against a rock wall with the dolly next to him and ate voraciously but every few minutes he filled his tea cup with alcohol and toasted something in his outlandish Korean babble. Fugimora watched for nearly two hours at which point the liter bottle contained only a quarter of its original measure and 3-1-27 had been unconscious and immobile for 30 minutes. It was time for the young lieutenant to do his part.

He unsheathed his sword, silently unlocked the barred gate, and approached the sleeping figure still propped against the coral wall. Like a big-league baseball batter Fugimora assumed a crouched stance, pawed the floor to secure his footing, and swung the Katana with both hands aiming at the neck; the blade went through tissue and bone with no discernable resistance and actually sparked as it knocked a chunk of coral out of the wall behind the man. The torso twitched grotesquely, causing the severed head to topple from its seat to the floor and roll a short distance. A fountain of blood spurted from the neck of 3-1-27, more blood than a dentist sees in a lifetime of surgery. The young dentist stared, mesmerized by the shocking sight of the twitching torso and displaced head, his sandals soaking in his victim's blood.

He clumsily removed his sandals and retreated from the body and the open-eyed head that mockingly grinned at him. Fugimora grabbed the bottle of alcohol from the dolly and took a major hit.

When he set the sword down he noticed that it bore only the slightest trace of blood. He also noticed that his hands were trembling as if by palsy. He took another drink and then another until the bottle was empty.

By the end of the following day, Dr. Fugimora had cleaned up the scene, placed his sword with the torso and the severed head in the new vault along with the crates containing his platinum hoard. Then he mortared in the blocks of coral to form a new wall. He allowed the mortar to set for what he guessed was 24 hours and then plastered and painted the new wall to match the rest of the interior. All in all, Dr. Aoki Fugimora considered it was a job well done.

CHAPTER 7

Longstreet Performs

The Gomez da Silva and Martin families had a tradition involving what Dona Modesta is pleased to call "mating day". Doc Martin and her husband Felice call it *"dia p'ra fudar as cabras"* which is quite impolite. Dona Modesta does not approve of this kind of language, especially in the presence of her children, which is not to say she has not heard such phrases all of her life. She understood perfectly well that the female goats, usually referred to as does, must be bred at this time of the year, and that this is essential to their livestock enterprise. But she did not think it had to be the spectator sport that Felice made of it. She knew that "men will be men" and that her husband was an extremely good and hardworking man. So, Dona Modesta was wise enough to not voice opposition to the approaching ritual and was even permitting her 13-year-old son João to participate for the first time. João, for his part, had seen goats breed plenty of times, but he was very keen on seeing the behavior of his father and Dr. Martin. Dona Modesta and Maria planned drive into Austin to spend the night with her married sister. A pot of her famous Portuguese chick pea soup waited on the stove.

Female goats usually enter their heat cycle about mid-October and their gestation is on average 150 days followed by about 305 days of lactation. Thus, Felice phoned Martin on the evening of October 14 and asked Doc to bring Longstreet to the Gomes da Silva ranch the next morning after the milking was finished. Accordingly, Martin loaded General Longstreet into the back of his pickup truck around 9 a.m. Neither Doc nor Felice would get much work done this day.

General Longstreet, although trained in "dog sentry duties", was never the less a virile Boer buck at the peak of his powers and considered himself a masterful lover in the fashion of goats. He knows he will be the star attraction of mating day and is not expected to pick up the paper on this morning. He will need his full strength. Martin signals for Longstreet to jump in the back of the truck and the General does not have to be asked twice. Longstreet stands proud during the short ride to the Gomez da Silva ranch. He knows exactly where he is going.

In this annual ritual, Martin fills his dad's role with Felice; it is his third mating day but Jack Martin participated in the seven previous events. When Martin arrives, he exchanges greetings with Felice and João while Longstreet descends from the truck bed and regally struts though the open gate of the 10 x 10-foot breeding pen. Felice has placed lawn chairs on the flat-bed trailer drawn up next to the enclosure. The view will be unobstructed. A beach umbrella shades the chairs; an ice chest sits ominously between them. The stage is set.

Felice has set a lofty target for the General. Last year Longstreet successfully serviced 15 does (a record incidentally) without a break in the action. This year, 20 Boer does in heat wait impatiently in an enclosure next to the breeding pen. It is, perhaps, an unrealistic number but all present know Longstreet will do his best. Two other bucks are held in reserve in a nearby shed and will take over for the General if he falters today; otherwise they will see action tomorrow. After all, nearly 200 does must be serviced this week.

João works down in the pens with a wooden cane in his hand. His job is to send one doe at a time into the breeding pen and then escort her to another pen after she is bred. He carries a can of red spray paint and puts a red spot on the back of each bred doe.

Felice and Martin climb up onto the trailer and seat themselves in the lawn chairs. A minor adjustment is made in the position of the umbrella; two glasses are retrieved from the cooler and filled with ice. The cooler also yields a bottle of Talisker 10-year-old single malt from the Isle of Skye. Felice and Jack Martin initiated this part of the ritual but Doc the younger is well pleased with it as he has fond memories of the Talisker distillery and haggis during a field trip on Skye some years back. The glasses are filled, Felice gives João a wave, and doe number one enters the pen where the General waits. The men clink glasses and say *"ao a dia p'ra fudar as cabras"*. The show has begun.

They will be drunk on this day before noon.   By the zenith, the score is Longstreet seven does, Felice and Martin one bottle of single malt.   João informs the pair that dinner waits in the kitchen and with some difficulty the men descend to the ground.   The General takes a well-earned rest and a long drink of water.   After a hearty bowl of chick pea soup and a loaf of Modesta's home-made bread, the gentlemen are prepared for round two and again mount the platform and seat themselves.

The umbrella must be adjusted again and a second bottle of Talisker makes an appearance.   The former scene is repeated.   The conversation switches from English to Portuguese unpredictably, there are whistles and applause for Longstreet, there are nasty shouts meant as encouragement in both languages.   João is fully entertained as the count rises to 15.

General Longstreet cannot count, of course, but from the raucous behavior of his audience he can tell he is in record territory.   He can see that four more does remain in the adjacent pen.   He pauses for a few moments after number 16 and takes a very long drink.   He is exhausted and knows that he is about finished for the day.   He looks up to the men in chairs.   He is a proud gladiator and his audience wants more.   He walks slowly around the pen twice, pauses for another drink and then faces the men on the platform again.   He stretches his neck, rolls back his upper lip and lets out a mighty bleat that rattles windows.   He is ready and Felice orders another doe sent in, number 17, and the men go crazy.   Longstreet finishes the job knowing that it is not his best work; as number 17 is guided away, he totters and finds himself leaning against the fence to keep on his feet. Martin tells Felice "I don't want to kill my dad's goat, amigo. He's had all he can take." The same might be said for Martin and Felice. "Let's call it a day."

João offers Longstreet more water and slowly guides him to a shady spot where he lies down. His tongue is hanging out. This time the two men nearly fall off their platform. By helping each other they finally manage to get on solid ground. There is enough Talisker for one more drink but João must climb onto the platform to fetch the bottle, fill the glasses with ice, and bring them to the men who are also leaning against the fence for support. They toast to number 17, *ao dezessete*, and to Longstreet. Mating day ends in an entirely predictable way.

João escorts his dad to the couch in the living room of the house. Martin yells "Dinner at my place tonight, around seven." Not much chance of this. João returns to the pens and he and Martin are both required to lift Longstreet into the bed of the pickup. He is dead weight and unable to stand. Martin manages to get behind the wheel without help but it is a good thing he has only one mile to drive on the highway. João must milk the goats alone this evening but he is already looking forward to next year's mating day.

CHAPTER 8

Tokyo: 1945

One of the singular proclamations arising from the Potsdam Conference in July of 1945 was the decision to allow Japanese military forces, after being disarmed, to be repatriated to their homes with the opportunity to lead peaceful and productive lives. This lenient policy meant that Japanese subjects on Guam, Saipan, Truk and elsewhere in the Pacific were not prisoners of war; they were merely disarmed military personnel. On 2 September 1945, commanders of Truk's remaining Army and Navy garrisons, reduced in number by battle, suicide and starvation, officially surrendered on board the U.S. cruiser *Portland*. This was the same day as the formal, well-publicized surrender ceremonies presided over by General Douglas MacArthur, took place in Tokyo Bay aboard the battleship *Missouri*. Each repatriated man would be allowed to carry home the equivalent of one ordinary sea bag, subject to inspection. In addition, dental and medical officers were allowed to carry a bag of their instruments back to Japan.

Dr. Aoki Fugimora had been very busy in the Truk dental lab during the days prior to the surrender of the island. He made an unauthorized withdrawal of 146 ingots stamped with *Credit Suisse, one-ounce fine gold, 999.9* from the vault of the Imperial Naval dental lab. The value of these ingots at the official exchange rate of $35 US per troy ounce was $5110 US. Fugimora thought that a higher price might be obtained on the black market. He melted and cast 100 troy ounces of this gold into 25 sets of dentures artfully camouflaged to appear as dental porcelain. He placed an additional five ingots into the soles of each of his naval dress shoes, five more were cast into a new belt buckle covered with a thin film of brass. The remaining 31 ingots were concealed under a false bottom in his dental sea chest.

Inspection on the day of departure for Japan was so ludicrous that Lieutenant Fugimora had to strain himself to keep from laughing in the face of the military inspector. The marine police sergeant who opened his dental chest instantly recoiled in horror from the array of false teeth and wicked-looking surgical utensils. He slammed the case shut and waved Fugimora onto the ship. One would have thought he encountered a venomous snake rather than dental instruments.

Aoki Fugimora stepped off the repatriation ship in Tokyo Bay into a Japan reeling in economic, social and political chaos. It was not the Japan he had left behind in 1941 and it was not a Japan that he could recognize. The harbor area and downtown Tokyo itself had been desecrated and transmuted into an inconceivably monstrous phantom of its former self. Block after block after block of former dwellings and bustling enterprises of this ancient city were now simply charred ruins endlessly scavenged by starving, mindless, faceless zombies.

Attired in his naval dress uniform, he arrived at his parent's house in a decrepit and shabby taxi driven by an elderly woman. This was the house he had been born in, the house he had grown up in. Although he carried 146 ounces of gold on his person, he was forced to accept 50 yen from his mother to pay his taxi fare. His father had died during the war years and his mother lived in the family home with an elderly lady servant. This formerly prosperous house had no income because his father's considerable wealth, like that of countless thousands of Japanese, had vaporized with the collapse of the Japanese banking system. The two elderly ladies of the home lived by selling furniture and family heirlooms to unscrupulous traders who called upon them weekly.

In the days that followed, the former naval dentist easily found used dental equipment at cheap prices belonging to deceased practitioners. He negotiated for a chair and electric dental drill and had them installed in his mother's house. From a defunct jewelry business, he purchased a small metallurgical furnace with graphite crucibles, tongs, and melting ladles. The melting point of gold is 1064.58 °C and this furnace would reach 1100 °C and melt 10 ounces of gold in 50 minutes. He obtained a used, high quality balance for measuring gold weights from the same source. The first use of the furnace involved liberating the 100 ounces of gold stored in the dentures smuggled past the military police on Truk. This metal was recast into one ounce ingots for use in his practice.

Within two weeks Fugimora opened a practice catering to patients who could pay with US currency, gold or food commodities. You may be quite sure there were not many such patients in Tokyo in late 1945 and Dr. Fugimora drilled out more than one cavity for a skinny stewing hen. There were not many of these in Tokyo either.

The advertised specialty of this practice was gold fillings, bridges, implants and crowns. Dr. Fugimora kept in touch with black market gold prices but he found it was far more lucrative to use the gold from Truk in repairing bad teeth which were not in short supply. He worked hard and performed high quality dental work and within a few months the cash inflow was sufficient to meet the domestic needs of his household and pay installments on his equipment. Any funds remaining were devoted to buying more equipment. Dr. Fugimora yearned passionately for one of the new X-ray machines that were beginning to come onto the dental market.

The post-war years saw the Japanese yen fall drastically in value against the US dollar from 15:1 in 1946 to 360:1 by 1949, but at least the latter rate remained fixed by law for the next 22 years. The dollar itself was pegged to gold at $35 dollars US per troy ounce by the Breton Woods Agreement which locked yen, dollar, and gold prices to each other until 1971.

These circumstances motivated the astute, gold-financed dentist to gradually expand his one-man laboratory into a small metallurgical refinery employing both an extractive metallurgist and a physical metallurgist to develop capabilities for refinement of silver, gold and, of course, platinum concentrates. This business, Fugimora Dental Laboratory, was licensed to import precious metals for the dental industry, so clearly Dr. Fugimora had not forgotten about Truk Atoll.

The dental practice also expanded during this period from two chairs in 1947 to five in 1949. In this year, Dr. Fugimora opened a private dental school, Fugimora College of Dentistry, and began training dental students who could afford high tuition rates; these were the sons of Japan's emerging elite, which is to say, the rising post-war criminal class who made their wealth from black market activities. Dr. Fugimora reluctantly realized that he was now a member of this growing new social class.

These expansions made inroads on the Truk gold supply, of course, but he was now able to buy gold ores on the world market, pay himself to refine them, and install his product at a profit in people's mouths. He was becoming wealthy and he needed to be wealthy in order to buy a sea-going ship that could bring his platinum hoard from Truk to his refinery in Tokyo.

Beyond these notable post-war business activities, Dr. Fugimora also took it upon himself to become an expert on the economic aspects of platinum group metals. He studied their chemistry, mineralogy, metallurgical applications, global distribution, production statistics as well as the marketing strategies of the producing nations of South Africa, Russia, Canada, the US and Colombia. He became aware of the many applications of platinum group metals in the chemical and petroleum industries but naturally it was the dental applications that he was most interested in.

Gold dental work had historically been the choice for Japanese people who could afford it. Dr. Fugimora himself had two gold crowns and they frequently had to be repaired because of the inherent softness of dental gold. It was annoying, but it gave him the idea of redirecting the public's preference to platinum dental work. As president of a dental college he began by publicizing the fact that he had replaced his own gold dental crowns with much harder platinum crowns. He directed the dental school to work only with platinum metals and to initiate research on further applications of these metals to dentistry.

In 1951, he expanded his small dental laboratory into a true refining operation under the new name Fugimora Precious Metals Ltd.; he ordered his metallurgical staff to prepare for refining platinum placer concentrates and to perfect their techniques on 100 kilograms of ore, the equivalent of 3,215 troy ounces; this order was placed with Goodnews Bay Mining Company in Alaska.

This Alaskan purchase was Dr. Fugimora's first play in the precious metals market. One could buy refined platinum, palladium, osmium, iridium, rhodium, and ruthenium on the New York Commodities Exchange at the free-market daily price or at so-called "producer prices" set essentially by South Africa, the world's major source of these metals for contract customers. This producer price, per ounce of platinum, had climbed from $36 US in 1945 to $92 US in 1948 and while this increase pleased the dentist who was holding 450 kilograms of illegal platinum ore it was not a wise investment for a man who owned a precious metal refinery. His research had revealed a post-war drop in demand for the unrefined concentrates produced by Goodnews Bay Mining; this made them vulnerable to price negotiation. Dr. Fugimora was a very good negotiator, even without his Samurai sword, and ended up with a contract with this Alaskan mining company for one thousand kilos of concentrate delivered to Tokyo over a ten-year period at a very cheap price relative to refined platinum. Of course, he realized that this meant he could sell his own refined platinum on the New York exchange but he did not wish to become a market speculator in platinum group metals. He had his eye on a larger and more lucrative objective: he wanted to install platinum in every mouth in Japan.

The president of Fugimora Dental College wanted platinum to replace gold in Japanese dentistry and was not long in devising a plan for his school to host an annual conference organized around the topic "The Role of Platinum Group Metals in Modern Dentistry: An International Symposium". He spent money to advertise his conference in all the international dental journals and invited Goodnews Bay Mining to send people to display colorful posters showing how platinum was mined and, of course, reach new customers. Behind the scenes, he made arrangements that insured each attending dentist would have access to all the sex and whisky he wanted at Fugimora expense. This maiden conference was a complete success as any attendee still alive will tell you; so were the annual conferences that followed.

Dr. Fugimora was successful at each and every business endeavor that he undertook and was already rich by post-war Japanese standards. But he still faced two very difficult problems. The first involved the unforeseen political status of Truk. In 1947 the United Nations mandated the Truk Islands as part of the Trust Territory of the Pacific Islands to be administered by the United States; this was a serious problem that his growing wealth could not solve. The second problem was related to the National Bank of Colombia which claimed ownership of all platinum smuggled out of the state during the war years. His platinum could be claimed by this bank if the source was ever revealed. Dr. Aoki Fugimora was no dunce when it came to problem solving and had given much thought to these particular issues; he had concluded that patience would solve the first but deception would be required to solve the second. He was quite sure that he was equal to the tasks before him.

CHAPTER 9

Deer Hunt in Llano

The first Saturday in November is a sacred day in Llano County, Texas and nearly every business closes its doors. This magical day marks the opening of the general deer season and all red-blooded men, boys and not a few gals take to the wilds with their favorite rifle in pursuit of the noble whitetail buck. For those who are successful in this endeavor it will be a day of festivity and carousal. For those not successful it will be exactly the same. This is the case with our friends who patronize the Grey Parrot Bar and Grill which is, naturally, closed on this very special occasion.

It happens that Doc, Felice and Nestor are first class hunters who take pride in bringing in their bucks before noon on opening morning. Doc takes his deer at 7:57 a.m. and drops it off at the Gomez da Silva ranch at 9:30, hanging it up on a beam with a block and tackle especially erected for this purpose. When Felice returns from the field he will hang his deer next to Doc's. Felice is a skillful butcher and will quickly deal with both animals. Dona Modesta will help by wrapping the cuts of meat, labeling the packages and taking them into their walk-in freezer used to store their butchered goats.

Meanwhile Doc returns to his ranch and begins preparing for the banquet to come in the early afternoon. He will cook two boneless venison loin roasts larded with bacon and rubbed with olive oil, garlic and herbs from the garden maintained by Dona Modesta. For those not caring for venison there will be two chickens grilled by the beer-butt method and two more roasted in Dutch ovens with onions, carrots, peas, potatoes, celery and a jalapeno. He will make a very large pot of pinto beans with green chilies in the New Mexico style, grill 20 ears of corn, and heat up large stacks of corn and flour tortillas. Dona Modesta will bring a giant bowl of coleslaw and several loaves of bread. She had to foresight to send her children on the bus to her sister in Austin; they will not return until Sunday afternoon. The stock tank will be filled to capacity and no one, not even Dona Modesta, anticipates going home on this night.

Doc gets his beans boiling in the Nesco cooker and begins chopping vegetables and herbs. This traditional festival of the hunt began before he was born. Different times and different people of course, but his dad had loved deer hunting and having his friends over on opening day. Doc had used his dad's rifle since his return to Llano, an old Savage model 99 chambered in .308 Winchester. He always took the old jeep to the rock quarry and settled in on the quarry wall about an hour before daylight. His dad had taken him to this spot on his first hunt when he was 12 years old; their last hunt together came when Doc was 18 and a freshman in college.

After that he had not been able to get back to the ranch in November during his 10 years of schooling and 20 years of university teaching. Six years, it was not much time to spend with your dad when you think about it. Sitting with your ass on a chunk of cold granite waiting for the sun to rise gave you time to think about it.

Felice drove up at that moment. Doc greeted him with the traditional query on this special day "How many points?"

"Only six, same as your buck" answered Felice with a smile. "Here are your loins and the antlers of both of our bucks and I have ice in the bed of the truck." They loaded blocks of ice into the stock tank which contained a formidable quantity of beer and wine, covered the tank with a heavy tarp, and then Felice left to get his morning milking done. The beans were boiling hard so Doc turned them down to a slow simmer, dropped in six roasted and peeled green chili peppers of the Anaheim type and four cups of chopped white onions and placed a lid over them. The two sets of antlers were placed on the granite wall in a prominent spot for inspection by the guests. Felice had tied tags on each identifying the respective hunters.

Doc lit one bag of charcoal in the fire pit and a second in his grill before turning to his venison loins. First, he cut six pieces of bacon into narrow two-inch strips then used his larding needle to insert them at one inch intervals in both loins. He crushed some garlic in a large mortar with coarse kosher salt, added black pepper, Spanish paprika, and cayenne pepper and ground the mixture in the mortar. The dry ingredients were poured into two cups of olive oil and stirred. Doc had learned this recipe in Portugal from displaced Angolan refugees who called it *Piri-Piri* sauce. He used a brush to paint the loins with his sauce and placed them on a rack in his grill well above the hot coals. He trussed the wings and legs of two of his chickens and painted them inside and out with the same mixture. Then came his favorite culinary step, two cans of cold beer chugged down to the half way mark and shoved into the cavity of each bird. The trussed chickens were then carefully balanced on the beer cans and placed on the main grill away from the live coals and the lid closed. This part of the dinner would take about two hours.

Next, he laid two Dutch ovens on live coals in the fire pit to pre-heat while he placed an onion in each of the cavities of the remaining two chickens and inserted thin slices of lime under the skin of the breasts. These were then painted with *Piri-Piri* and set in raised pans in each of the Dutch ovens. The chopped potatoes, carrots, celery, peas and a thinly sliced jalapeno chili were added to each pot and the pre-heated lid placed over both. A shovel full of hot coals was placed on each lid and the deed was done. For these the estimated cooking time was also about two hours.

Doc awarded himself a cold bottle of Shiner Bock as he surveyed the situation. Only the beans remained. They were soft enough to mash so he removed about four cups of the boiling beans crushed them with an old-time potato masher and returned them to the pot with a big dollop of Crisco. He added four cups of chopped onions, a big can of Ro-Tel tomatoes, four cloves of crushed garlic, and two thinly sliced jalapenos; he liked his beans spicy. The cooker was set for a slow simmer and all was in readiness except for the corn and tortillas and these could be dealt with after the guests arrived. He sat down in a lawn chair, put his feet up, and awarded himself another beer.

About this time, Nestor's truck could be seen coming up the dirt lane. A perceptive observer would have noticed this truck weaving in a somewhat irregular fashion. As he pulled into the yard Nestor shouted, *"Bon jour monsieur l'docteur!"* On this special day, it was permitted to be drunk at any hour and this Nestor Gallegos was. As he dismounted from the truck, General Longstreet took the opportunity to charge the unsteady hunter in camouflage cover-alls and succeeded in knocking him to the ground. The General was rather pleased with himself but, Nestor was not, and pulled out his hunting knife.

Doc was forced to interrupt this entertaining scene with "Now, now boys, let's all play nice. Longstreet, you go to your pen. You are forbidden to knock Nestor down again until this time next year." Longstreet readily retreated and Nestor was forced to laugh at himself. Doc cooled him down by saying "Let's have a drink while you tell me how your hunt went." Nestor placed his 10-point rack next to the other trophies and the men sat themselves in lawn chairs parked next to the stock tank.

"Something tells me you are drinking whiskey today Nestor." As he said it, Doc reached under the prep table and pulled out a bottle of Talisker; he found two, more or less clean glasses, put a chunk of ice in each and filled them with three fingers of single malt. The men exchanged their morning success stories embellished with only very minor lies.

Nestor was a traditional Texas hunter who always used a saddle horse and an old beat-up Winchester .30-.30 with iron sights. Not many men did these days.

"Need any help with the cooking Doc?" Nestor asked.

"You could check my chickens in the Dutch ovens Nestor while I baste the meat on the grill. Be careful now and don't fall in the fire pit."

"I think I can stay out of the fire. The chickens look ok. I'm going to add some more coals to the lids."

With these minor tasks accomplished, the men retired to their chairs and violated the Talisker bottle once again. They admired the three pairs of antlers that now adorned the granite wall. It was 12:15 p.m.

Rhoda arrived next in her red beetle. Longstreet wanted to greet her but thought better of it; he could feel Nestor's eyes on him. Doc got up to welcome her and carry her casserole of cheese and jalapeno grits. "Howdy Doc, looks like you and Nestor are getting a head start on the party."

"I suppose we are but we have plenty to celebrate and practically all the preparations are done. Shall I put your grits in an electric skillet on low to keep them warm?"

"Yeah, that will be fine. What are you boys drinking?"

"A little Talisker, but what can I get for you Rhoda?"

"Cold white wine would hit the spot, Doc."

"Ok, check out the antlers, Rhoda. The big set is from Nestor's buck, the two smaller ones are from mine and Felice's." Doc handed her a glass of wine and they both sat down facing Nestor who had helped himself to the Talisker. They were thinking it might be a short night for the former master sergeant.

At that moment, an old white Ford pickup drove up to the ranch house. General Longstreet, forgetting his recent scare, ran to the truck snorting in his most ominous manner. The occupants were the Ryder twins from a ranch about a mile away, close neighbors by local standards. Longstreet retreated when he noticed Nestor was glaring at him. The twins, Roy and Jerry, were 20 years old and drunker than Cooter Brown at a country picnic. "Howdy Dr. Martin" one of them said "We just dropped by to see how you and Mr. Nestor did this morning."

"We have six, six and ten points on our side, how about you boys? I can see some antlers sticking out of your truck bed." The whole party walked over to the truck to examine the deer, a nice ten-point buck and a smaller four-pointer. Doc had known their dad since high school where, predictably, he was known as "Red" Ryder in spite of the fact that he did not have red hair. Red was a big boy and played offensive tackle on the same football team as Doc and Nestor. Red had been a wild and reckless lad in those days but grew up to become a respectable and successful cattle rancher. Roy and Jerry followed Red's path in academics but did ask for Doc's guidance on a school science project they worked on two years before. Doc asked, "How are things going for your dad, boys?"

"He's fine Dr. Martin and sends his regards to you and Mr. Nestor and Miss Rhoda." The twins beamed as Nestor examined their ten-pointer and nodded with approval. They knew about Nestor's reputation as a deer hunter.

"You boys come on over to the patio, check out our racks and have a drink with us. You all are welcome to stay for dinner" offered Doc. The twins followed the group back to the patio and knocked down a Shiner Bock each as they examined the antlers on the wall.

"Thanks Dr. Martin, but we gotta get back to the ranch and take care of these deer. Maybe we can come back when we get finished. We just dropped by to show off our deer and see how you guys did" said Roy.

"Sure boys, bring your mom and dad back with you."

Doc walked with them back to their truck and warned them to drive straight to the ranch, no going to town today. As they were leaving, Dona Modesta and Felice arrived in her yellow truck. General Longstreet greeted them in a conservative fashion without pawing or snorting and received a loving pat on head from Dona Modesta but was ignored by Felice as usual. He sulked back to his pen maintaining a watchful eye on Nestor.

"*Boa tarde,* Dona Modesta!" shouted Doc Martin as he rose to help carry in the food items she brought. Felice carried the loaves of bread made by his wife and headed straight for the stock tank. He was ready for a drink and selected a cold Shiner Bock to start. He and Nestor exchanged success stories of their morning hunts. Dona Modesta put her coleslaw on the table and exchanged an embrace with Rhoda, then Nestor who was a bit unsteady, and then with Doc who was still in good shape.

"Modesta, you must try Doc's white wine. It is very cold and wonderful" said Rhoda and handed her a filled glass.

"Thank you, Rhoda. How are our hunters behaving this day?" asked Dona Modesta with a knowing wink.

"I am thinking that Nestor might be down for the count if Doc does not serve the food soon. He is drinking scotch" returned Rhoda.

"Yes, he is a bad boy, our Nestor, is he not?" replied Modesta with a mock look of disapproval meant for Nestor to see.

Nestor, who followed their conversation, smiled broadly and said, "I'll be putting you girls to bed before this night is over." Everyone laughed at this unlikely scenario.

During this conversation, Doc checked his chickens in the Dutch ovens. They were done so he lifted the heavy pots off the fire with his claw hammer and removed their lids. Inside the grill, he also pronounced the beer-butt chickens done, removed the beer cans from their cavities and placed the birds on an upper rack. He made a small slice on one of the venison loins and decided they needed another 15 minutes. He basted them, put 10 ears of corn on the grill, placed a stack of tortillas on the upper rack as far from the fire as he could and closed the lid. Next, he checked the beans and then went to the house returning with all the large platters he had. These were spread across one of the picnic tables.

Returning to the grill, Doc rotated the ears of corn and removed the chickens to one of the platters. He quickly quartered both chickens and spread them on a platter. Then he placed one of the Dutch ovens directly on the table and quartered its chicken as well and placed a large ladle in it. The corn was finished at this point and was stacked on another platter. He was satisfied now with the boneless loins and withdrew them from the grill and sliced them onto another platter. Rhoda scooped about two quarts of beans out of the Nesco cooker and into a large bowl, placed the tortillas next to them and her cheese grits next to the tortillas. Modesta, in the meantime, sliced up a loaf of bread and placed serving spoons in everything that required one. More beans, 10 ears of corn, a second loin and chicken and loaf of bread stood in reserve. Doc opened two bottles of red wine from Mealhada, Portugal with four more in waiting. It was 5:15 pm and dinner was served.

The Grey Parrot group was still eating when the Ryder twins reappeared and obliged Doc by fixing themselves a plate and helping themselves to beer. The older people looked on in amazement as the twins put the food away. Doc was laughing to himself as he cut up the second loin, grilled the back-up corn, and added another two quarts of beans to the table. He had worried that he might have prepared too much, but now he was pleased that his guests were happy and that he had enough food and liquor to keep them in that state.

Nestor was unsteady but still on his feet. The Talisker bottle had become a casualty of war around 6 p.m. and the Army cook had switched to drinking beer with the Ryder twins. The boys pumped Nestor about his hunting experiences and his 30 years of duty overseas. It was educational for them without a doubt.

At about 8:30 Doc suggested that the twins might want to call their dad to come over and take them home. The boys were definitely not keen on this idea so, after some discussion, it was decided that Jerry was in the best shape and should drive the pair home.

By 9:30 the table was cleared and the friends sat around it talking and drinking wine, all except for Nestor who was, by now, confined to his lawn chair. No one wanted coffee. Doc put on some music which drifted softly over the patio and the revelers.

Doc watched Dona Modesta carefully as the music changed from Brazilian jazz to Coimbra-style fado. Her eyes widened as she caught the strains of the distinctive classical guitar style and the low, mournful voice of the male singer. Doc had bought this disk on his last trip to Portugal intending to give it to Modesta but had forgotten to do so. He could see that Modesta knew the song and was silently mouthing the Portuguese words. Then she was on the table dancing and singing the words aloud with the recorded voice. Felice covered his eyes in embarrassment at first but his wife had a good singing voice, rather deep for a woman. He smiled when he saw that the audience was watching intently. Her movements on the table were graceful, particularly if one considered the amount of wine she has taken in this night. There was a moment when she nearly tumbled but she managed to recover her balance and continue.

Doc translated the words of the singers as best he could for Rhoda's benefit. He explained that the song was a mournful story of students in love under unbearable academic pressures exerted by hard-ass professors. After the fado piece finished, Felice helped his wife down from the table and all could see tears in her dark eyes but no one cared to mention it. The party wound down quickly at this point and Doc guided Felice and Modesta to the guest bedroom at about 11 p.m. Doc and Rhoda followed suit soon thereafter leaving Sergeant Nestor to spend the night in his lawn chair.

Nestor had cashed his chips in around 9:30 and missed the dramatic fado scene. When he awakened at daylight, he was blessed with an extremely dry mouth and a well-deserved headache. After a failed attempt, he managed to pry his eyes open only to find himself staring into the unblinking amber irises and baleful rectangular pupils of General Longstreet.

CHAPTER 10

Washing Dirt

Doc Martin was reading the morning edition of the Llano News-Deer Capitol of Texas and drinking coffee on the front porch when the telephone rang. He didn't get many calls at 6:30 a.m. "Hello."

"Hello Doc, Monty Simmons here. I just boarded a plane for Tokyo via Dallas and I am planning to overnight with you. Is that ok?"

"Yeah sure, when should I expect you?"

"I get into Dallas at 8:50 a.m., your time, and will rent a car and meet you at the Parrot around 5:00 p.m. I have some questions about dealing with the refineries. By the way, I have made contact with the National Police there and have arranged to travel with an English-speaking cop. Better yet, this cop has a brother who is a metallurgist for the Japan mint branch in Osaka."

"Perfect, Monty. See you this afternoon."

"Right, tell Nestor to go easy on the red pepper for the eastern dude tonight."

Doc finished reading his paper and had more coffee but his

mind was on the platinum problem. The bad guys must have gotten their hands on an illegal supply of platinum placer concentrate somehow and could not import it to Japan in the usual way. But what would make it illegal? If it were stolen from an active mine site directly it would be news and every one would know about it. It would be like stealing a Van Gogh, you could never sell it. It would be worth a shit-pot of money on today's market, something in excess of $1500 US per troy ounce of refined metal. But a placer concentrate was not money in the sense you could spend it. It could only become money if you sold it to a refinery or mint and that requires a legal source with a full paper trail back to the point of origin. Even if you paid refinery fees and took delivery of the bullion, you would still need that paper trail. Any lies about the source would be quickly discovered by the metallurgists as soon as they made a test assay and the scheme would unravel quickly. So, why would the beheaded guy be smuggling a small amount of placer concentrate into Japan rather than just selling it on the black market outside of Japan and avoiding the risk of Japanese customs?

It had to mean that a large amount of illegal concentrate destined for Japan was stock piled out there, somewhere. That somewhere had to be in another country. But what would the 4.5 kilograms of ore be worth? Doc got out his calculator and began pushing buttons. If the platinum comprised 82% of the sample by weight that would make 3690 grams of platinum and at 31.1 grams per troy ounce this would equate to 118.6 troy ounces of platinum metal. Then, say at $1500 per ounce of platinum, the 4.5 kilo bag would be worth $177,960. Not a trivial amount of money but definitely not enough to be worth losing your head over; evidently, the sailor on the slab in Tokyo did not see it that way. But it did not make sense to Doc Martin, since the sailor would still have the problem of getting the ore refined into pure platinum before it was worth any amount of actual money.

Neither the seller, nor buyer, can set a price on placer ore without a mutually acceptable, reliable assay to determine weight percentages each of the six platinum group elements which all sold at different market prices and that fluctuated daily. A lot has to happen before placer concentrate turns into actual money. It was not at all like rural oafs cooking up dope in a sleazy motel room; refining platinum ore takes real professionals, modern labs with high temperature electrical furnaces and a bunch of fancy equipment. Kitchen chemistry it was not. To get an illegal ore refined, the bad guys would need an inside guy, a metallurgist fairly high in the pecking order at one of the commercial refineries, or maybe even one of the national mint labs. A sailor, dumb enough to get his head cut off for 180 K, probably would not be on this team.

Doc Martin could not ponder the question too long. He had a lecture and lab to plan. Today it was silver mineralogy and he began sifting through his collection for good examples of silver minerals. His personal favorite was a beautiful specimen of proustite and native silver from Fresnillo, central Mexico.

Proustite was often called "ruby silver" because bright sunlight diffracted through the crystals as intense ruby-red beams.

Special agent Simmons walked into the Grey Parrot Bar and Grill in Llano, Texas at precisely 4:30 p.m. This time he was wearing cowboy boots, blue jeans, a short sleeved western shirt and a straw cowboy hat all purchased at DFW airport that morning. In spite of this disguise, Rhoda recognized him immediately. "Beer cowboy?" she quipped with a broad smile and full X-ray treatment.

"Yes, please ma'am. How's business, Rhoda?"

"I can't complain. You're early if you are looking for Doc."

"Yes, I know but I'd rather be here drinking beer with you than sitting on my butt at the Dallas airport. I'm on my way to Japan and stopped by to talk with Doc before I go on."

"Sounds like you two might be cooking up something. Is it a mystery, are there dead bodies?" she asked, her eyes widening with interest.

"No, it's nothing as interesting as that" Monty replied. Special agent Simmons found it difficult to tell even a small, innocent lie under the heat of those penetrating X-ray beams. Fortunately, Doc Martin walked in at that moment.

"Hi guys, what's happening in the Treasury Department, are we going back to the gold standard?" he asked. Evidently the lecture on silver minerals had gone well and Doc was in an excellent mood.

"All is well with your government, but they want you to pay a 10 percent surcharge on your income tax" Monty joked.

"Sure, no worries mate, as soon as I get my refund. Hi Rhoda, is this federal agent hitting on you?"

"Not yet, but I believe he was working up to it. Glass of wine, Doc?"

"Oh yeah, definitely." Doc walked over to the kitchen entrance and shouted his usual greeting to Nestor over the din of fans and banging pots. "What do you have for us, Master Sergeant Gallegos?"

Nestor smiled broadly, gave his standard reply in French and added pithily "I have Catfish Laffite and fried okra for the paying customers, sautéed cat shit and ketchup for you." Evidently, all was well at the Grey Parrot.

Doc and Monty had a pleasant dinner and then drove out to the ranch in their separate vehicles. Longstreet had recovered his health by this point and put on a good display for agent Simmons who seemed to be easily intimidated by farm animals. Monty grabbed his overnight bag, and with Doc between him and the goat, quickly walked to the door of the ranch house. Once inside, Doc grabbed two bottles of Portuguese red wine from the *Dão* region, two glasses and led the way to the lab. They sat, as before, on opposite sides of the table with the microscopes. Doc opened the first bottle, filled the glasses and waited for Monty to speak.

"Well Doc, here is what has happened since our last talk. I am in communication with Inspector Hisashi Kuno, Bureau of Criminal Investigations in the National Police Agency. He will meet me at Narita Airport in Tokyo and has obtained the sample found with the gentleman who lost his head. He tells me the sample is about 5 kilograms and that he has the decapitated body in question in a police morgue. I can examine it, if I want. As I told you on the phone, Kuno has a brother who is a senior metallurgist at the Japanese mint branch in Osaka. Kuno told his brother that we are looking for odd occurrences or assays of platinum samples passing through the mint labs. By the way, the National Mint has branch labs in Tokyo and Hiroshima in addition to Osaka. The brother has already found one really weird thing."

Agent Simmons paused then took a sip of wine, waiting to see the effect his statement had on Doc Martin but could read nothing on Doc's impassive professional face. He continued "So, the brother finds that someone recently dropped off a small sample of what turns out to be platinum ore for analysis at the Tokyo mint. The mint does gratis analyses on small samples as a public service, you know. Well in this case, no one ever called on the mint to get the results of the test which is a little weird in itself, but not really the weirdest thing." Simmons paused again and looked intently at Doc.

"Ok you have my attention Monty, what is the really weird thing?"

"The guys in the mint lab were mystified as to the origin of the sample. None of them had seen that particular platinum signature. They had to go back into the mint archives all the way to WWII to find anything comparable. They decided that the sample came from the Chocó Province in west-central Colombia, South America and they tell us that this type of ore has not been seen in Japan since the war years. What do you think about that, Dr. Martin?"

There was another long pause in the conversation before Doc said "That really is interesting Monty. Did you know that the element platinum was first discovered in Chocó around 1557 and that the word platinum comes from the Spanish word *platina*?

"I know Colombia is famous for other things these days but this helps with some of the questions that have been bouncing around in my head. I suppose everyone knows that since Russia, South Africa, Canada, and the US were all on the same side during the war, Germany and Japan had their asses in a sling to get platinum. Germany was able to get a little out of Finland but not nearly enough to meet their needs.

"Both Axis countries were forced to buy it through Colombian fascist agents who could deal with the miners and get it smuggled out of Colombia. Most of the platinum probably went to Argentina, then to Franco's Spain by ship and finally to Germany. In the Chocó district, you had 20,000 to maybe 40,000 native miners working independently by old time hand methods to wash out very rich platinum placers. It was inefficient, but that number of men can produce a hell of a lot of concentrate and during the war years there was virtually no government oversight or paper work on production. I read somewhere that Chocó production was estimated to be in the neighborhood of something like 50,000 troy ounces per year during the war. That's equivalent to about 1,555 kilograms a year, Monty."

"I don't understand why platinum was so vital, Doc" replied the Treasury agent. "Doesn't it just go into jewelry and dental crowns?"

"No Monty, the Axis powers needed it to make contact ignition points and spark plugs for high performance aircraft engines, is that vital enough for you? To some extent they substituted tungsten for platinum in car, truck and tank ignitions but tungsten corrodes faster than platinum at high temperature and that is not so good in airplanes. There were other important uses as well, thermocouples, high temperature furnaces and crucibles, and catalysts used in petroleum and chemical industries. It is a textbook case of a rare mineral controlling the destinies of millions of people who have never even heard of the mineral."

"Doc, I have been reading a book on placer mining and I have some questions that you can help me with. Can you tell me what 'washing dirt' means? It sounds simple enough, if you have dirt, you wash it off, but I think it may have another meaning. Does it?"

Doc had to laugh in Monty's face at this, but when he got himself under control, he said "Sorry Monty, I know you are a fish out of water with the business of mining but that was really very funny. 'To wash dirt' is what placer mining is all about. The 'dirt' is the input, or feed, containing all the material, rocks, sand, clay and ore as it comes from mine site. 'Washing' refers to using water to separate out the valuable minerals like gold or platinum."

Doc was still having a problem trying to keep from laughing at the look on the Treasury agents face.

"I don't see what is so damn funny, Dr. Asshole".

"Ok, I am sorry. To understand washing you first have to understand the physical property of density which is mass per unit volume. Almost nobody gets it from that definition so I usually use the analogy of two bricks of equal size. One brick is an ordinary construction brick which has a density of 1.92 grams per cubic centimeter; the second brick is identical in every way except it is made of pure lead which has a fixed density of 11.34 grams per cubic centimeter. Which brick is going to have the highest mass? Or to put it more simply, which will be the heaviest?"

"The lead brick of course" answered Monty without hesitation.

"Yes, that's right G-man, but why is lead heavier than an equal volume of clay brick?"

"I don't know why, but I know that it is" replied Marty growing a little peevish at Doc's instructional tone.

"It is because the mass of the lead atom is far greater and the atoms are more closely packed than is the case for the atoms comprising the ordinary brick. That means there is a lot more mass crammed into the lead brick than the ordinary brick. This is one way of saying the density of the lead brick is 5.92 times greater than the density of the clay brick" explained the geologist still trying, valiantly, to keep a smile off his face.

"So, what does this have to do with washing dirt?" Monty replied now trying hard to understand Doc's point.

"Look, when sediment on a flat surface is washed by a gentle stream of water the minerals of lowest density are mobilized first and minerals with higher density remain in position. By increasing the flow rate, minerals of higher and higher density are mobilized. That is washing. A common mineral like quartz has a density of 2.65 grams per cubic centimeter; it is a light mineral and easily washed out of the sediment; a mineral like platinum, on the other hand, with a density range of 14-19 grams per cubic centimeter is considered a very heavy mineral. So, placer mining for platinum is all about adjusting the water flow to remove everything with a density less than something like 13 grams per cubic centimeter which then leaves you with a nearly pure platinum or platinum-gold concentrate. That is what 'washing dirt' means. Get it?"

"I think I do get it, now. It seems so simple when you explain it and so complicated when I read it in a text book" said Marty.

"Well, it is simple enough from the theoretical viewpoint, but to actually do it is another thing. Guys who wash dirt on dredges for a living are called 'table-masters' because they perform magic on their riffle tables. They are not college boys I can assure you Monty. It takes years operating a particular table for them to perfect their technique and get really good concentrations of gold and platinum. It's not something I could do, or any other geologist for that matter." Doc stopped the conversation to open the second bottle of wine while agent Simmons reconsidered the subject of 'washing dirt'.

When Martin had a full glass in front of each of them, Monty asked "Why do you say that lead has a fixed density and platinum has a density variation?"

"That, agent Simmons, is the best question you have asked me yet. The answer is that lead has a fixed composition, it is nothing but lead; every atom in it is exactly identical to all others and this produces constant density. Platinum on the other hand almost always contains variable amounts of iron plus minor substitutions by other PGE's for platinum and this produces variations in density. That's why it is called an 'alloy' or ferro platinum. Since iron has a lower atomic weight than platinum, high iron content in the alloy reduces its density in proportion to the iron present. If we look at absolutely pure platinum, we have a density of 21.46 grams per cubic centimeter but platinum this pure is virtually nonexistent in nature. So, you have to understand that density is a function of both composition and atomic packing in a crystalline substance."

With this both men drained their glasses and looked across the table at each other for a few moments. Each man was thinking he was beginning to trust the other. They were beginning to appreciate how very different were their special fields of knowledge and expertise.

After this pause, Simmons resumed the dialog with "I made some calls down to Bogotá on the federal dime. I started with *Banco Nacional de La Republica* and eventually got in touch with their precious metals expert. He told me that bank records for the war period are very poor but that they estimate that at least 30 percent of the total platinum output was siphoned off by smuggling operations and that all such ores were, and still are, the property of the Colombian government. He was quite adamant about that. I also discovered that we, meaning the US government, were all over Colombia during the war years. The FBI, the OSS, and something I had never heard of, the BEW, the Bureau of Economic Warfare, were active down there and very busy as a matter of fact. I checked out the records for this BEW group. They were platinum cops essentially and their records are so heavily redacted I have to suspect J. Edgar Hoover himself had his fingers in the Colombian pie."

Martin filled the glasses. Clearly, he was thinking about the implications of this conversation. Finally, he said "What are you going to do when you get to Japan Monty?"

"Well, the first thing is to see if any progress has been made towards identifying our headless guy and then I am going to try to get that five-kilogram sample, or at least as much of it as I can, to bring back to you. Kuno and I are going to visit the lab that analyzed the Chocó material and see if we can get a lead on the person who brought it in. After that, we are going to visit all of the commercial labs that do platinum refining. I already have a list from the brother. There are not many, but they are scattered all over Japan. I guess I will ask them if they have seen any material from Chocó, Colombia in the post-war era."

Doc considered this statement for a few moments and said "That sounds very good, Monty. Since you have a metallurgist at your service, tell him to make a split of the five-kilogram sample for analysis here in the states. He will know how to divide the sample and package it for transport. Ask him to make an analysis of the other half of the sample in his lab and send a copy of the results to me so I can compare the two. I will also need a copy of the Chocó analysis performed by the Tokyo mint. I think that will do it, Monty, at least for now. You have done some good work here."

Monty beamed. He was proud of himself. There were a lot of chemistry and mining terms that he did not fully understand involved in this investigation but there also was smuggling, murder, and deception and these things he did understand. "Have I got everything straight, Doc?"

"It occurs to me that you might be better off not mentioning the Chocó thing. I'm thinking the bad guys must have corrupted someone at one these metallurgical labs to get their ore processed into bullion. Mentioning Chocó might tip your hand. I suggest you ask about unusual samples, samples from supposedly new deposits, or samples from inactive mines claimed to have been in storage for years; examine the paper work for fraudulent claims regarding source and shipping history. What do you think?"

Agent Simmons considered the question while he sipped his wine. "Yeah Doc, I think you are right about this. You have the makings of a good cop." Both men chuckled over this delayed riposte and finished off the second bottle.

CHAPTER 11

The Chuuk Free Dentistry Clinic

1979 was an important year in the history of Fugimora Enterprises. This was the beginning of self-government for the Truk Islands. The islands were now an independent member of the Federated States of Micronesia and no longer directly under the watchful eye and authority of the United States.

Aoki Fugimora was then 59 years old, a very successful business man and less of a dentist than in his younger days. His one-man dental practice had grown to a ten- man operation now known as Fugimora Dental Associates. The dental school, Fugimora College of Dentistry, was similarly successful and had achieved a level of prestige that rivaled, in a small way, that of his alma mater, Nippon Dental University. These enterprises had made him wealthy, wealthy enough to buy an ore hauling ship that he re-named after himself. This ship was a full-hull, single-screw, rear-house bulker with four cargo holds and loading booms for each. When it was not busy hauling his ores, it could transport unpackaged cargos such as cement, grain, coal, and salt for others. It would be the center-piece of a new business to be called Fugimora Maritime Transport Limited. His pride and joy, however, had always been the dental laboratory that had grown from one small, used, jewelry furnace into a modest, but very capable precious metal refinery, Fugimora Precious Metals Limited.

Each of these spokes in the Fugimora wheel of fortune functioned as a self-sustaining legitimate business. In aggregate, however, they were purposefully designed to achieve a single clandestine goal… to import 450 kilograms of platinum ore cached in a World War II bunker on Truk Atoll. Dr. Aoki Fugimora smiled to himself as he contemplated completion of the final step in bringing his obsession to reality. True, 34 years had elapsed since this plan was conceived, but there was consolation in the fact that the market price of platinum had increased at least 50- fold during this period. It was better than money in the bank from his perspective.

Fugimora Enterprises was now ready to establish a free dental clinic on the island of Chuuk, the newly chosen name for Truk Atoll. Dr. Fugimora had sent two new graduates from his college to Chuuk with all the necessary equipment to set up the clinic. He gave them a month to get the clinic operational and then sent two very pretty dental nurses to help his dentists through the trials of their two-year commitment at the clinic. It amused him to think of these educated ladies as comfort women with hypodermic needles.

After independence from the US became official, he donated in the name of Fugimora Enterprises, the yen equivalent of one half million dollars US to the Chamber of Social Equality of the state of Chuuk. He knew that most of this money would be gobbled up by the new governor of the state but this was part of the plan because he wanted a very special favor from this new governor. He wanted his clinic to be located, in due course, on the site of the old Imperial Navy dental facility.

Aoki Fugimora had been far too busy with his business interests to marry and raise a family. Nevertheless, he had a son, Ryota who was born in this banner year of 1979 and was destined to inherit the entire Fugimora Empire. This son was illegitimate, an intentional consequence in this particular case. The mother was a Kyoto *geisha* of the highest caste, the *gion kōbu* who traced their traditions from the 19th century *oisans*.

Fumiko Hatori was always addressed, even by Dr. Fugimora, as Lady Fumiko, a name meaning child of treasured beauty in English. She was a socially adroit woman of exceptional beauty, wisdom and poise who played important roles in many of Fugimora's business dealings.

Lady Fumiko consented to have Fugimora's child and raised the boy to the age of five when he was taken by his father to be educated. For the next nine years, Ryota lived with his father and received English language lessons and instruction in traditional Japanese subjects from private tutors. He was a willing and disciplined student but he yearned for adventure. When adventure finally arrived at age 14, it came in the form of attending a martial arts academy in Okinawa for four years to learn karate, judo, kobudo, kick-boxing and the use of Japanese weapons including the Katana, the long curved feudal sword.

After Okinawa, it was a shooting academy in Northern Ireland for a year where he became proficient with a variety of hand guns, shot guns and rifles and where he managed to acquire an Irish accent and seduce a lass of sixteen years in Belfast.

Ryota returned to his native country at the age of 19, his training nearly complete. It only remained to take a year-long course in business management, at which point, his father placed him in a management traineeship in his shipping company, Fugimora Maritime Transport.

The Chuuk Free Dentistry Clinic had long ago moved into the old Imperial Navy dental facility where all dental services were offered without cost to Chuuk Islanders. The structure, still completely underground in coral bedrock, had been extensively renovated and equipped with modern X-ray facilities, plumbing, electrical systems and air conditioning. A new façade, surrounded by a professionally designed Japanese garden, proclaimed the structure to be The Fugimora Dental Building. Six dentists and six assistants, all new graduates of the Fugimora College of Dentistry in Tokyo, now worked full time on the teeth of Chuuk Islanders. The "comfort women with hypodermics" were still chosen personally by Dr. Fugimora for each two-year rotation.

The renovation plans for the clinic were drawn by Fugimora himself and specified that the old dental lab was to be walled off and a new lab was to be constructed in a central position within the former imperial facility. The costs of renovation, operation, and the salaries of the dentists, their pretty assistants, and local workers were completely borne by Fugimora Enterprises. This altruism propelled the name Fugimora to almost royal status among the common people and politicians of the Chuuk state from the governor on down.

On the occasion of his 79th birthday, Dr. Aoki Fugimora decided to throw himself a gala. Senior executives, dentists, and scientists of his various companies and their wives attended as did a number of parliament members. The governor and a handful of subordinates were flown in from the Chuuk Islands for the occasion on the dental magnate's private jet. Of course, Lady Fumiko came from Kyoto for the grand event and played the role of hostess.

Lady Fumiko was attired in an exquisite hand-stitched white silk kimono of the *furisode* style. This gown was adorned in a hand painted black floral motif with five crests or *kamons*. It drew admiring glances from all present and some ladies estimated its cost in excess of $20,000 US. Their calculations were low. Her son Ryota, now 20 years old, was to be installed as president of Fugimora Maritime Transport. It was a proud moment for Lady Fumiko.

In truth, old Dr. Fugimora was not much of a party man or public speaker and he knew it. But on the arm of Lady Fumiko, the hosting couple flitted from one guest to another chatting, charming and complimenting each as if this were their life's work.

Actually, Lady Fumiko had simply memorized the guest list and few accomplishments of each of the male guests but her personal beauty coupled with her exquisite *geisha* manners and grace charmed the sox off of everyone in attendance.

At about the midpoint in the party, Lady Fumiko, by request of course, sang a geisha song accompanied by the traditional Japanese flute and zither. When the heartfelt, ovation concluded she introduced Dr. Fugimora who liked public speaking considerably less than he liked parties. The dentist rather brusquely announced his decision to appoint his son, Ryota Fugimora, to be president of Fugimora Maritime Transport. Mandated applause followed, even by those who were disgusted by this undisguised nepotism so common in Japanese business.

When Ryota took the podium, he demonstrated that he was not only a handsome, poised young man but, also, a far better speaker than his father. He thanked his father and mother, begged indulgence of his employees-to-be, and offered a prayer that his father would have many more birthdays. Naturally, this sparked well-concealed snickers from the more cynical members of the audience. A number of *pro forma* toasts were then offered by various guests and then the party resumed it former, less formal atmosphere.

The dentist asked Lady Fumiko and his son to join him in the library adjoining the ballroom where the festivities were becoming more boisterous. When Ryota arrived, his parents were seated on an ornate futon. His first thought was that this was the first time he had ever seen them seated together. His mother handed him a rather heavy oblong package wrapped western style in flowered paper with a crinkly bow. Ryota bowed solemnly to his mother and asked mischievously "What could be the occasion for a gift for your unworthy son?"

Lady Fumiko smiled and said "A present is in order because today you assume the role of a man in the world of business. This is a world fraught with danger and I know that your father will soon send you on a dangerous quest. Perhaps this gift will prove useful. The man I bought it from swore that it has a long history of good luck."

Ryota removed the wrapping and opened the box revealing a wavy damascene blade of a 200-year-old Javanese Kris; the glistening 38-centimeter blade exhibited seven waveforms of declining amplitude and terminated at a point of exquisite sharpness. It was in perfect condition; its ivory handle and sheath were inlayed with intricate patterns of gold filigree. This dagger was a work of amazing artisanship and historical significance and Ryota was speechless. He loved his parents, despite the distance at which they had always held him, and the many unusual aspects of his childhood. He knelt at his mother's feet and told her he loved her to her face for the very first time. Geishas do not cry, of course, but the eyes of Lady Fumiko were certainly glistening.

When he had recovered somewhat from his emotion, Ryota asked "Mother, I know that these old Javanese daggers are said to possess magical powers, can you tell me if any such legends are associated with this piece?"

"Yes, my son, there is such a story. I was told that more than one hundred years ago, this dagger saved its masters life when he was attacked by a wounded tiger during a hunt in Malaya. Without human assistance, this knife is said to have disengaged itself from the sheath and repeatedly stabbed the tiger in the heart until it fell dead. The master of the knife was badly mauled but his life was saved. It is a silly story of course, but it pleases me to think that this Kris might protect you in a moment of danger" said Lady Fumiko with a heart-felt motherly smile.

Dr. Fugimora was proud of the young man but uncomfortable with the intense emotional level of this scene. He cleared his throat nervously and spoke "I must tell you about the mission I wish you to undertake." Ryota rose to his feet and dabbed his eyes with his handkerchief.

"Yes, father I am ready to go anywhere and do anything within my power to please you and mother."

"Very well, my son. I wish you to take our ship *Aoki Maru* to Alaska and buy some platinum for our refinery. On your return to Japan you are to stop at Chuuk Island and retrieve some items stored in our dental clinic there. As you know Ryota, your mother and I are both already quite wealthy. This voyage will be one that will make you wealthy in your own right, wealthy beyond your most extravagant dreams."

CHAPTER 12

Inspector Kuno

Special agent Monty Simmons returned his rental car and got some breakfast at the Dallas-Ft. Worth airport. He checked his bags with American Airlines at 10:30 a.m. for flight Am 61 departing Dallas at 12:40 p.m. and arriving in Tokyo at 4:10 p.m. local time the following day. The flight would consume 20 hours and 40 minutes, a brutal experience even for first class passengers. His boss would not have approved a first- class ticket so Monty did not bother asking permission for the purchase. He would try to bury this necessary extravagance in his monthly expense report which would be a whopper. Reading up on Japanese etiquette and platinum metallurgy ought to keep him busy during the long flight but the 14-hour time difference meant serious jet lag, a problem he could not afford; he had pills to help him sleep during the long flight.

Inspector Hisashi Kuno glanced at his watch and then up at the large arrival board which told him that flight Am 61 had just set down 20 minutes early. He awaited the American treasury agent at the point where deplaning foreign passengers show their passports before undergoing customs inspection of their bags. He paced nervously, rolling and unrolling the placard on which he had printed 'Mr. Monty Simmons'. After fifty or so passengers had lined up to show their passports he spotted a man whom his police instincts told him was a brother lawman. He held up his sign and the other man gave him the international thumbs up signal. The two men approached each other with Kuno offering his hand and Simmons performing the traditional Japanese bow. Both men had to laugh. Kuno spoke first saying "Good afternoon Special Agent Simmons. I am Inspector Kuno and I hope your long trip was not too wearisome. I can take you to police guest house if you require sleep."

"Thank you very much inspector, that is very kind, but I am feeling rested and am anxious to begin our work."

"Very well then, if you will give me your passport I will speed up the rather tedious process of entering our country. By the way, are you carrying a weapon or have you one in your luggage?"

"Neither inspector, if there is to be any shooting, you will have to protect me."

Kuno nodded, smiling at this, and took the passport. He proceeded to the window of the closest customs booth, flashed his badge and handed the agent Monty's passport which was immediately given the arrival stamp and returned. They then went to the international baggage claim where Monty picked up his two bags. Kuno again showed his badge and Monty's passport at the final customs booth where it was run through an electronic scanner. Since no one asked him any questions, or examined his bags, Monty concluded that Kuno's badge carried a lot of weight.

Inspector Kuno was of usual height for a Japanese man, about 5 feet six inches, dark eyes, 150 pounds at most, and clean shaven. He did not wear coke-bottle glasses and his teeth were straight. There was no sign of grey in his hair. Monty estimated his age as early forties and he appeared to be in excellent physical condition.

The two policemen walked to Kuno's black Toyota sedan parked in a special space outside the main entrance of the terminal reserved for police. There was confusion created by Simmons getting in the driver's side of the car. Kuno laughed outright and asked, "You wish to drive in downtown Tokyo traffic, Special Agent Simmons?"

"Certainly not, inspector, I forgot that you drive on the left in Japan."

"You must be careful during your first day as a pedestrian here in Japan. We lose a few newly-arrived Americans every year because they look the wrong direction for on-coming traffic. Now, what is your priority for the rest of today?" As he spoke Kuno pulled the car onto the Higashi Kanto Expressway and they headed west at high speed toward Tokyo, leaving Narita International behind.

"I would like you to give me an update on the headless Caucasian man and to take a brief look at his body in your police morgue."

"Yes certainly. We still have no identification but I have received a DNA profile and run it through Japanese national data base without result. I suggest you send it to your people in US to run against your own data base. The data is on a disk and, if you send it electronically tonight, I think we can have results by tomorrow."

"Excellent idea inspector, now give me the details on when and where this body was found."

"Yes, of course, Agent Simmons. The body was reported two weeks ago, near the US Naval base in Yokosuka city. Yokosuka lies at end of a peninsula about 50 kilometers south of Tokyo at the narrow entrance to Tokyo Bay. It was major naval base for the Imperial Navy during the war and also big shipyard, anchorage, and arsenal as well as site for many special naval schools. Of course, it was occupied in 1945 and has been important forward base since then for your navy, especially during the Korean and Viet Nam conflicts."

"And this man had in his possession 5 kilograms of platinum black sand?" Monty queried.

"Not exactly, Agent Simmons. A 4.5-kilogram bag of what we call 'black sand' was found in trash receptacle not far from body. We think the dead man hide it there before he was killed by man with sword. We also think dead man was sailor in US Navy during Viet Nam era from his tattoos and age."

This prompted Monty to ask, "Are there are many ex-patriot US sailors living in Yokosuka?"

"Yes many, perhaps several thousand. Many have been in Japan since the late 1960's. They mostly run small bars or get jobs on merchant ships. Some are thieves, some are panhandlers and some are violent criminals. Perhaps some are honest, but not too many. They live in a law enforcement crack between US naval authorities and Yokosuka police. If we get name and picture of dead man, we can interrogate these ex-patriots and maybe find link to platinum."

"How is it they can stay in Japan without US passports and working visas inspector?"

"It is relatively simple and perfectly legal. They can get international seaman passports issued in Hong Kong or Macao. These are valid for three years and can be renewed without limit as long as they claim one merchant voyage in that span of time. It is easy to fake voyage certifications. Another way is to marry Japanese girl which gets them permanent work-type visa. Many do this."

At this point in the conversation they had been driving in downtown Tokyo for 20 minutes and Kuno pulled the car into the police morgue parking lot. "Let us see our headless sailor man, Agent Simmons."

The dead guy was certainly 60-ish in age and obviously Caucasian judging by size, body hair, skin tone and tattoos favored by American sailors and marines in the 1960's. His size in the present state was, of course, somewhat abbreviated. Simmons d one tattoo on the man's forearm that read 'Born to Lose' above a pair of dice showing 'snake eyes'. Another tattoo showed a rooster with a rope around his neck placed on the inside of the left leg below the knee. Monty wondered if Kuno understood the meaning of this crude and, in this case, quite misplaced humor. He hoped not. But there was no missing the laser precision of the cuts that removed the head and hands.

After his examination of the body Simmons said "Thank you, inspector, I agree totally with your assessment of the corpse. It is nearly 7 p.m. now and I don't think there is much more we can get done tonight. Why don't you take me to my apartment for the night and help me order some dinner? I'll get the DNA profile running through our federal data banks and maybe we will have a hit by morning."

"Of course, special agent, I have made arrangements to visit the mint branch here in Tokyo where the odd sample was submitted. My brother has already arrived from Osaka and is at my house. You will meet him tomorrow and we will proceed to investigate as policemen and metallurgists."

Simmons smiled appreciatively at the inspector's attempt at a little joke. He understood it was not easy to express humor in a foreign language and he was beginning to like Hisashi Kuno very much. "Yes, inspector we will make a two-pronged attack on the bad guys."

The next morning Simmons was up early. The room in the police apartment was furnished with instant coffee, tea bags and an electric pot to heat water and he was drinking his third cup of instant when his lap top signaled in-coming email. It was his office notifying him of a positive ID on the DNA profile submitted the night before. The headless corpse belonged to one Donald Richard Atkins, born in Peoria, Illinois September 1, 1946. He served in the US Navy from 1965 to 1968 and was dishonorably discharged for desertion in Yokosuka, Japan in November of 1968. At that moment, Simmons was interrupted by a knock on his door.

Inspector Kuno introduced his brother Dr. Katsu Kuno, senior metallurgist of the Osaka branch of the Japanese National Mint, to Special Agent Simmons. The brother was almost a carbon copy of inspector Kuno but a few years younger and he wore bifocals. His English was perfect; the accent was American and included fairly current slang. Simmons complimented the metallurgist on his language skills "Your English is better than mine, Dr. Kuno."

"Thank you, Agent Simmons, it's because I lived in the states for six years while I was getting my Ph.D. at Colorado School of Mines. I've been back here in Japan for five years now and I feel like my English skills are going to hell. Not enough practice and my brother will only speak Japanese with me."

Monty nodded appreciatively and then said "Inspector Kuno, I have good news. We have identified the headless man as a navy deserter by the name of Donald Richard Atkins, born 1946, formerly six feet two inches tall, 180 pounds, blue eyes, and blonde hair. He has probably been in Yokosuka since his discharge in 1968. At least we have no record of his re-entering the US. Do you think you can track down his residence and associates?"

"All I needed was a name, Agent Simmons. Will you write it for me? I will inform Inspector Komatsu of the Yokosuka police who investigated the original crime scene. Komatsu will have no difficulty in tracing our sailor. More than likely, this man has had contact with Yokosuka police and they will be able to provide recent photograph and finger prints." Kuno took out his mobile phone, pushed a few buttons and spoke authoritatively in Japanese to a person on the other end. All Monty understood were the words 'American', 'Atkins, Donald, Richard', and 'A-T-K-I-N-S'. "I think we shall know all about Mr. Atkins by the end of the day."

Monty offered his guests cups of instant coffee which they declined in favor of tea bags sitting on the counter of what was positively the smallest kitchenette on earth. Dr. Kuno did the honors and the three men sat down and began discussing their plan for the day. The Tokyo mint was expecting them at 10:00 a.m. and a request had been made to interview the person who received the sample and the metallurgist who performed the analysis and identified the source of the material as Chocó, Columbia.

As they sipped their tea, Dr. Kuno told them "I have personally analyzed material from the 4.5-kilogram sample associated with your dead man. The grains were coated with carbon in an effort to disguise their nature and my analysis definitely matches up very well with the unrefined Colombian platinum that was imported into Japan during the war years."

"That would suggest the sample analyzed by the Tokyo mint

branch was part of the material found in Yokosuka and that a connection exists between the person who delivered it and our unfortunate Mr. Donald Atkins" observed the inspector.

"Indeed, it does" said Monty, increasingly pleased with the progress being made. "Dr. Kuno, can you send your analytical report, in English of course, and about half of the large sample to my consultant in the US for confirmation of your results?"

"Sure, who is your consultant?"

"His name is Dr. P. Martin of Llano, Texas. He said you would know how to split the sample in a scientific way."

"Martin, wow, yeah I know of him. I have read his articles on geology and chemistry of platinum deposits. In fact, he published a paper in the Mineralogical Journal of Japan a few years back, so people in my lab are big fans of Dr. Martin. Being a metallurgist I think of myself as half chemist and half mineralogist. I will get the stuff shipped to him first thing tomorrow morning. That's ok isn't it big brother?"

"Yes, as long as you furnish me with a copy of your report and the remaining sample for evidence" replied the inspector drily. The inspector looked at his watch and rose. "It is time now to leave for the mint interviews."

The director of the mint branch met inspector Kuno's party at the front door. Introductions and formal bows were exchanged all around and then the director guided the group to a private office where the interviews were to take place. The first to be interviewed by inspector Kuno was a 20-year-old intern named

Chika Oshiro. She looked terrified. Kuno asked the nervous intern "Please describe your duties here at the mint, Miss Oshiro."

Her voice broke on the first attempt but on the second try she managed to get out "At mint I receive and log in samples submitted to analytical division. I fill out requisition form with information about customer and source of the sample. Then I assign our laboratory number to sample and place sample in a special container. Sample then picked up by one of analytical metallurgists for analysis."

"Very well Miss Oshiro, do you have the form dealing with the platinum sample NMJ-122-K that was submitted about two weeks ago?"

"Yes inspector, this is requisition form for sample."

Kuno studied the form for about a minute and then said to the young girl "It appears that the sample is from Okinawa and was submitted by a Miss Suzie Wong. Are you aware, Miss Oshiro, that the name Suzie Wong is not Japanese? It is a Chinese name from an old Hollywood movie starring William Holden and Nancy Kwan and the address given here, 'number 10 Downing Street, London', is obviously false as well. Also, did you know there are no platinum mines on Okinawa?"

"N-no inspector, I am so sorry, so sorry. I just fill form with the information lady give me. I do not question honesty of customers" sputtered the frightened girl.

"Very well, Miss Oshiro, calm yourself, you are in no trouble here. Please tell me what you recall about this woman. Was she

Japanese? Did she have an odd accent? Did she have any distinguishing physical features?"

"She was Japanese, perhaps 40 years, native speaker but grammar not so good. Not educated, I think, maybe from rural area originally. She was pretty with long hair put up in traditional way. This lady give me sample in handkerchief. She not dressed appropriately for downtown business."

"What do you mean about her dress?" asked the inspector sharply.

Miss Oshiro began tearing up but managed to say "She not in business suit or uniform. Her clothes like those jo-san girls wear and she smell of alcohol and tobacco smoke."

"Are you saying she was dressed in a slutty fashion? Surely she was not dressed in the traditional kimono?"

"Kimono no, she dress like bar girls I see in movies and, sometimes, on street at night."

"Thank you, Miss Oshiro. You have been very helpful, now dry your eyes and sit down" said inspector Kuno with a kindly smile.

Kuno signaled for the next person to be ushered into the interview room. He introduced himself as Dr. Riku Nakamura, metallurgist at the National Mint Branch of Tokyo. The two metallurgists knew each other and exchanged brief formal greetings. Kuno eyed Nakamura for a few moments and then began with "I understand that you are the man who analyzed sample NMJ-122-K, is that correct?"

"Yes, inspector Kuno. I remember the sample quite well because it is extremely odd to get a submission from the public that is not in the form of jewelry. It consisted of 20 rounded grains, about five millimeters in diameter, that were probably hand-picked from a larger sample. With a density of nearly 20 grams per cubic centimeter, magnetic character, and a whitish metallic luster, the material could only be placer platinum; the weird thing was that the grains were carbon coated."

"And what did you make of this carbon coating Dr. Nakamura?"

"I thought the sample must have been smuggled into the country and the carbon was meant to deceive customs."

"So, you analyzed the sample and what did you find?"

"I found that it was platinum-iron alloy with a composition of about 87 % platinum and 7 % iron. The source of the sample could only have been the Chocó district of western Colombia, the first locality in history to mine platinum."

"I suppose there is no possibility of error about the source?"

"No, I analyzed five individual grains under the electron microprobe with identical results for all grains. After I figured out that they were from Colombia, I went into our sample collection which goes back to the late 19th century. I pulled a few grains from a war-time Chocó sample and analyzed them by the same methods. It was a perfect match; there is no doubt."

"Thank you very much, Dr. Nakamura. Special Agent Simmons, do you have any questions for Dr. Nakamura?"

"Yes, I do. Dr. Nakamura, outside of samples submitted to the mint by the public, do you know if the mint has processed any ores from the Chocó region since the war years?"

"I checked on this point very carefully, Agent Simmons. No Colombian platinum has been received or assayed at any of the Japanese mint branches or at any of the commercial refineries in Japan in the post-war era. Virtually everything any of us get, these days, is from South Africa or Russia and this usually is in bullion form rather than placer ore; on rare occasions, we get concentrated placers from Alaska or Canada which we refine."

"Thank you, Dr. Nakamura. If you will provide a copy of your analytical work, the remains of the sample, and the handkerchief that contained it, I think our work here is finished" said Inspector Kuno. A brief discussion ensued between Dr. Nakamura and Miss Oshiro who left the room and returned a few minutes later with the sample, handkerchief, and a copy of Nakamura's report. Both policemen were smiling by this point.

"What the hell do you two cops have to smile about? You didn't get much here, did you?" asked Katsu Kuno with a puzzled look.

Inspector Kuno gave a wink to Agent Simmons and replied, "After I make call to Yokosuka police, little brother, I think it will not be long before we speak with Miss Suzie Wong of number 10 Downing Street, London."

CHAPTER 13

Mystic Kris

Ryota Fugimora did not appreciate full scope of his father's plan on May 22nd, when he boarded the *Aoki Maru* for the first time. As the new president of Fugimora Maritime Transport he had sent the captain instructions to prepare the ship for a voyage from Yokosuka, Japan to Goodnews Bay, Alaska to Vancouver, British Columbia to Weno, Federated States of Melanesia and back to Yokosuka. His father had told him that Captain Satoshi Hiraki was a "Fugimora man" who could be trusted in all things, even those that might be considered illegal. From this, and the fact that his father trusted so very few people, Ryota concluded that the captain was, either a close relative he did not know, or was very strongly indebted to his father for some mysterious reason.

The voyage was rough, stormy and unpleasant for Ryota who had never traveled in a ship on the open ocean. He was quite seasick during the first four days but gradually acclimated to shipboard life by the time they entered the Bering Sea. He was feeling quite well when the ship entered Goodnews Bay, or Kuskokwim Bay as natives called it, and tied up at the village of

Platinum, Alaska on the southeastern shore. A car sent by Goodnews Mining Company was waiting to take him to their office to make a very large purchase of platinum ore concentrate. The driver was a geologist who introduced himself as Dr. Reuben Tobey.

The sea and sky were grey, the mountains were grey and the village of Platinum was grey. Ryota saw no sign of life except a dozen or so indolent dogs in Arvig, the native village that was loosely attached to Platinum. A cold grey mist was falling and the total impression was dreadfully depressing here in the land where platinum was scratched out of the dirt.

Sitting across from the chief geologist of Goodnews Mining Company, Ryota asked for a glass of whisky. Tobey smiled and said "I get that reaction every time a customer sits in that chair, so we keep the bar well stocked. We all need whisky to survive here. By the way Mr. Fugimora, how in the world did pickup your Irish accent?"

"I spent a year at a school in Belfast, an interesting and productive year. I think it must be difficult to retain employees under such conditions as you have" observed the president of Fugimora Maritime.

"It is. People are initially attracted by the high salaries but no one stays for long except the native workers living in Arvig. At the moment, we have only one accountant, one engineer, one dredge crew, and one geologist, me. None of us can be relied on to stay. The whole bunch of office people flew into Anchorage yesterday to get drunk. Imagine leaving a geologist in charge of a multi-million-dollar business. If you have a couple of hours, Mr. Fugimora, I can take you out to the dredge and we can pick up another 20 or 30 kilos of concentrate gathered since our last delivery. That is, if you want any more than the 550 kilos. The diggings are on the Salmon River, about 11 miles from here" replied the geologist pouring two large glasses of scotch from a nearby crystal decanter.

"I would very much like to see your mining operations. But first let us finalize our transaction, that is to say, I will give you my signature on a note of credit drawn on the Bank of Japan. We are an old and, I hope, valued customer so I expect my signature will suffice and that the ore will be delivered to my ship."

"Your order is quite large Mr. Fugimora, 550 kilos are a little less than 18,000 troy ounces and that is about half of our yearly production these days. But we have it loaded on a truck and ready to deliver to the dock. I was told to offer you more."

"No thank you, Dr. Tobey. My order is for 550 kilograms, no more but certainly no less. I will go to see your mining operation on the condition that you bring a bottle of your scotch whisky. Please order the lorry delivery. Meanwhile let us have another drink to the Bank of Japan."

Dr. Tobey and Ryota Fugimora bounced and skidded along the rough muddy forest road leading to the dredging operations making frequent stops for whisky. They saw two cavorting black bear cubs at one such stop which pleased the young Fugimora immensely. "Do they eat humans?" asked the wide-eyed Japanese.

"They do sometimes but garbage cans are their preference" offered Tobey. Both men were moderately drunk by the time they reached the company dredge. Ryota was astounded at the gigantic size of the machine with it impressive 70-foot boom extended below the water line and generating a huge rooster-tail of water and red mud above the steel digging buckets. This old, rust-covered dredge reminded one of a monstrous, prehistoric beast, a beast that gobbled sediment with its gigantic, rotating 20-bucket mouth and shit out a stupendous stream of sand, pebbles and boulders by conveyer belt into the water 200 feet to the rear. Tobey explained that the rusty sheet-metal, three-story structure housed a mill, engine and boiler room, machine shop, sluice room, living quarters and galley for the operators and mechanics, as well as offices and quarters for an accountant and a crew of surveyors. The dredge and its equipment sat on a large, low-profile, flat-bottomed wooden barge which allowed the dredge to travel at a glacial pace, eating and shitting, up and down the Salmon River.

Everything on this corrugated colossus operated directly by steam power or by steam-driven electrical generators. The resulting repetitious boom of the piston strokes, augmented by furious screeching and clanking of gears, levers, drums, pulleys, chains and cables operating in disharmonious unison, could only be described as maddening.

Dr. Tobey handed Ryota a pair of battery-operated aircraft head phones equipped with a small microphone and donned one himself as they made their way past a rusty pickup truck used to transport ore concentrate back to the office in Platinum.

The pair made their way up the gang plank a little unsteadily and entered the door of the mill. Tobey's voiced crackled through the ear phones as he explained what was before them. "Platinum was discovered in 1926 on Fox Gulch, a tributary of Platinum Creek which then drains east into the Salmon River just west of where we are now. The discoverer, Walter Smith was a native guy but he didn't make a dime out of his discovery. Goodnews Mining got started here in 1934 and by 1940 they controlled every claim worth having".

Tobey declared a drink break and then resumed his monologue. "This dredge was built here by GNM in 1937. It features 20 digging buckets at the end of the boom and they supply about 7 tons of feed per minute. This feed ranges from boulders to mud and travels into that giant rotating drum you see there. We call it 'the screen' because it is perforated with hundreds of holes, 0.75 inches in diameter. The stuff that is rejected by the screen rides out to the rear on a belt and is dumped behind the rig as tailings. We hope there are no large platinum or gold chunks in those tailings but it has been known to happen. The minus 0.75-inch material drops down through the screen holes into a sluice system below this floor which we will see next. It's all 19th century technology, of course, and works on the same principle as the miner's gold pan but on a massive mechanized scale. We estimate that it does the daily work of a thousand miners in just one hour and that it has produced half a million troy ounces of platinum for us since 1937. The first dredge in this part of the world was introduced in Yukon Territory during the Klondike gold rush in 1899; by 1912 there were 42 of these dirt-eating babies working placer gold in Alaska and the Yukon. This dredge is a relative new-comer. Now, let's have another drink."

After this short pause the men descended a flight of spooky, perforated metal stairs to the "washing room" and Dr. Tobey resumed his role as tour leader. "This sloping table is where all the interesting things happen. The little barriers you see on the table are shaped like the letter L; they are removable riffles and do the work of catching the gold and platinum while the lower-density gangue, or waste material, is washed on over the riffles, down the table and out to join the coarse tailings at the back of the rig. Below the riffles are expanded metal screens and below that a thin layer of so-called 'miners moss' that traps the extremely fine metal grains. Most of the valuable stuff is captured by the first three riffles. Are you with me on this, Ryota?"

"Yes, Mr. Geologist, I understand how gravity works."

"Ok then, by adjusting the table slope and the rate of flow of the wash stream we can be very selective in terms of the density of the minerals that are retained by the riffles. Since platinum-iron alloy and gold both have densities greater than 14 grams per cubic centimeter, we adjust the table and flow to retain everything with a density above 13 and pass on everything below this density. The mass ratio of platinum to heavy waste minerals starts out on the table at about 1: 233 and we try to get a concentrate close to1: 1 and, when the system is right, we get a concentrate of platinum with a little gold and very little black sand. The guys here will clean out the riffles and wash the miners moss at each shift change and the new concentrate will be collected by the accountant and locked up in a special safe-room until we have enough to justify trucking it into Platinum. That is usually a period of two or three days when things are running well. Want to see more?"

"No, this is enough Reuben. I do not wish to become a geologist. Let us look for bears and drink more whisky on the road back to my ship."

The purchased platinum ore had been loaded into a cargo hold of the *Aoki Maru* long before the bear-watchers returned to Platinum in an advanced drunken state. Dr. Tobey retired to his office, wobbly but under his own power; Captain Hiraki's services were required to assist his boss aboard the ship.

The ship's course was set for the port of Vancouver, British Colombia and every soul on board breathed a sigh of relief to be sailing south and seeing the last of dismal Kuskokwim Bay. *Aoki Maru* arrived in Vancouver on the afternoon of June 4 and immediately took on a cargo of 10,000 kilograms of unsorted dry river sand delivered to the dock by Emerson Quarry Operations. Four hours later the *Aoki Maru* was sailing southwest for the Federated States of Micronesia.

During dinner with Captain Hiraki, Ryota informed him that the cargo manifest record must be made to show that only 100 kilograms of placer ore came on board at Platinum, Alaska and that the official documentation must show that 900 kilograms of platinum ore came on board at Vancouver. The point of origin of this nonexistent ore was to be listed as Tulameen, British Colombia.

The Captain looked intently into the eyes of his young boss before saying "I was a smuggler for 20 years before your father hired me. I ran every kind of contraband you can think of between Pusan, Korea and Kitakyūshu, Japan. I was wanted by police in both countries and also by some unhappy competitors. My life and that of my family were under threat when your father gave me a new identity and a well-paid position in Fugimora Enterprises. I always thought he hired me for my smuggling skills, so now, I am honored to help his son. The ship's records will read exactly as you wish."

"Thank you, Captain, my father said you would be helpful. There is another matter of an equally serious nature. When we dock at Weno I will need two men to assist me ashore. It is rather unlikely that they will be alive when the ship departs for Yokosuka. Can you provide such men?"

The captain rolled this thought over in his mind for a minute or so and then, at last, said "Yes, I believe so. There are two Filipino men on this ship. They keep to themselves because they do not speak Japanese. They do not have proper seaman's papers to work and are not listed as crewmen on the ship's papers. They are known to be poorly-trained, stupid and careless sailors and there have been disputes between them and the regular crew. Such men might fall into one of our large cargo bins and require burial at sea. Would such an arrangement be satisfactory?"

"Perfect Captain Hiraki, perfect if no suspicions arise among the crew and there are no difficulties with customs or law enforcement when we get to Yokosuka."

The captain again paused and then said "Such accidents are common on ore haulers. There will be no problems in Yokosuka, Mr. Fugimora."

At mid-day on June 11, the *Aoki Maru* tied up at a dock in the village of Weno on Chuuk Island in the Federated States of Micronesia. There was much activity in and around the lagoon where international tourists in scuba gear were diving to see the remnants of the once invincible Japanese Imperial fleet. This was a new and welcome industry for these poor island people.

Captain Hiraki was on deck overseeing the lifting of five crates of cargo grossing 5000 kilograms from one of the ship's cargo holds onto a flatbed truck waiting on the dock. A sixth box containing tools and a four-wheel dolly was also loaded onto the truck. The captain had assigned two Filipino sailors to dock work in which they were to detach the ship's boom hooks, secure the load to the truck, and accompany it to its destination. This truck belonged to the Chuuk Free Dental Clinic.

Ryota Fugimora assigned himself the duty of driving the truck to the clinic and supervising the off-loading of the expensive dental equipment in the crates. The truck was parked on a small loading dock, hidden from the street, where a small electric boom efficiently loaded the crates onto the four-wheel dolly which his men pushed into the clinic. The Fugimora dentists directed the crates to their new homes with smiling faces. They loved working with the most modern equipment.

Ryota directed his men to remove the packing materials, break down the shipping crates, and place the debris on the loading dock. He then sternly asked the dentists and their lovely assistants to assemble in the main office of the clinic for an announcement from Fugimora Headquarters in Tokyo. The dentists were not smiling now, they were thinking about recent sins and wondering how Tokyo could possibly know of them. Ryota had to work at restraining a smile as he looked into the grim faces of his youthful audience. "We have had reports in Tokyo of after-hours parties, involving liquor and sex, in this clinic" he said in a feigned harsh tone. "And I am here to make sure that such things continue. I am going to give you $1000 US, the currency of these islands, to make certain that happens." By this point, Ryota was smiling and holding up a wad of bills in his hand. The dentists and their lovely assistants were awestruck. "You must cancel all appointments for the rest of today and all for tomorrow and you must promise that you will not return to work before the day after tomorrow. My father, Dr. Fugimora, orders this."

There were smiles all around now as it dawned on the staff that Ryota was giving them time off from their arduous work routine and was actually ordering them to party it up at Fugimora expense for two days. "There is one condition, however" continued the young Fugimora, again in his stern voice, "if you do not spend every dollar of this money on food and drink you will be fired and sent back to Japan in disgrace." Of course, the mood instantly changed to a party atmosphere and the receptionists grabbed the phones and began rescheduling appointments. Ryota handed the money to one of the dentists and promised that his men would clean up the mess left in the clinic. Believe it or not, within 10 minutes the clinic was empty except for Ryota and the Filipino sailors.

The young president of Fugimora Maritime had his men load the four-wheel dolly with the box of tools and led them into the bowels of the clinic, periodically referring to a map provided by his father. It took about an hour to locate the former dental lab and break through the new wall concealing the its entrance. When the debris was cleared, Ryota inserted his father's old key. The lock was stiff but turned, the door opened with a shuddering, high-pitched creak for the first time since July of 1945.

They proceeded by flash light to the rear of the old lab which was in darkness, electrical power having been cut off from the old facility decades before. Evidently looters had not disturbed the lab in any way and all seemed in order beyond a thick coating of dust and insect dung on everything and the myriad of cobwebs dangling from the ceiling. Ryota consulted his map, made a number of measurements with a pocket tape and directed the sailors to break through the rear wall at a specific point.

After 15 minutes of destruction, they had produced an opening large enough for a man to step through. The appalling stench issuing from this breach recalled to Ryota's mind the unfortunate boyhood incident of falling into a farmer's stercorary on Okinawa. But of course, in this instance, President Fugimora was quite aware that this nauseating odor was the gaseous by-product of human decomposition trapped in an air-tight vault for sixty years. It was a smell well known to the older residents of Truk.

Young Fugimora entered the dark interior space with the flash light and immediately saw the skull and otherwise fully-articulated skeleton of 3-1-27 as well as the family sword. He stepped back into the lab proper holding the skull and the sword and watched the two sailor's faces blanch ashy grey in horror. It occurred to Fugimora that he might have to kill them on the spot. In his sternest manner, he ordered one man into the opening and directed him to carefully lift the wooden cases through the opening to the second man who was to place them on the dolly. They were hesitant but could not fail to notice the way their boss was holding the samurai sword; ready to draw. Slowly, reluctantly and fearfully, one man took the flash light and entered the vault.

The ten wooden boxes were small at 10 by 25 by 32-centimeters but they were exceptionally heavy, more than 45 kilograms or 100 pounds each. Because of their age, they had to be handled carefully. Young Fugimora helped his men with the transfer of the 10 boxes to the dolly. When all were loaded, the group returned to the outer entrance which was well illuminated. He closed the old door, locked it and ordered the sailors to rebuild the wall sealing off the old lab. He had the paint, mortar, and the tools needed on the dolly.

While the Filipinos busied themselves with the masonry work, Ryota strained to push the now heavy dolly down the hallways and out to the loading dock. He loaded the boxes onto a pallet from one of the dental crates and then used the electric boom to carefully lift the pallet onto the truck bed. It would not do to break one of the boxes open at this point. He was beginning to think about the value of 450 kilograms of platinum at $1,500 US per ounce.

It was turning dark on Chuuk Island and Ryota was hungry. He bought a selection of food items and 12 bottles of beer from a passing food cart and returned to his men in the clinic with the dolly. They had restored the wall and were waiting for the mortar to set before applying paint. The sailors ate and drank beer and joked about the skull in the stinky dark hole. No one was afraid now, now that the hole was on the other side of a 12-inch-thick coral wall. Ryota had left the skull and sword in the truck, he would not need a weapon to deal with these imbeciles even if they became troublesome. Besides, he had a 200-year-old Kris dagger on a shoulder sling under his windbreaker.

The Chuuk Free Dental Clinic truck returned to the dock and parked about midnight under the still-extended loading boom of the *Aoki Maru*. The captain was waiting on deck and ordered the hooks lowered. The pallet of 10 small, but heavy, wooden boxes ,along with the toolbox and dolly went up, over the rail, and down into the hold containing the ore from Goodnews Bay in less than three minutes. Ryota told his two sailors to meet him in that cargo hold to secure the boxes and retrieve their tools. The decks of the *Aoki Maru* were deserted.

Fugimora entered the cargo hold before the sailors who had made a detour to relieve themselves. He stood in the dark, near the newly arrived pallet, holding his 200-year-old Kris with seven luks on a damascene blade; this blade glistened with newly applied poison. The first sailor approached and bent over to pick up the toolbox. The Kris blade entered his back below the left scapula and pierced the heart chamber. There was a heavy grunt but no other sign of protest. Ryota had the definite impression that the dagger, rather than he, guided this deadly strike. The second man saw it all, but was paralyzed with horror, his eyes wide and unblinking, his mouth gaping as Ryota stepped closer. By its own volition, or so it seemed to young Fugimora, the knife thrust itself into the hapless Filipino's heart from the ventral side encountering no detectable resistance.

Ryota had read Javanese legends about magical Kris daggers that could kill enemies of their masters unaided by human hand or mind. He did not believe such nonsense, in spite of his mother's tiger story, but this dagger did seem to have a will of its own and definitely found the hearts of its victims. Perhaps it did have mystical traits. The blade had been coated that morning with a film of traditional knife poison known as *Buta Buta* throughout Malaysia. Obviously, it worked, it worked very well.

Fugimora wiped his blade with a piece of cotton waste and returned it to its sheath. However, unknown to the young president of Fugimora Maritime, a pair of eyes, blue western eyes, observed these unholy proceedings from a dark passage above the cargo hold, their owner immobilized by terror and yet acutely excited by greed.

The ship put out to sea on the 5 a.m. tide and, when Ryota went out on deck around 7 a.m., the Chuuk Islands were a dirty grey smudge on the horizon. He greeted a passing sailor with "Good morning."

"Honorable president hear about excitement last night?" inquired the sailor.

"No, you are the first person I have spoken with this morning. What has happened?"

"Captain say two Filipinos get in knife fight last night and fall into open cargo bay. They dead. Not worth shit as sailors, ship better off."

Two bodies could be seen on a heavy plank on the fantail of the ship. They were encased in white canvas bags with weights attached. After the crew had eaten, all hands were called aft for the burial. The captain gave a brief traditional Shinto prayer and then nodded his head at two sailors who lifted the plank and the bags slid noiselessly into the foaming sea.

CHAPTER 14

Born to Lose

He heard the strike of the bell signaling the end to the first watch at 12:30 a.m. He shut off the metal lathe he had been working to turn out parts requested by the second engineer, Mr. Suguchi, wiped up around the machine and turned out the lights in the machine shop. As he was ascending the ladder leading from the shop to the main deck he noticed a rather peculiar thing. A boom was lowering a pallet of cargo into the hold at this very unusual hour. It was one thing to deliver cargo to Weno and quite another to take cargo on. What the hell was produced on Chuuk Island worth carrying to Japan? He paused in the darkness above the cargo hold and observed three figures dimly illuminated by beams from the ship's lights passing through the open hatch on the main deck. When the net and boom were raised, he could see a number of small crates and the ships tool box sitting on a wooden pallet.

Able seaman Donald Atkins was easily the biggest man on the crew of the *Aoki Maru*. His six feet-two inch, 180 pound-frame towered above his Japanese crew mates. This, combined with the fact that he was the only American on board and had blue eyes and short blonde hair, meant he stood out from this crew like a goldfish among creek minnows. Atkins was a good worker for being 61 years old, was particularly talented in the machine shop, and thought he could make damn near anything from metal. He spoke passable Japanese but, beyond this, Donald Atkins did not have much to brag about. He was married, one might almost call it a state of indenture, to a Japanese hooker and spent all of his free time and most of his money drinking at the Shit-Kickers Bar in Yokosuka, Japan. This bar had been fun and exciting during the Viet Nam days when he was a young sailor in the U.S. Navy but he had screwed that up and just about everything else in his life as well. He could not even go back to his own country. Nowadays, sitting at this same bar was no longer a wild holiday or a spree to let off steam and get a woman. Drinking and getting drunk was now his profession and this made him feel like the loser he knew he was. Peering over the rail from the darkness, he saw one of the figures bend over to pick up the toolbox; there was a rapid flash and sound like a boxer's punch. That figure slumped silently to the deck. The two other figures seemed to approach each other and there was another flash and a second figure also fell to the deck. The man that remained upright stood over the prone men for at least a full minute then calmly wiped the blade of his knife free of blood; Donald could clearly see now that it was a knife in the man's hand. For Christ's sake, he had just witnessed a double murder!

Atkins pulled back from the rail to the bulkhead behind him and remained absolutely frozen in both mind and body in the darkness. The murderer sheathed his knife under his jacket and stooped to pick up one of the crates. This box was rather small but evidently quite heavy as the man had to struggle to lift and carry it off into the darkness. Clearing all of these boxes from below the hatchway required ten round trips. Think of it, ten crates of very dense material that was worth killing two men for; it had to be gold! Donald's body was still frozen but his mind was rapidly thawing and he was beginning to think his bad luck had finally changed. But like all losers, Donald so easily forgot that, by definition, a loser's luck never changes for the better.

The big American remained in his hidden position, hardly daring to breathe, but carefully keeping track of the number of boxes being removed into a distant corner of the dark cargo bin. During this action, Donald became aware of the identity of the killer; it was none other than the president of Fugimora Maritime, Mr. Ryota Fugimora himself.

Donald Atkins was uneducated and knew he was not the sharpest tack in the box but, below him in those wooden crates, was the opportunity he had been waiting for all of his life. Ten boxes of gold, each as heavy as a grown man could carry. It was a fucking dream coming true.

Of course, Donald knew that he had to make very wise decisions from this moment onward if he did not want to end up in a pool of blood like the two sailors on the deck below. Obviously, he had to wait until Fugimora cleared out of the cargo bin to get at the gold and he must not take so much that the killer would notice the theft. After all, he had to remain on the ship until it docked at Yokosuka and he did not wish to be hunted down by this ruthless man with a knife. Then there would be the problem of getting his gold off the ship. Donald was already thinking of the treasure below him in the darkness as his own. He realized the ship's log would show his presence in the machine shop until the end of the first watch and that meant he would be questioned by the captain about what he saw and heard during his watch. These were all life-threatening problems that he must confront very soon; failure meant his death. It made his head spin, but he was determined not to let this opportunity pass him by. He wanted and he needed a drink.

Atkins waited a full hour after the last sound and movement below had ceased before he re-entered the machine shop and grabbed a small pry bar, flashlight, and hammer. He removed his heavy work shoes, hung them around his neck, and descended the ladder into the cargo bin with excruciatingly slow and meticulous steps. He paused on the last rung for a full five minutes listening acutely for the slightest sound. He had to be sure, absolutely sure, that he was alone and that Jap bastard was not lurking in some dark corner ready to pounce on him with his knife.

Donald warily circled around the spreading blood pools oozing from the two corpses. He tried to avoid looking at their faces but, in spite of the attempt, he recognized them as the two Filipino sailors ostracized by the crew. He followed the path taken by Fugimora away from the hatch opening into the black recesses of the bin and with a one- second flash of his light managed to locate the crates now stacked five wide and two deep. When he approached, he tried to lift one of the small boxes and was amazed. Christ, they weighed a ton!

Feeling for the lid edges of one box in the dark he found it to be solidly constructed of strong smooth wood and securely nailed. Another one-second burst from the flashlight was enough to show the American sailor where to insert his pry bar. When he lifted the bar the withdrawal of the rusty nails produced a piercing screech that echoed through the entire cargo bin. The sailor nearly went into coronary arrest from fear of discovery but the lid was off, at least at one end of the box. He waited a full five minutes to see if the noise attracted anyone's attention. Evidently it did not, and he shot a quick beam of light into the crate.

The box was full of dusty white canvas bags. He slipped his hand in and removed one bag; it was magnificently heavy for its size. He was sorely tempted to take a second bag but managed to beat back his metastasizing greed by thinking of the men on the deck a few feet away. He replaced the lid, carefully tapped the nails back into their original holes, and placed this box in the lower tier with another box above it. He gave the stack of crates a five-second inspection with his flash light and was satisfied that everything appeared as he found it.

Atkins slithered along the walls, avoiding both light and the corpses, to return to the ladder leading up to the machine shop. When he reached it, he deposited his tools and turned on a small lamp over the work bench. With a pair of needle-nosed pliers he removed the sealing wire and poured the contents of the bag onto the bench. The grains were whitish-grey and not yellow!

This sailor was not a high school graduate, or a guy who split atoms in his basement, but he sure as hell knew what gold looked like and this was not gold. What the hell could it be? It was obviously a dense metal but not as white as silver coins or silver solder which he had worked with many times. Maybe it was platinum or tellurium or tin. He had heard of these metals but never seen them. But whatever it was it must be damned valuable and he would have to take extreme care to get it off the ship and past those slimy bastards in Japanese customs.

Atkins thought for a moment and decided to spray the grains with light machine oil and coat them with powdered graphite. It made a black soupy mess, but after he dried it under a heat lamp, the mystery metal looked like coarsely crushed charcoal rather than a shiny metal. He would tell customs, if they asked, that the material in the bag was the remains of a burnt bearing that he had replaced in one of the ships engines; just a mechanical trophy, nothing more. Donald carefully replaced the blackened grains of mystery metal into the bag, resealed it with the wire, and put his shoes on. He would tell Captain Hiraki he had seen the murders but, of course, without mentioning the name of President Ryota

Fugimora. Seaman Atkins was confident that he had devised good solutions to his very pressing problems and was rather proud of himself, as we might expect a loser to be.

CHAPTER 15

Captain Satoshi Hiraki

Captain Satoshi Hiraki stared down into a tumbler of single malt scotch and contemplated the situation. Two worthless Filipino sailors were in transit to the bottom of the Pacific and he was thinking that it was no great loss. He was well aware that these men did not stab each other in the heart. Hiraki had seen what a Kris dagger does to a man in his younger days as an ordinary seaman on cargo ships trading between Singapore, Borneo, Java and Sumatra. He did not believe in magic daggers but he certainly believed in their killing power and he had seen just such a weapon in Ryota Fugimora's room. After inspecting the corpses of the Filipino sailors, he had an old and trusted sailor stitch them up in canvas before slinging the bodies up to the deck where a silent but curious crew waited and watched.

No, he was not concerned about these murders, the things that concerned him were his orders to under-report 550 kilos of legal platinum as 100 kilos and then to fraudulently report 10,000 kilos of Canadian river sand as 900 kilos of platinum ore from

Tulameen, British Colombia. Of course, there was no thought of disobedience of these orders from the Big Boss's son but as a professional smuggler he needed to understand the mechanics of the transaction he was involved in.

It was clear that the *Aoki Maru* was going to enter Japan declaring 1000 kilos of platinum placer ore. But there was, in fact, only 550 kilos on board that the Captain was certain of, but only 100 kilos of this would be declared as originating from Goodnews Bay. The simple mathematics of the constant sum led the Captain to conclude that the remaining 450 kilos of Alaskan placer would be used to disguise another 450 kilos of platinum that could not be legally imported into Japan. This second 450 kilos had to have come aboard while the ship was docked at Weno and that was why the Filipinos had to die, of course. Extending this logic led the former smuggler to presume that the platinum from Weno would be, or already was, mixed with the legal Alaskan platinum.

Captain Hiraki had never heard of Tulameen, British Colombia but assumed that Aoki Fugimora knew that it was a potential source of platinum that would not be questioned by Japanese customs when they sampled the ore aboard his ship. It was all very clever, very clever indeed. Satoshi Hiraki approved of such cleverness but was left wondering how platinum in such amounts came to be in a remote place like Chuuk Island and why it could not be imported in the usual and legal way. Satoshi Hiraki was not young but he was of a generation that studiously avoided learning Japanese Imperial history and, consequently, knew nothing at all concerning the history of Chuuk Island and the role it played in the destruction of the Empire of Japan.

Captain Hiraki had to smile when he thought of how easily Japanese customs inspectors could be duped. They really were complete dumb shits and he had proved this many times during his smuggling career. He would follow the standard procedure of taking the senior inspectors into his comfortable cabin and pouring them very good whisky while their youngest and least experienced men went below decks to examine the ship and cargo with his first officer. A pair of these youngsters attired in white coveralls, armed with the ship's manifest, flash lights, and clipboards listing the inspection points to be checked off were sent with his first officer who led the neophytes below decks and into every dark, hot, and filthy corner of the ship, especially the bilges, ore bins, sailor's head, and the greasy machine shop.

Hiraki knew full well that these nimrods would be concentrating on keeping their overalls clean and getting back to the captain's cabin before the whisky hour was over. The captain purposefully extended his whisky fest until the first officer returned with the two youthful, grease-spattered, and disheveled inspectors. He personally poured each of them four fingers of premium 30-year-old scotch. Captain Hiraki considered this was the least he could do since, of course, they had found nothing amiss. Complete dumb shits. Tradition demanded that each senior inspector leave the ship with a bottle of this excellent whisky in his brief case. It made for efficient inspections and minimal paperwork all around.

CHAPTER 16

Mine, All Mine

No sooner had the Filipinos slipped beneath the briny waves than Ryota Fugimora was down in the cargo hold of the *Aoki Maru* examining his fortune in platinum. He opened the strong wooden crate containing 550 kilograms of black sand from Goodnews Bay, Alaska. He weighed out 100 kilograms in 10-kilogram increments on a portable scale borrowed from Captain Satoshi Hiraki, himself a former smuggler. This ore was placed in a smaller crate and labeled 'Goodnews Bay, Alaska'. Then he began opening the 10 by 25 by 32 centimeter boxes taken aboard the ship at Weno, Federated States of Micronesia.

These boxes were well built and despite their age, were difficult to open. His father had told him what they contained but now Ryota wanted to see his fortune with his own eyes. He withdrew the 10 white canvas bags sealed with tightly wrapped wire and set them side by side. Using wire cutters, he opened the first bag and poured the contents into a bucket. He let the nuggets drip through his fingers again and again. The feeling it gave him was better than sex, at least the sex he knew about. True, the so-called black sand was not as attractive as gold, but so what? He began calculating the value of this one bag in his head: 4.5 kilograms is equal to about 145 troy ounces which *at a minimum* would sell at $1500 US per ounce of pure platinum. Since this ore was about 82% platinum it meant that a single bag was worth about $180,000 US; each box contained 10 such bags which made a box worth $1.8 million US and there were 10 such boxes! He would need a calculator, a good assay and market prices for the various platinum group elements to actually compute the true value of this treasure but for now it was enough to know that it was in the neighborhood of 20 million US and it was his, *all his*; it made his head swim.

Ryota had to force himself back to his appointed task. All 450 kilograms of the Colombian ore had to be emptied into the crate now containing 450 kilograms of Alaskan black sand purchased in his father's name. The total value of this 900-kilo mixture had to be in the neighborhood of 40 to 45 million US dollars but the immediate need was to get the ore bin thoroughly homogenized before the ship entered Tokyo Bay.

He emptied the first 10 bags into the crate and then climbed into the container with a large scoop shovel to stir the black sand. It was hot, hard physical work but the smile never left young Fugimora's face. Everything went smoothly until he got to the eighth box; the lid was cracked and the nails were missing from two holes. Clearly it had been tampered with after his careful inspection of the boxes on the loading dock in Weno. When he opened this container, and laid out the bags, there were only nine! Someone had discovered his hoard!

He had already killed two men and did not mind, in the least, killing a third. But who should he kill? Could it be the captain? Not likely, the captain was wise enough to figure out the operation based the fraudulent entries Ryota forced him to make on the ship's manifest, but he also wise enough to know his life and that of his family would be forfeit for such an action. No, not the captain, someone else, it had to be a crew member.

Ryota finished mixing the two placer ores, secured the cover and labeled the crate 'Tulameen, BC'. Next, he bundled up the bags, wires, and boxes the Chocó ore had arrived in and placed it all in a cargo net. On deck, he asked the bosun to lower a hook into the hold, pull up the net and discard the contents into the sea.

Early the next morning, the day the ship was due to arrive in Yokosuka, Captain Satoshi Hiraki knocked on the door of Fugimora's cabin. "Good morning Captain, what brings you to see me before breakfast?"

"I have information that will not please the honorable president. May I come in?"

"Certainly, may I offer you tea, Captain?" Ryota poured two cups of tea and motioned the captain to sit down. "Now what is the problem, Captain?"

"Unfortunately, a crew member may have witnessed the proceedings in the cargo hold two nights before. This seaman is an American by the name of Donald Atkins and he reported seeing the Filipinos attacked by a third man whom, he says, he cannot identify because of darkness. I think the latter statement could be a lie but he must have been present to know as much as he reports. Perhaps he hopes I will arrest you."

"I see" said the young Fugimora after a pause. "Can we arrange for Mr. Atkins to have a fatal accident before we enter Tokyo Bay?"

"No, this is impossible because this man is a listed and licensed crewman and an unfortunate accident will cause an inquiry by both the naval police and the investigators of the Maritime Union. You must deal with him after he leaves the ship. He lives with a prostitute across the street from the Shit-Kickers Bar in Yokosuka. Do you know this bar?"

"No Captain, I do not, but with a name like that it should be easy to find. Who on earth would give their bar such a low-class name?"

"It is a hangout for sailors of low degree, particularly American ex-patriots from the Viet Nam era" returned Hiraki with a wry grin.

"Thank you, Captain, I think I can deal with the situation after we dock as you suggest."

Later, after the ship had docked, passed inspection by Japanese customs and discharged her crew with pay, Ryota Fugimora threw his gear into the armored truck waiting on the dock and supervised the lowering of the Goodnews Bay and Tulameen crates which were loaded into the back of this truck. He directed the driver to a secure warehouse in Yokosuka owned by his company. This truck carried 1000 kilograms of Fugimora platinum concentrate. After unloading the 900-kilos of platinum marked *Tulameen* he directed the security guards to transport the remaining 100 kilograms labeled 'Goodnews Bay, Alaska' to the laboratory of Fugimora Precious Metals in Tokyo.

President Fugimora made himself a pot of tea and began making inquiries on the telephone concerning the location of the Shit-Kickers Bar. He placed the skull of the unfortunate 3-1-27 and the family sword on his desk. The sword needed care after its long interment; sadly, 3-1-27 was beyond earthly care.

For three nights in a row a man dressed in black waited patiently across the street from the Shit-Kickers Bar with an elongate bundle in his hands. In the early evening of the third night Donald Atkins emerged from the kitchen entrance below the apartment he shared with Ayame Watanabe. Instead of walking across the street to the bar as usual, he turned and walked briskly towards the naval yard. The man in black with the oddly shaped bundle followed at a discreet distance.

CHAPTER 17

The Shit-Kickers Bar

The Shit-Kickers Bar, located near the Yokosuka naval yard, was world famous for two things in the wild Viet Nam days: the best jo-sans and a band that played nothing but Johnny Cash songs with perfect mimicry. Ayame Watanabe made her living in this establishment from the age 15 to 31. She was a pretty, but uneducated, girl from a poor rural Japanese village. At age 14 she had never heard the Japanese word *keikoku,* which means prostitute, but only a year later, she was one. She worked the Shit-Kickers Bar as a jo-san during the peak days of the Viet Nam war and a good many years afterwards.

Ayame picked up bar English from sailors over the years and, of course, could sing Johnny Cash's entire repertoire from memory. Her personal favorite was *Folsom Prison Blues* and, although the lyrics were meaningless to her, she soon discovered that the incongruity of a tiny oriental woman in stiletto heels belting out southern English with a Japanese accent drove drunken sailors crazy. She made more money in tips for these performances than she did on her back. In those days', jo-san girls in Yokosuka bars charged 600 to 650 yen, less than two dollars US, for what was called a "quick date" and this pitiful sum had to be split with the house.

Ayame lived as frugally as a working girl could but had little to show for "fucking more sailors than a one-eyed street dog has flees" as she expressed it to the other jo-sans. At length, she was able buy a small kitchen and overhead apartment across the street from the bar and began selling soups and ramen noodles to the staff and customers of the bar. She was 31 then, and her looks were beginning to fade, but the kitchen made up for her declining income in the jo-san trade.

Naturally, Japanese men do not marry jo-san girls, but American sailors do. So, when Ayame went into the soup business she decided she needed the help of a husband. She had many offers of marriage from sailors during the Viet Nam era but these opportunities declined as time passed. In the latter phase of her career she met a former American sailor who needed to marry a Japanese woman to stay in the country. He was making a living as a merchant sailor and was not a bad looking man for a Caucasian. Ayame did not love this foreigner, jo-sans really do not fall in love, but she did marry him as part of her business plan.

Donald Richard Atkins was a dishonorably discharged navy deserter whose life goals were to remain in Japan and hang out at the Shit-Kickers Bar. Marrying the Watanabe whore fit his plans perfectly. They lived together in a tiny two room apartment above her soup kitchen which he worked at night while his wife worked customers across the street. Occasionally he worked as a bartender when business was good but was more often found on the other side of the bar. His wife permitted this because when he did take a job on a ship for a month, or two, his income was many times that which Ayame and the kitchen brought in.

Ayame Watanabe-Atkins waited impatiently on the dock for the arrival of the ship *Aoki Maru*. She had arrived an hour early taking no chance of her husband and his pay check getting away from the dock without her. She knew better than any woman alive the mischief a sailor with money can find. She met him at the gate and took him straight to the apartment by taxi. She had a case of Jack Daniels black label whiskey waiting in the apartment and he would have all the sex he could handle this night. But she would deposit his check for three thousand US dollars from this voyage into her account in the morning. The sex and whiskey went on for the better part of two days, about average for a two-month voyage by Ayame's calculation. On the third day, she insisted that they return to their normal work routine. A haggard Donald was quite willing to please her in this matter.

Ayame had noticed an odd thing about this particular home coming. Before Donald opened his first bottle of whiskey, generally the first item of business after he passed through the door, he had stowed his sea bag in the closet without removing the padlock that secured it. Normally the contents of the sea bag were dumped in a corner so she could add his dirty clothing to the regular laundry. It was so curious that she decided to examine the contents of the bag during one of Donald's numerous Jack Daniels naps.

It was an easy matter to find the key to the padlock and spill the contents of the sea bag onto the bed. The only unusual thing she found was a small but very heavy white canvas bag sealed with wire wrapping. With the aid of a nail file she managed to pluck out the end of the wire and carefully unwind it. She examined the contents meticulously. It was some kind of sand, not very pretty at all, and covered with black stuff that smudged her fingers. She got a magnifying glass and studied the material rolling it between her thumb and fore finger. As the black coating rubbed off she could see the grains becoming white and shiny. It was not yellow, so it could not be gold, she had seen plenty of gold in her life, but it might be silver. She removed 20 of the larger grains and wrapped them in a handkerchief. Then she carefully resealed the bag with the wire and restored the contents to the bag, locked it, and placed it in its original position.

What was her husband up to? Should she confront him about this mysterious sand? Should she ask the jo-sans if they thought the sand grains were really silver? If they turned out to be silver, the bag would be worth a great deal of money.

Ayame arranged to have Donald work as a bartender on the third night after his return while she worked the kitchen. She knew he would come back to the apartment around two or three in the morning and he would be drunk.

Ayame pondered the black sand until the late hours when she expected Donald. Three o'clock came and went and he had not returned; probably he had passed out in the bar which would be locked up by this time. It would not be the first time for such a thing. No matter, the cleanup crew would send him home in the morning when they got to work around eight o'clock. But when eight o'clock came, there was still no husband. Ayame walked over to the bar and inquired. He was not in the bar. She waited there until mid-day when the bar reopened to the public. No one had seen her husband last night, not the other bartenders on duty, not the jo-sans, not the owner. He had not shown up for work.

Ayame Watanabe became progressively more concerned for her husband each day that he remained missing. She discussed the matter with the jo-sans at the Shit-Kickers Bar. The girls advised against notifying the police on the grounds that Donald might be involved in some criminal activity. Ayame considered this sound advice but Donald claimed he had long since given up such pursuits. Still, he did have a record with the Yokosuka police as well as the US Navy, so no police.

After seven days, she decided to take her black sand to the Tokyo mint to find out if it was worth anything. Jo-san girls frequently received gifts of jewelry from sailors which they usually sold to local dealers but only after the items had been evaluated by mint scientists. It was a free service and the mint people were always very nice to the girls.

Ayame boarded a Tokyo bus at the Yokosuka station and

made the hour trip to Tokyo with her handkerchief of black sand. She filled out paper work for the prudish Miss Oshiro in the mint office and submitted her sample for analysis, promising to return in a week for the results.

Later this day it occurred to Mrs. Watanabe-Atkins that, should the analysis indeed prove the sand to be silver, it would be wise to store the canvas bag in a place safer than Donald's sea bag. She went to the closet and was surprised to see that the lock was not on the bag. She was quite certain that she had left the bag locked. She dumped the contents on the bed for the second time. Everything was there as before, except the white canvas bag.

CHAPTER 18

Grotto of the Golden Snake

Ju-long, an 80-something-year-old ethnic Chinese gentleman, grew up from early childhood in the waterfront streets and sailor dives of pre-war Yokosuka, Japan. He had no memory of his parents, he did not know his age precisely, he never attended any school but the Oliver Twist Academy of Pick-Pockets and he could not speak a word of Chinese. An old China sailor who did speak Chinese once told him the name, Ju-long, meant "The Power of a Dragon". Ju-long liked this translation and repeated it to anyone who asked about his foreign-sounding name and appearance.

Japanese prejudices against ethnic Chinese are well-known but they did not deter the youthful Ju-long from growing a fine Fu Manchu mustache, a long queue and adopting a Mandarin outfit based on the cheap Republic movie serials of the nineteen forties when yellow-peril entertainment was in vogue. This costume, combined with a menacing hatchet and broken English babble about Chinese tongs and dragon's teeth, were quite effective in persuading deadbeats to pay their gambling debts. Of course, that was years ago, during Ju-long's strong-arm career and long, long before he settled into his present legitimate business.

In spite of the many obstacles facing him, Ju-long eventually became a rich and powerful figure in the Yokosuka underworld by virtue of disciplined work habits, frugal life style, and innate intelligence. With a university education Ju-long might have entered any profession from medicine to nuclear physics, but circumstance declared otherwise, and the lad was forced into street crime to fill his rice bowl. Over a fifty year career this intelligent boy grew to manhood and climbed the ladder of crime from a lowly artful dodger to a dealer and artisan in fine jewelry. Jewelry and precious metals were his passion, his chosen field of study, and the source of his wealth and influence within the Yokosuka crime community.

His shop, known as The Grotto of the Golden Snake, was a more or less legitimate business by the time of this story and located on a narrow, poorly-lighted back street with hideous, foul-smelling gutters that backed up with frequency. From the roof of the Golden Snake, Ju-long could with some difficulty see the Womble Gate of the U. S. Naval Shipyard, one of three gates that controlled access to the 579-acre restricted peninsula. From this same vantage, he could quite easily see the glowing golden arches of McDonald's restaurant on the naval base. With a little more difficulty, he could also see a portion of the campuses of Mikasa Kindergarten, Shonan Junior College, and the Kanagawa Ladies Dental College; all, of course, are well-known attractions to visitors of Yokosuka.

During his long life, Ju-long had witnessed great changes in the part of Yokosuka where he lived and worked. When he was very young, this same naval yard was the beating heart of the vast and powerful Japanese Imperial Navy but by the end of the war it was a smoldering inferno of what was, or might have been. But from these ruins there soon arose a phoenix in the form of what is now the thriving home of the U. S. Seventh Fleet; a model of modern American life, administered and governed by Americans, policed by Americans, and hermetically isolated from the people of Yokosuka, Japanese culture, and the language of Japan.

The Grotto of the Golden Snake was a long, narrow, two-story edifice with bars over both the door and the single external widow at ground level. A sign, swinging over the doorway, proclaimed the name of the shop in both Japanese and English. Naturally, this sign featured a realistic cobra with flared hood, poised and ready to strike but this snake was composed of cheap brass rather than gold in deference to the low economic circumstances of the neighborhood. Not that there were many locals who would contemplate stealing from Ju-long; his underworld connections were known to all and made such an idea almost the equivalent of suicide.

Ju-long lived above his shop under extremely Spartan conditions; a simple pallet bed, an electric hot plate for boiling tea and rice, a bucket of potable water for cooking and washing, and another bucket for the body functions. This life style was not dictated by financial necessity because Ju-long could afford to live wherever, and however, he wished. But he chose to live in this manner simply because he could not bear to be more than a few steps distance from his shop, his tools and the objects he loved.

From the front door, the shop offered a single narrow passage between floor-to-ceiling shelves of jewelry, watches, and insanely ticking clocks of all sorts and sizes. These goods were arranged to become systematically more expensive as one approached a barred cage at the rear of the building. The cheaper goods were much in demand by sailors who comprised the majority of Ju-long's customers.

Within the cage, the work benches presented the patron with an astonishingly disordered riot of trays, boxes and jars filled with tiny parts scattered amidst torches, furnaces, metal cutting tools, drills, bits, dies and clocks in mid-repair. All these were essential to the jewelry trade, naturally, but it was fortunate that some of these tools were speechless and without memory.

Only Ju-long was permitted behind this cage and he remained there during business hours and often long into the night making repairs or constructing custom jewelry pieces in demand by the socially elite ladies of Yokosuka. Old Ju-long did not require much sleep and never wearied of his claustrophobic surroundings; they reminded him daily of his difficult journey from a starving, abandoned foundling, forced to shit in the public streets, to a respectable, or let us at least say, semi-respectable, business man and artisan that he now was.

Behind this cage, Ju-log was normally occupied with his work.

He would almost invariably be found wearing a magnifying jeweler's visor tilted above his regular old-fashioned rimless spectacles. But at one end of the cage there was a secret, securely-locked steel door leading to a fire-proof vault where gold, silver, and platinum bullion were stored along with very expensive jewelry items and diamonds both cut and un-cut. This was Ju-long's real wealth and no one was ever permitted to know of its existence.

Donald Atkins emerged from the soup kitchen entrance just as darkness began to fall. He wrapped the heavy white bag of black sand in a newspaper and carried it securely in the inside pocket of his pea jacket. He considered crossing the street and having a drink or two at the Shit Kicker's Bar but he knew he would need to be in top mental shape in order to deal with old Ju-long. He had negotiated with the master jeweler many times in the past but tonight he needed Ju-long's advice in a bad way. That old bastard knew everything there was to know about gems and precious metals but he was justly famous for screwing sailors, including Donald himself, out of their last buck.

Donald had formerly been into small-time burglary and, in those days, the old Chinaman fenced practically any type of stolen property. So, they were old business associates in a way. Both had been on the straight and narrow for the past few years but they certainly shared many secrets that would interest the Yokosuka police.

Donald simply had to find out what was in his white bag that was worth killing two men over and yet was not gold. He walked at a steady pace but took an indirect route to the Chinaman's seedy shop and paused several times to study the street behind him. But he saw only the normal crowd of pedestrians rushing along their various ways toward home and dinner.

Standing outside and peering through the barred door of the Golden Snake, Donald could make out a faint light coming from the cage in the rear. He pushed the buzzer with three short pulses, then a five second delay, then one extended buzz. It was the secret signal between brother criminals and Donald had to smile as he recalled how many times he had made this very signal when he brought his stolen goods to master jeweler, Ju-long.

Ju-long knew from the buzzer signal that one of his former criminal associates was at his door. A hidden camera, whose lens was coincident with the eye of the cobra on his shop sign, informed him that his visitor was one Donald Atkins, formerly of the U.S. Navy, and person of interest to detectives of the Yokosuka police force. He had dealt with Mr. Atkins on many prior occasions and found him to be a reliable master of ignorance but otherwise as honestly dishonest as most petty criminals he dealt with. He pushed a button that released the lock of the front door.

"Good evening Mr. Atkins" smiled Ju-long with a token bow which could only be taken as an obvious imitation of Charlie Chan. "What brings honorable Navy man to humble Grotto of the Golden Snake?"

"Hello Ju-long, it has been a long time since I was here last.

You screwed me on five watches I brought to you, as I recall."

"That was only business, Donald. The street tells me that you are an honest man these days, a soup entrepreneur, and in partnership with the beautiful Ayami Watanabe."

"Yes, and that woman treats me like a god damn slave when I am ashore; my only escape is going out on merchant cruises. In fact, that's why I came to see you, old friend. I picked up something on my last cruise and I need your help in figuring out its value. Don't worry, I am not here to sell or pawn any of my belongings, you old rascal." With this, Atkins pulled the parcel from his coat and removed the newspaper wrapping. "It is a heavy metal of some kind but not gold. I know it is valuable but I need to find out what it is to figure what to do with it."

Ju-long eyed the cotton bag on the table from behind the cage but did not reach for it. Years of experience with sailors had taught him to never exhibit interest in the items they brought in; reluctance was always the best policy, especially if a valuable article was on the counter. "It seems you have a cotton bag of the type miners often use for storing their ores. I have no interest in such bags."

"God-damn-it, Ju-long, it's not the bag I want to know about; it's what is in the fucking bag. Open it and tell me what you think" responded Donald with some heat.

Ju-long, of course, realized he already had the upper hand if there was to be a negotiation between himself and the sailor. He knew very well that he was sitting across the bars from a loser at the top of his game, a loser borne under the well-known brown star. Atkins pushed the bag through the slot beneath the bars and impatiently waited for the Chinaman to pick it up. Ju-long delayed about 30 seconds and then finally picked up the bag with an obsequious smile and said "Yes, very heavy, very heavy" resuming his Charlie Chan imitation. Then he reached back to a work bench and retrieved a pair of needle-nosed pliers. "Shall we open bag and examine contents, Donald?"

"Yes, of course, you have to look at it to tell me what it is in it, old man" replied Atkins who was growing more and more exasperated with the deliberate pace of the elderly master jeweler. This Chinaman was demonstrating less interest in his bag than he would in watching a street dog shit.

Ju-long used the pliers to meticulously unwrap the wire and opened the bag at last. He directed an intense beam of light from his jeweler's visor into the contents. "Hmmm, yes, very interesting, you have some kind of black sand, Donald, not gold or silver, not brass or bronze, not tin. Definitely back sand, Donald."

"What the hell do you mean by black sand? What is it and how much is it worth?" cried Donald in a voice that clearly reflected his growing irritation.

Ju-long had already guessed from the heft of the bag that it contained platinum concentrate but he was enjoying the sport of playing with this big American fish. "Did you know, Donald, that someone has covered these sand grains with powdered graphite?"

"Yes, I did know it, you old scoundrel, because I did it myself to get the stuff past customs if they decided to search my sea bag. Now please let's get on with it, Ju-long" the sailor said, making an obvious effort to calm himself. The old Chinaman always pulled this shit, getting a guy so pissed-off he couldn't keep his eye on the ball.

"I am truly sorry if I upset you, Donald, but you cannot expect an old man to identify an unknown mystery material with a single brief glance. Permit me to make a crude calculation of the density of this black sand. It may resolve the mystery." With this, he resealed the bag leaving a single pea-sized grain on the table. He smashed this grain and quickly passed a small pen magnet over it which attracted the flattened grain. Then he weighed the bag on a nearby scale; it was exactly 4500 grams or 4.5 kilograms. Next, the jeweler measured the length of the bag at 15 centimeters and then rolled the bag between his hands into a cylinder with a circular cross-section from which he measured a diameter of five centimeters.

The mater jeweler then pulled out an antique Chinese abacus from behind the counter and began clicking beads this way and that in very rapid succession. Ju-long knew how to use a Chinese abacus not because he was ethnic Chinese but because he had studied a book on the subject for over a year. This abacus routine was a display he very much enjoyed presenting because the stupid sailors watching it were always so bedazzled and impressed. Besides, in the hands of an expert it was as accurate and fast as any modern electronic calculator when it came to arithmetic operations. In less than 10 seconds, Ju-long said "The volume of a cylinder with the dimensions we measured is 294.52 cubic centimeters but this must be reduced by 25 % to account for open spaces between the sand grains. Thus, the approximate volume of the metal grains is …" here he paused and batted more beads along the abacus wires while noting the zombie-like expression on Atkins' face … "ah yes, the corrected volume is 220.89 cubic centimeters. Now we compute a crude density value by dividing the mass of 4500 by the corrected volume of 220.89 and arrive at estimated density of 20.3 grams per cubic centimeter. Did you follow that calculation, Donald?"

"Fuck no, I didn't follow that calculation. Who the hell could understand all this Chinese mumbo-jumbo mathematical bull shit? Just tell me what it means before I come into that cage and pull your arms and legs off."

Ju-long smiled, within himself of course, he had taken Mr. Atkins as far as he could, just short of violence, so he said in a soothing, obsequiously-polite, Charlie Chan manner "Why Donald, this means you are rich man because the bag contains high-grade platinum ore."

"It's platinum? God-damn-it, Ju-long, you are alright. I am fucking rich!" Donald cried out in an ecstasy of greed. "Quick, tell me what it is worth, Ju-long!"

"This is not so easy my son because assumptions have to be made as to the percentage of platinum in the ore and the market price of the platinum which changes all the time. Then there are the other platinum family elements which we cannot evaluate without an assay" responded the jeweler with a cunning twinkle in his eyes that was shielded from the sailor by the visor.

"Ok, ok, I get that, Ju-long, but you can give me a rough estimate, can't you?" begged Atkins.

"Yes, yes a very rough estimate of the *intrinsic* value of the platinum alone if you wish it" and Ju-long picked up the abacus and repeated the previous routine. "In what currency, do you wish to express the value, Donald, Japanese yen or Hong Kong dollars?"

"Jesus Christ, Ju-long, cut the horse shit and tell me what the sack is worth in US dollars."

There were additional bead movements designed to increase Donald's agony but at length Ju-long relented and said, "The *intrinsic* value is something in neighborhood of 180,000 US dollars."

Donald Atkins sat in awed silence for once. This was an astronomical number as far as he was concerned, far beyond his greediest speculations, and he was already beginning to regret that he had not stolen a second bag.

"I sense this is welcome news for you, Donald, but at the same time I fear there is also some bad news" said the old Chinaman now in a sincere and gentle tone.

"What the hell can be bad about a 180-thousand-bucks, Ju-long?" the now smiling sailor quipped in joyful response.

"Just this Donald, to get money for your platinum ore it must be refined to a state of purity, to what is called 'fine platinum'.

Only then, can it be traded commercially and you will not be able to have such a small amount of ore refined by any commercial refinery. A small refinery perhaps, one affiliated with the dental industry might be persuaded to do the job, but they will charge a significant commission for this service. I have heard that Fugimora Precious Metals does such small jobs but perhaps you do not wish to deal with Fugimora Industries."

At this, Atkins expression changed from radiant to something approaching cadaverous. He swallowed hard several times causing his Adam's apple to bob in a ridiculous way. He could not speak for a few moments, but at last croaked out "Fugimora Industries? No, no I can't do that at all, it is impossible because it's their platinum we are looking at!"

"Ah yes, I thought as much Donald. This compounds your difficulties my lad as they will certainly be looking for you and they will be very insistent for the return of their property; very insistent. I trust you follow my meaning."

"Jesus Fucking Christ, Ju-long, are you are telling me I can't sell it, I can't keep it, and either way the Fugimora's want to kill me?"

"I am afraid that is my view of your situation, Donald. I do not know what you can do except return their property and pray for mercy. As the matter stands you are a walking corpse and even that is merely a temporary state."

Donald, by now, was at least on familiar ground, the ground tread by losers; a place from which there is no path to redemption.

He needed to think, he needed a plan but, most of all, he needed to get drunk. He snatched the bag off the table and thrust it back into the inside pocket of his coat. He stared wildly at the inscrutable face of Ju-long behind the cage in his spectacles and jeweler visor. "You have been a big fucking help, you crooked old bastard. Thanks a-fucking-lot. Now buzz me out." He rose from his stool and raced to the door. When the lock released he peered out the door way into the darkness of Yokosuka and looked keenly in every direction. He saw people, of course, but he saw no one who looked like an assassin and no one who resembled Ryota Fugimora.

Ryota Fugimora had no difficulty following a six foot two-inch-tall Caucasian with blonde hair through the narrow streets of the waterfront district to the door of The Grotto of the Golden Snake. Fugimora was not familiar with Ju-long, his establishment or his underworld reputation but it did not require a brain surgeon to deduce the business being conducted through the cage at the rear of the building.

Donald Atkins walked rapidly, thinking only about the first drink he would have at the Shit Kicker's Bar. After two blocks, he mechanically stopped and looked back over his shoulder along his route from the Golden Snake. A shock, like that delivered by the electric chair, pulsed though every part of his body and momentarily paralyzed him.

It just could not be, it must be an alcoholic nightmare, life could not possibly end in such a fucked-up way. Yet, there he was, 30 yards away, dressed in black like some fucking Samurai warrior with a sadistic smile on his ugly, yellow oriental face. He knew this face. He feared this face. He had good reason for this fear. It was the monstrously impassive face of Ryota Fugimora.

Ryota watched calmly as sailor Atkins plummeted into a state of raw terror and then began to run down the street. Young Fugimora was enough of a hunter to know that a rabbit in full panic mode will soon make a fatal mistake. He did not bother to run after the fleeing 61-year-old sailor, he merely pursued him at a normal walking pace keeping his elongate bundle securely under his arm.

Atkins turned right into the first narrow alley he came to and raced through the darkness amidst the litter, overflowing garbage cans and scurrying rats. Ryota paused at the entrance to this alley and very nearly broke into an actual smile which would have been an extreme rarity for this damaged, misanthropic young man. At eye level, there was a sign in Japanese warning pedestrians and drivers that this was a blind alley. But, of course, he knew that Donald Atkins could not read Japanese.

Donald ran as he had never run in his life. Thank God, he was wearing his athletic shoes instead of his clunky seaman shoes but he was getting a stitch in his side and his lungs were on fire. The dead weight of the 4.5-kilogram bag in his coat felt like an anchor; he retrieved it and found its weight repulsive; this bag now seemed to be ugly, repugnant, and odious to his soul. It was like holding a hideous writhing snake and he realized, in this moment of peril, that his black sand was a worthless, filthy, and vacuous thing; an evil, oppressive, mass that was not at all worth dying for. He flung it wildly aside into one of the hundreds of seething, rat-filled cans of garbage as he flew past. He immediately felt lighter, faster and almost like a better man.

He now ran with abandon; he ran for absolution for his poorly-lived life; he ran for the fragrant flower of life itself. He knew he was increasing the distance between himself and the man in black. Now, if there could just be a crossing alley that he could turn into then, perhaps, escape would be possible. But there were no crossing alleys and the alley he was confined to terminated 20 yards straight ahead of him with a crazy disorganized stack of garbage receptacles. The race of races was over and he knew it.

Ryota walked steadily and, of course, without emotion. He knew what he would find at the alley's end. At 30-yards distance from this dead end he drew his 400-year- old samurai sword and dropped the sheath to the pavement.

Donald waited for him, trembling, at the extreme corner of the alley, holding up the lid of a garbage can for defense. Ryota assumed the offensive crouching position of the Samurai warrior with the two-handed sword held horizontally over his right shoulder. At three yards' distance, he made a feinting slash at the sailor's torso causing Donald to lower his shield in response. In less than three seconds the head of sailor Donald Atkins was spinning away amidst the filth and darkness of a Yokosuka waterfront back alley.

Ryota calmly restrained each arm of the still-twitching corpse with his foot and deftly removed the hands with a single cut for each. He wiped his blade on Donald's pea coat and then thoroughly searched through the clothing of the quivering torso. He did not find the all-important white bag of black sand. Young Fugimora did not care about the monetary value of this bag; no, his concern was that this bag was a dangling thread that, if pulled, could unravel the fabric of the Fugimora wheel of fortune.

CHAPTER 19

The Broom of Despair

Ryota Fugimora did not panic when he was unable recover the missing 4.5- kilogram bag of black sand from the body of the unfortunate sailor. Logic dictated that it must be hidden somewhere in the apartment of the prostitute. He kept close watch on this woman and entered her apartment on three occasions during her absence to search for his white bag of black sand. He was not successful. Young Fugimora was quite unhappy with this turn of events and, on the fourth visit, he awaited her return. She would be made to tell him where his property was hidden.

By the fourth night of watching and searching, Ryota knew every inch of Mr. and Mrs. Donald Atkins's small apartment. He had looked in at the Shit Kicker's Bar on several occasions and knew that Ayame performed as both singer and hooker; he also knew that she usually returned to the apartment between 1:00 and 2:00 a.m. It was about midnight when he entered and he made himself a pot of tea and seated himself in their only comfortable chair to wait in darkness for the prostitute. Of course, he knew her troublesome husband would not be making a surprise appearance on this or any other night. He sipped his tea while the 400-year-old gleaming Katana blade rested across his knees, its sheath on the floor beside him.

Ryota Fugimora had no experience with prostitutes and little, beyond the Belfast lass, with women at all. Parting with that 16-year-old girl in Ireland had been a tearful and emotional affair that he did not ever wish to repeat. He did not understand boy-girl love, or any other kind of love, beyond that within his own family, and really, he considered this filial love simply as his duty to the parents who brought him into being. He had no public-school experience at all, only private tutors and exclusive academies for rich boys. The consequence of being raised in this manner, as a solitary and privileged lad under the Fugimora model of child-rearing, was that Ryota's capacity for human empathy approached that of a turtle. Understandably, this young man was totally unaware of his own personality aberrations. He simply considered himself a warrior, not a lover.

Perusing Ayame's bureau drawers, which were crammed with sexy bras and panties, did cause him to become aware of something however. The scent of this woman was a sensory delight of the first magnitude and it aroused him more than anything he had experienced in rainy Belfast. He leisurely and meticulously sniffed every intimate garment the lady owned. He was particularly attracted to a bra-panty combination which featured sparkling blue sequins arranged in an ornate fish-scale pattern. This olfactory form of masturbation was a singular weakness in a young man who could, otherwise, be considered a fighting machine and a true descendent of the Samurai cult.

Ayame Watanabe sensed the stranger's presence as soon as she switched on the light. Her profession had taught her to be an unemotional and calculating woman and so she was not tempted to scream at the sight of a strange man, a man dressed in black with a glittering medieval sword across his knees. She intuitively knew that the appearance of this stranger was the consequence of Donald's mysterious bag of black sand and his sword was a certain indication that he meant business. She knew now why her husband, Donald, had not returned to her.

The man remained sitting and holding her tea cup, a faint suggestion of a smile on his lips. He was handsome in the Japanese way, had a quite athletic build, and an extremely confident bearing that told her it was useless to attempt running for the door leading to the stairway; he would reach her with the sword in less than two seconds. The same for screaming; her head would be off before the sound reached the noisy street below. Her only chance, and she was quite aware that it was not a particularly good one, was to use sex to distract this malevolent stranger from his intended mission. Perhaps, only just perhaps, she could find an opportunity to make her way to the small unbarred, second story window above the busy street. Then what? Jump or scream?

She immediately adopted her sexiest smile and bearing and approached within reach of the ominous blade and said, "If you have come for sex with me, you will not need that sword."

"I did not come for sex, Ayame-san. I came for property that your husband has stolen from me" replied the stranger in a grim tone. "And I suppose you know very well what I am referring to."

"I think you may be talking about a bag of heavy black sand that Donald brought back off the *Aoki Maru*. I did see such a bag when he first arrived home but I have seen neither the bag, nor my husband, in the past seven days."

This, of course, was perfectly true but Ayame was finding it difficult to speak even the truth in her sexy voice under these menacing conditions. She put a hand on her tilted hip and turned a little so the stranger could see her breasts to advantage. She was certainly aware that this man was no drunken sailor; his precise and perfect Japanese grammar told her he was of the wealthy, educated class of Japan's elite, not at all like the classless American sailors she was used to dealing with nightly at the Shit Kicker's Bar.

Ryota Fugimora looked at her steadily without speaking for a full minute, he thought she might fall to pieces under this stare and was pleased that she did not. He appreciated bravery in a woman. Finally, he said in a commanding tone "I have seen thong panties and a matching bra with shiny blue sequins in one of your drawers, I wish you to put them on. Do not close the door of your bedroom."

Because of her trade, Ayame, naturally, had a large and expensive collection of risqué matching underwear; she had to admit that she approved of this stranger's choice because she knew she looked quite well in blue sequins. Standing in the doorway, she removed her dress in the most alluring manner she could muster, letting the intruder see her naked from every angle without being overtly obvious about it. She bent over more than was necessary to put the panties on; a maneuver that she called her "one-thousand-yen ass-shot" and one that never failed to inflame the man watching it. It briefly occurred to the always calculating Ayame that because the blue sequin panties were of the thong-type, maybe she should call it the "fifteen-hundred-yen ass-shot".

She took more time than was absolutely needed to hook the blue sequin pushup bra and position her breasts in it. Ayame also took her time in finding the matching blue heels, bending over several times before she found the pair she wanted. She stood on one foot and feigned a struggle to get them on; she knew this made her breasts sway and jiggle in a most provocative manner. It was a slow-motion burlesque show that would have driven a sailor crazy but, when she returned to the living room, the man with the sword remained stoic and unmoved.

This uneducated, rural-class working girl stood in the light in front of him with her hands on her hips and smiling in her most seductive manner. With her practiced eye, she was expecting to see the obvious indication of arousal in this stranger but there was nothing to indicate success in this calculated maneuver. Looking directly into his dark eyes, she had the disturbing feeling that she was staring into the deep black, unblinking pupils of a hideous reptile. Her natural courage began to drain and she was aware of the dry, coppery-taste of fear in her mouth. Her cheap sex act was clearly not working on this strange, horrifying young man. She could sense her life ebbing away like the tide.

After a lengthy period of stare-down, the man unexpectedly asked her to sing one of her bar songs. This was a God-send from Ayame's perspective as it provided additional time for her to ponder the calculus of survival. She simply must find a way to force this monster to set aside that wicked-looking blade. She said "Ok, I will sing for you, but I must have my music and that means I must step back to turn on my karaoke box." He nodded his assent and she turned on the machine to one of her favorite performance pieces and took up the wireless microphone.

A plan was forming in her head but it required that the grim visitor become aroused to be successful. She made certain that the switch on the microphone was in the on-position and set the volume on the karaoke machine to the maximum she thought the man would allow. He forced her to lower this setting twice but it was still fairly loud when he nodded his permission. She would service this evil, home-invader orally and this act would force him to set his blade aside; then at the explosive moment she would run to the window, jump through it regardless of the consequences, and scream for her life through the live microphone. Ayame realized that this was a most desperate plan but she found herself now at the wicked end of the broom of despair.

Ayame Watanabe had been a prostitute for more than twenty years. If anyone knew anything about blowjobs it was she, and no man, drunk or sober, young or old, sailor or landsman had ever declined this service during her long career. The suggestive rhythm of *Tulsa Time* and the southern voice of Don Williams began coming through the speakers and she opened the most important stage performance of her life with well-practiced, serpentine gestures.

The irony of the repeated lyric *Living on Tulsa Time* was lost on this Japanese prostitute but she was certainly aware that she and Don were harmonizing for her very life. She put supreme effort into each of her dance moves, stroked the microphone in an obscene manner and even repeatedly took the bulbous head of the microphone into her mouth. Ayame breathed heavily into her microphone trying to suggest an approaching female climax. She was gratified to observe, finally, a growing bulge in the stranger's trousers. Her final move at the song's conclusion was to drop to her knees with her inviting mouth open and her soft, white throat only one inch from the gleaming Katana blade.

Ryota watched the woman wrapped in deep fascination which eventually evolved into sexual arousal but he did not want this attractive lady in the normal way. He had already enjoyed as much of her as he needed or wanted. He knew he was not going to get his property back on this night so there was no reason that this sailor's whore should live a minute longer. When she dropped before him he simply drew the blade rapidly from left to right a few inches and watched the blood spurt from the thin red line onto his crotch and spill onto the floor.

It would be a Yokosuka police matter now, of course, up until this Atkins couple entered his affairs it had not been. Ryota continued to live in his office at the security warehouse and reading the Yokosuka daily newspapers carefully for a number of days. But there was no mention of the fates of Mr. and Mrs. Atkins, and no mention of his missing bag of platinum. This struck him as odd, but understandable, since identification of people without hands and heads no doubt posed a problem for the police. The missing canvas bag troubled him most. It was a loose end and he definitely did not like loose ends.

It gradually occurred to him, during these days of inactivity and reflection, that there was another loose end. Dr. Tobey, that arrogant dung-eater of a geologist in Goodnews Bay, knew too much. He was a loose end that would require remediation in the near future.

CHAPTER 20

Caribou Valley: West Side

When he exited the hotel bar of Circle Hot Springs, Alaska, he was more than a little drunk. He had bought just one round of drinks for the five men at the bar but failed to anticipate that each of these men would feel honor bound to follow suite. Consequently, young Fugimora was forced, out of simple courtesy, to drink six double scotches. It was a very friendly crowd that drank here at the end of the world. Evidently, they represented the social class described in American novels as "red necks" but he could see no physical evidence of this condition under the bright midnight sun. Ryota Fugimora managed to drive his rental car about 500 yards to the airstrip where he was informed he could leave it for his projected four-day fishing trip along the river known as the Yukon Fork. On this fishing trip, he was not taking a rod and reel but he was taking a scoped Weatherby Mark V Deluxe rifle in caliber .30-06. He was after a very big salmon; a fish that knew too damned much about his business.

He climbed unsteadily from the car next to the airstrip and read his altitude as 906 feet above sea level and his latitude as

65.48° N from his I-pad. He lashed the rifle to his back pack, locked the rental car and set a bearing on his compass for due south toward the confluence of the Yukon Fork and the South Fork of Birch Creek. The initial walking sobered him and was easy since it followed a level trail through thick clumps of small birch and willows populated by cute little arctic hares. But within a mile of the car, this trail gave out, low brush became denser, and he was completely dependent upon his compass to keep to his course. The sky suddenly became overcast and blocked the sun but it did not block the mosquitoes that swarmed on his face, ears and hands. In his ignorance of arctic summer conditions, he had neglected to bring either a head net or insect repellent.

The terrain was now wet, swampy and difficult to walk over. His expensive leather hiking boots were quickly saturated and his socks were wet after the first few hundred yards. As Ryota plodded on, he thought about the warning given him by the men in the bar. "Watch out for grizz" they had told him. By this, they obviously meant the ferocious, big-brown grizzly bears he had read about in books on Alaska. He had seen black bears at Goodnews Bay but they were small playful cubs, not giant man-eaters. He had explained to those men at the bar that he was armed with a .30-06 but they laughed and said, "Too small". He worried a little about this.

Five hours of hard, uphill walking brought him to the junction of the South Fork of Birch Creek and the Yukon Fork and a long-abandoned miner's cabin situated at 1300 feet elevation. Looking south, into the Yukon-Tanana highlands and up the valley of the north-flowing course of Birch Creek, he gazed upon a stark, treeless, ever-frozen landscape of barren rounded mountains with elevations ranging between 3000 and 4600 feet. It was amazing to see patches of snow still clinging on in the north-facing ravines in July. The many streams in this region were nourished almost exclusively by snow melt.

Ryota was unfamiliar the word "tundra" but indeed this was the land he was entering. A land of permafrost where cold, wind, and 60-day growing seasons limited vegetation to dwarfish, shallow-rooted, clumping tussock grasses, mosses, liverworts and lichens; a land that was marshy and wet in summer from snow melt that could not drain down though the frozen soil; a land where sloping soil layers were deformed by gravity into curious, rumpled lobes extending from the steep valley walls to the banks of the streams. This creeping soil action is the dominant form of erosion at extreme latitudes where brief summer heat melts only the upper few inches of frozen soil.

The young Japanese man was tired, his feet hurt from walking in wet socks and boots, and his face was unrecognizable from welts produced by mosquito bites. It was ten o'clock p.m. by his watch, still broad daylight, and Ryota Fugimora was already cursing this horrid land where bears haunted the mountains, beastly insects made life unbearable, and the sun never sets.

He was ready for rest, hot tea, some nourishment and the comfort of a goose down sleeping bag. So, starting his one-burner gas stove, he put a pot of water on to boil and then removed his wet boots and socks and hung them to dry; of course, the mosquitoes instantly forced him to dig into his pack for more heavy wool socks and place a towel over his head and face as make-shift netting. It was awkward but he managed to drink tea and munch trail-mix while keeping his head wrapped in the towel. Ryota was very tired and decided to crawl into his mummy bag, both for warmth and to escape the endless swarming insects. He did not even think about removing his clothes. The mosquitoes had been joined by even more obnoxious biting flies. Inside the bag, he could still hear the mindless buzzing of these ravenous creatures but, except for one lone individual who was soon dispatched, he was free from their contact. The fully-zipped bag presented the unexpected virtue of blocking out sunlight which was still quite bright at 11 p.m.

Fugimora slept soundly for five hours and awakened to a sun still resting at 30 degrees above the horizon. He immediately started water to boil for tea and began repacking his gear for the long traverse he knew this day would bring. It took him five minutes to realize the mosquitoes and flies were gone. The sky was grey and the stiff wind blowing out of the west had dispersed the carnivorous insect hordes. Ryota felt the urgent need for a certain body function and with it he discovered the axiom every Alaskan knows "If you need to shit in the woods, find an exposed place in the wind; otherwise save it for another day."

By 5 a.m., the Japanese business man was on the trail south

along the east bank of Birch Creek. He forded the Yukon Fork in sock feet for the sake of his boots and put them back on with dry socks on the other side. Four hours of steady walking in sand and gravel adjacent to the creek with loaded rifle in hand brought him to the confluence of the northeast-flowing Puzzle Gulch Creek and the northwest-flowing Caribou Creek. His map, compass and I-pad GPS locator confirmed his position and he shifted his course to the southeast and followed the valley of Caribou Creek. The icy waters of this new creek flowed swiftly over almost continuous rapids and was enclosed by a rugged, narrow, V-shaped valley.

Ryota was hiking upgrade and could feel it. He stopped at 9 a.m. to make tea and eat two candy bars and some trail mix. During this respite, the sun emerged from the clouds and the wind dropped to nothing. Mosquitoes appeared instantly, of course, but the young man was learning. He pulled a pair of boxer underwear out of the pack, tied the leg openings shut with string and placed this garment over his head. With his baseball cap on and his collar securely buttoned over the waist band of the shorts he had a passable head net. Unfortunately, these underpants were blue. Fugimora did not know that blue is the favorite color of arctic mosquitoes and caused them to swarm his new head gear with renewed and fanatical frenzy. He could see through his underwear in spite of hundreds of insects perching a centimeter or two beyond his eyes and by continuously waving his rifle back and forth just beyond his nose he kept most of these in flight.

Ryota was conscious of the ridiculous figure he would pose to another human as he proceeded up Caribou Creek; but he knew there was only one other human within 30 miles in any direction. He pushed on nearly seven miles and was nearing the headwater of Caribou Creek when he spotted three moving dots on the slope of a mountain on his left. He threw up his rifle and brought the three dots into focus in his scope. They resolved into a mother grizzly and two half-grown cubs. He pulled out his binoculars and studied the bear family in earnest for a few minutes. They were about a mile distant and meandering down the side of hill 4531 towards Caribou Creek and towards him; as far as he could tell, the mother was unaware of his presence. Consulting his topographic map, Fugimora saw that he could avoid the bears and put himself onto the north rim of Caribou Valley by heading due south. It meant a tough uphill climb of 1200 vertical feet but three "grizz" gave him plenty of incentive.

His first uphill pull brought him to up to about 3500 feet elevation where he stopped to catch his breath and survey the progress of the bears. They were much closer now and at about his elevation but still on the opposite side of the valley. A moderate breeze was blowing at his present elevation and Ryota decided to remove his underwear from his head and place them in a pocket for ready access.

He rose and began trekking up slope again. The tundra vegetation was thick, wet and difficult to walk through because the unstable tussocks bent under his weight in an unpredictable manner and threatened his balance. His boots and socks were saturated again.   He pressed on, wanting to put a ridge between himself and the man-eaters on the far side of the valley.   He stopped again, briefly, at about 4000 feet elevation and studied the bears through his binoculars.   They were well below him at this point and still seemed oblivious to his presence.   Another two hundred yards up-slope and Ryota was on the ridge forming the north wall of Caribou Valley.   Although he wanted to remain on the ridge to watch the bears, he did not wish to be outlined against the sky to anyone entering the valley from the south and he was expecting just such a person.

The ridges defining Caribou Valley described a crude letter U opening to the south and Ryota stood at the north end near the midpoint of the bottom of the U.   In this saddle, between hill 4240 and hill 4564, a cluster of large schist boulders perched precariously on the narrow ridge line and provided cover from anyone approaching from the south.   Ryota squatted behind these rocks, removed his pack and pulled out a camouflage rain suit.   He donned the suit and placed his binoculars, I-pad, gloves, spare ammo and some snack food in a small haversack.   Next, he wrapped his back pack in camouflage netting to prevent any glare off the aluminum frame if the sun should make an appearance and stashed the pack in a crevice between the boulders.

He was ready to swing into action and slung his rifle and haversack and headed west for hill 4240.   When he reached it, he assumed a prone position and carefully scanned every part of the valley below him.   He saw nothing but tundra vegetation and rocks. He also scanned the ridge north of him for the bear family but by now they would have descended to the creek and be blocked from his view.

Clouds were materializing from nowhere, reducing visibility, so Fugimora hurriedly made his way south along the western wall of the valley. When he reached the extreme southern limit of the ridge, a quarter mile south of hill 4216, he had an excellent view of the headwaters of the Salcha River Valley. Looking southeast, he could easily see the rough airstrip constructed there many years ago, and, even without binoculars, he could see a small blue dot which he knew to be a dome tent. The crowd at the Circle Hot Springs bar had, most obligingly, informed him that a geologist was dropped by helicopter at this very airstrip seven days before. Ryota knew this person was Dr. Reuben Tobey, the arrogant dung-eating bastard who had sold him 550 kilos of platinum ore and rendered him drunk at Goodnews Bay.

His man was even now wading across the shallow headwaters of the Salcha River. He quickly retraced his steps north along the ridge to a point about half the distance between the mouth and the head of the valley and then descended the east slope to some boulders situated at about 3500 feet elevation. This descent was necessary to reduce the cross-valley distance of the shot he planned to make.

He made himself a comfortable seat from the tundra plants behind the largest rock and then carefully wiped the moisture from his rifle and cleaned the lenses of the scope. Next, he removed two brown, heavy cotton bags and filled them with sand and fine gravel dug from the base of the boulder. The bags were securely tied and placed on the upper surface of the rock in front of his seat. A few adjustments to the seat and the sandbags and all was ready; a very comfortable and functional setup for a bench shooter and virtually invisible from the far side of Caribou Valley.

The range-finder in his Zeiss scope told him the horizontal distance to a point across the valley at his elevation was exactly 879 yards; a long shot under these conditions but one he had made in practice many times. Today, it would not be practice. He began entering the relevant data into the ballistics software housed in his I-pad; distance, temperature, humidity, wind speed, and elevation; bullet weight and shape, sight height, muzzle velocity, drag coefficient, zero range, barrel pitch were already entered into the program. Wind would be the only variable that might throw off the calculations. To solve this problem, Ryota scrambled down the wall of the valley about 200 yards and tied a small strip of plastic green survey flagging to a bush. This flagging would alert him to changes in wind direction and velocity. Ryota returned to his sniper nest and considered himself ready for Dr. Ass-lick. Final computation for bullet drop and wind drift would be made at the last possible minute when the target came down off the ridge and reached a point of 3500 feet elevation.

Fugimora did not have long to wait. A solitary figure soon appeared on the eastern ridge line and he studied this figure through his binoculars. He could not make out the facial features but the hunter orange back pack was clearly discernable even at this distance, a distance far too great for a shot even for an expert like himself.

The figure made his way north slowly, stopping periodically to bang his large hammer on rocks. Ryota could hear the faint ringing sound the hammer made on the stones and had to ask himself "How can this man, or any man for that matter, make a living by simply banging a hammer on stones?"

When the figure was directly across the valley from his position, but still on the ridge crest, Ryota checked the distance through the range finder. It told him the target was at distance of 1084 yards from his position. Too far and too high still; he must wait for Ruben-san to come down off the ridge both to reduce the distance and permit a level shot. An hour passed and the geologist was still banging around on the ridge but had worked slightly north of the shooter's nest. If Dr. Lap-Chicken did not come within range soon, it meant another night and day of camping in this hell hole of bears, wind, mosquitoes and permafrost, a thought that was unspeakably repulsive to Ryota Fugimora.

Suddenly, Tobey began a diagonal descent back to the south from the ridge crest. This was perfect for Ryota but not so good for the rock man. Evidently, the geologist was heading for a cluster of black rocks directly across the valley from his nest. Fugimora smiled and thought "Those black rocks will be unluckiest rocks that dumb, sister-fucking bastard has ever banged".

Visibility was deteriorating as clouds continued to close in on Caribou Valley and humidity was approaching 100%. Contrary to most shooters belief, increased humidity actually improved ballistic performance slightly but one still had to see the target. Ryota made his final calculations, set the indicated readings on the scope, and checked his wind flag below. Everything was in readiness so he placed the rifle on the sand bags, flipped up the two lens covers of the scope, and began lining up Dr. Reuben Toby in the eye piece at 16X.

CHAPTER 21

Caribou Valley: East Side

The bullet entered his hunter-orange back pack, passed diagonally through its contents and exited through his left shoulder. He remembered that the bullet splattered against the black graphite schist in front of him but could not remember hearing the sound of the shot. The impact rotated his body180 degrees and threw him against the rock ledge with enough force to knock him unconscious.

He did not know how long he was out, but he did know that he had been shot because blood was spurting freely from his shoulder into his face. There was no pain at the moment, that would come later, but he knew he had to get the orange ruck sack off his back before the shooter had time to zero in on it again. He carefully lifted the left strap off the injured shoulder with his right hand, unsnapped the belly belt and wriggled free of the pack frame. He used his legs to push himself on his back until he was two or three meters beyond the pack, and protected from the direction of the shot, by a large angular slab of schist. He rolled his handkerchief into a cigar and stuffed it into the exit hole in his shoulder. It hurt now.

The fact that the exit wound was a precise circular hole told him he had been shot with a full-jacketed .30-caliber round judging by the diameter. A hunting round would have expanded on impact within the pack and blown his shoulder to hell. The blood spurting had been stopped by the handkerchief but it was now becoming saturated. He would need something more for a bandage. He had a first aid kit in the pack, as well as a loaded revolver, but moving the pack would alert the shooter that he was still alive. No, the pack must remain where it was. As this thought passed through his racing mind, the pack made a definite movement. He counted a little less than three seconds before the sound of the shot rolled across the misty valley. Sound travels through dry air at 25 degrees Celsius at a velocity of 1126 feet per second. That nearly three second delay meant the shooter was set up at a distance of a little less than 3000 feet or 1000 yards, a very long shot. That meant a pro, someone with sniper training and knowledge of ballistics, someone who does not fuck around. It also meant that the shooter was on the opposite side of the valley and the drizzly-misty conditions necessitated a shot at the orange pack rather than a head or chest shot. For this he should be grateful but at this moment he was not.

If the shooter could not actually see him through his scope, he would have to either cross the valley from his position or walk north along the west ridge and around the head of Caribou Valley and then back south along the eastern wall of the valley to make certain of a kill. He would choose the latter to avoid exposing himself and to reach a place to scope out the situation that would be beyond pistol or shotgun range. He would want a relatively close, unobstructed "finishing" shot in case his victim was only wounded. The pack made another rapid jerk with the sound still arriving nearly three seconds later. The shooter was maintaining his position, perhaps hoping for the weather in the valley to clear. That would be a bad thing, a really bad thing.

Reuben Tobey was a contract exploration geologist who worked under the name of Bushwalker Enterprises, a small company he had started. Bushwalker specialized in remote area metal exploration. He was now on the Arctic Circle of east-central Alaska in July, near the headwaters of the Salcha River, and you can't get much more remote than that. Reuben had been in the field for seven days working on foot from a base camp on the Salcha River. The helicopter, operating out of Circle City, Alaska, had dropped him and his gear at the base camp but would not be back for three more days.

A light rain began and visibility closed down rapidly in Caribou Valley. It would take the shooter least two or three hours to make his way along the ridges to this side of the valley, maybe longer if he felt a need to be super stealthy. Reuben crawled apprehensively back to his pack. He could not help noticing the pattern of the bullet holes, three holes within a six-inch diameter circle; no doubt about it, the guy was a hell of a marksman. He closed his eyes, grabbed the pack and crawled back to his place behind the rock where he could safely extract the first aid kit. He laid the blood-soaked handkerchief aside and improvised a dressing for his wound. The result was not pretty but it effectively slowed the loss of blood. Now his shoulder was throbbing like a jackhammer.

He cut the legs out of his trousers at mid-thigh level with his belt knife and improvised a sling with one leg. The other leg was cut into irregular strips and patches using the bone saw on the back of his belt knife. He then squirted blood from the rolled handkerchief over the ragged remnants of his pants and threw them in every direction. He ripped the left sleeve out of his shirt; it was, by now, a bloody mess. Then he cut the right sleeve off at the elbow and used it to wipe blood away from his eyes and off his face. He took off his rubber knee-boots and raked them with the bone saw and cut a rough chunk out of one of the boots. He squirted blood over the boots and tossed them in different directions and then extracted a new leather boot lace from the pack for future use. That was a laugh. He was as close to no future as a guy could get.

From inside the pack Reuben retrieved two pairs of heavy wool socks and put them on his feet. It required a real effort with just one arm but using the rock as a prop, he managed to stand himself up. The loss of blood made him dizzy and he nearly fell, but after a minute or so, he recovered sufficiently to pull off his leather belt which held his sheath knife and Brunton compass. He scored the belt using both edges of the knife, jabbed a few holes in it, cut off the buckle; he did the same with the leather case of the compass and the leather sheath of his knife, and tossed everything into the blood pool that had formed next to the boulder. Next, he dumped the contents of the pack onto the ground, scored his ruck sack, and put a few whacks in the aluminum frame and tossed the pack back to its former position. Then he turned over a few large rocks using his big rock hammer and made a few gouges on its wooden handle. Reuben knew his holstered revolver, ammo, notebook, map board and especially his expensive camera were key elements in the scene but it was still a difficult thing to leave them. He retained his waterproof wrist watch and stuffed a waterproof container of matches and a space blanket into the front left pocket of what remained of his pants; the first-aid kit went into the right. He squeezed the last blood out of the handkerchief and splattered it onto the rocks and tossed his hat, pocket knife, and the 10 X hand lens, suspended on a thong around his neck, into the mess.

After tying his belt knife and compass onto the boot lace and hanging it around his neck, Reuben climbed back up his path of descent a couple of meters and surveyed his work. The rocks hurt his socked feet but the scene was not too bad, really. He knew he should leave the compass and big knife behind but he would surely need them if he was going to get out of this tundra hell alive.

It was a theatrically-staged scene that would not fool a real Alaskan and certainly not a geologist with much experience in tundra country. But it just might fake out a gung-ho, military-sniper-type, especially if the guy was a little worried about grizzlies which were as common as rats in a grave yard in this part of Alaska.

CHAPTER 22

Miss Suzie Wong

Inspector Kuno sat down at his desk with a cup of tea. It was 8:05 a.m. and the phone rang before he could take his first sip. It was Inspector Komatsu of the Yokosuka police. A rapid and lengthy conversation ensued in Japanese. Inspector Kuno then immediately telephoned the police apartment where special agent Monty Simmons was staying and said "Good morning, Agent Simmons. I send a police car to bring you to my office. We must go to Yokosuka immediately and maybe stay for overnight. Bring what you need. We have a new headless body. A woman this time, goodbye."

At 10:15 a.m. Inspector Kuno and Agent Simmons walked into headquarters of the Yokosuka police. They were met by Inspector Kazuo Komatsu who showed them to his office. Komatsu offered the men tea, which they accepted, and then began relating the details of the homicide. A Japanese woman in her early to middle thirties was found dead this morning in her apartment. She had been beheaded and her hands had been removed, probably by samurai sword. The head and hands were not found at the scene of the murder. It was the second such murder in Yokosuka in less than 10 days. Kuno and Simmons exchanged meaningful looks.

The inspector informed them that murder scene had been isolated, a forensic team was on site, and nothing had yet been touched by the police. "Would you esteemed gentlemen care to examine the murder scene with me?" asked inspector Komatsu with a slight bow.

By 10:45 a.m., Komatsu, Kuno and Simmons were staring down at the mutilated body of what had formerly been a beautiful woman. She was attired in a glittering blue sequined bra and matching panties. A ghastly amount of blood was on the floor, walls and even the ceiling. The forensic crew had photographed the body, the blood markings on the walls and floor, and laid narrow path of plastic so the body could be approached without disturbing the scene. Inspector Komatsu exchanged words with a uniformed policeman who consulted his notebook. When finished, the inspector turned to Kuno and Simmons who were wearing rubber gloves and forensic booties and intently examining the body. He told them "Woman's name is Ayame Watanabe, a jo-san girl, who works at sailor bar across street. She died about 1 a.m. this morning. She is married to American ex-patriot by name of Donald Atkins. Both persons are known to the Yokosuka police. Atkins not been seen in the bar or neighborhood for one week but, I suppose, he has been residing peacefully in your morgue, Inspector Kuno."

Inspector Kuno nodded to Komatsu in agreement and then signaled that he was finished examining the body. The Yokosuka inspector ordered the body removed by technicians. A large tarpaulin was laid over the blood area and police detectives began a meticulous search of the apartment. The salient item recovered in this search was an international maritime passport issued in Hong Kong in the name of Donald Richard Atkins. Kuno studied the document which was written in French and English and then handed it to Simmons and asked him to read it. Simmons examined the document thumbing through the pages several times and then said "Gentlemen, it appears that our headless friend, Mr. Atkins, had a rating of able seaman-unlimited and recently returned to Yokosuka from a voyage aboard the ship *Aoki Maru*. This ship called on ports in Alaska, Canada and the Federated States of Micronesia."

Kuno took the passport back from Simmons and said "I think that we should now leave this murder investigation in the most capable hands of Inspector Komatsu and return to Tokyo. We must find out what this ship *Aoki Maru* has been up to and who owns it. Do you agree Agent Simmons?"

"I quite agree, Inspector Kuno" replied Monty. "I think we shall need the resources of both of our countries to do it."

An hour and a half later both men were at their lap tops in Inspector Kuno's Tokyo office making inquiries of customs agencies of three countries. It was clear to both policemen that the two beheadings were related to the bag of Chocó platinum and the ship, *Aoki Maru.* It was probable that Atkins had pilfered this material from the ship and had paid for it with his head. It was equally clear that the mutilated female body in Yokosuka was both his wife and Miss Suzie Wong, formerly of London.

What was not clear, was where this ship could have gotten Colombian platinum or where that ore was now, but a search of the ship seemed to be the logical next move. Kuno had found that the ship was docked in its home berth in Yokosuka and that it was registered as a Japanese flag ship owned by Fugimora Maritime Transport Limited. He began the paper work to obtain a warrant to search the ship.

Agent Simmons was finding he liked Japanese cuisine and suggested that they should take lunch while they waited for information to come in. "Hisashi-san, if you pick the restaurant, I will buy the lunch. What do you say?"

"Yes, certainly, I have not eaten today. Would you care for fish Monty-san?" Both men welcomed the change to first names and dropping formal titles. Both were thinking they would like to buy the other a drink or two. Hisashi Kuno led the way down to the street to a nearby restaurant with a bar that specialized in grilled sword fish. They bought each other four shots of sake and ate their fish with a good deal of satisfaction.

It required two days to obtain legal documents to inspect the *Aoki Maru.* The ship owned and operated by Fugimora Maritime Transport Ltd. was empty and the search turned up nothing unusual. The *Aoki Maru* was a relatively small ore-hauling vessel used to transport unconfined, or bulk, maritime cargos which, in this case, meant gold, platinum and palladium placer concentrates to Japan for the dental industry.

The cargo manifest indicated that the ship picked up 100 kilograms of unrefined placer platinum ore purchased from Goodnews Mining Company on June 2. Two days later it picked up an additional 900 kilograms of placer platinum from Emerson Quarry Operations in Vancouver, British Colombia. The source of the ore was listed as Tulameen, British Colombia. Both ore shipments were bound for Yokosuka, Japan. The ship then proceeded to the port of Weno in the Chuuk Islands, Federated States of Micronesia and off-loaded five crates of dental supplies for the Fugimora Dental Clinic, with a gross weight of five thousand kilograms, on June 11. The voyage ended in Yokosuka on June 18 where Japanese customs inspected and sampled the ores imported by Fugimora Precious Metals Ltd., Tokyo. Everything appeared to be in order as far as the manifest was concerned but the agents still had no explanation for 4.5 kilograms of ore from Colombia and two headless and handless corpses.

Neither Inspector Kuno nor Agent Simmons had any notion of what quantities of platinum were used in the dental industry. One thousand kilograms sounded like a lot of platinum. What kind of money would it be worth? They called the inspector's brother, Dr. Katsu Kuno, senior metallurgist at the Osaka mint and asked.

"Japan is the largest platinum-group-consuming country in the world and most of it goes into dental applications. In fact, recent laws in Japan require substitution of 20 % palladium for gold and platinum in dental work subsidized by the government. This new compound is called "kinpala alloy" and is used in around 90 percent of all Japanese dental work. Did you get all that brother?"

"Yes, I got it, Katsu. Why is it necessary to have this "kinpala alloy" at all?" asked the inspector.

"It is because the prices of gold and platinum have reached astronomical levels. Over the last few years, prices of gold and platinum have fluctuated between $1000 and $2000 US per troy ounce. That means brother, that 1000 kilos of platinum are worth about $32 million US at $1000 an ounce and double that at $2000 an ounce. It is very big money brother, zillions of yen. The government subsidizes a large amount of dental work in this country so it has to save yen wherever and whenever it can. Palladium is much cheaper than platinum so, it is mixed with gold or silver in place of platinum in varying ratios to produce alloys for inlays, crowns and bridges. Ruthenium and iridium are sometimes used as well but they can be even more expensive than platinum. Most of these alloys go into crowns and implants, where the alloy forms the core and porcelain is bonded around it to make an artificial tooth. Platinum group metals provide strength, rigidity and durability; the gold or silver provides malleability. I can tell you these fake teeth are damned expensive, Hisashi. I just paid for one in my wife's mouth, it was 50,000-yen, brother."

"Yes, I see, Katsu. Thank you, this is most useful. One more question please. All the metals for these dental uses are imported,

I think. Is this a large amount? Is it large enough to require ships?"

"Yes, it is large enough to require ships, hundreds of thousands of ounces a year. But you should know that small amounts of gold can come from Japan but most is purchased through Hong Kong. However, all platinum group metals are imported."

"Thank you. One last question Katsu, do the platinum ores destined for dental use pass through the mints or commercial refineries on their way to becoming pure metals?

"Some do, but most do not. Many dental labs are sufficiently equipped to refine their own ores since they deal only with small volumes. They are permitted by law to import and refine precious metals from ores they purchase but strictly for dental use, of course. They must report the source and how much they refine in this way to our revenue people."

"Thank you, Katsu. Please come for dinner this Sunday and bring your family. I want to see your wife's 50,000-yen tooth."

CHAPTER 23

Tachikawa City

Monty was looking forward to an adventure on the Tokyo subway system as well as a Japanese cookout. The inspector had offered to come downtown to the central district from his home in Tachikawa City and pick him up but Monty insisted he was up to the challenge of getting there on his own. After all, he had ridden the subways of New York City and Boston, so how difficult could it be? Of course, he downloaded the English version of the Tokyo area train-route map, located both his apartment and the Tokyo Station, a few blocks away, on the map and had drawn his route between the two stations with a red marker. It was only 40 kilometers. He was ready.

Hisashi had instructed him to take the *JR Chūō* line, orange on his map, at 12:00 noon but, if he should miss this train, another following the same route would leave the station 25 minutes later. Monty was there in time and managed to get a round trip ticket for Central Station-Tachikawa Station but he needed help from a high school girl in a cute sailor outfit. This good-hearted teen took him to his train platform and pointed out his train car. Seated in this car, with a ticket he could not read, and map on his lap, his confidence was restored.

His map indicated that the train would pull out to the north and follow a circular route around the northern boundary of the great city, first veering west and then south to Shinjuku Station, diametrically 20 kilometers west of Tokyo Central Station. As he studied the map, he was alarmed to read that Shinjuku Station claimed to be the busiest train terminal in the world; then his heart nearly stopped when he noticed his train was leaving the station heading south, instead of north. He bit his nails until he noticed that the map showed trains departing, either north or south, all looped around the city and joined at Shinjuku Station. Kuno had instructed him to remain on the train, definitely do not get off at Shinjuku; these were his orders, so he admired the sights as the train pulled along.

He saw sky scrapers everywhere, government buildings and hotels, giant department stores for shoppers and expensive-looking night clubs for the younger crowd. It was a tourist's dream but he sat tight as hundreds of people scrambled to get on and off the train during its brief five-minute halt at Shinjuku Station.

When the train resumed its route, he was relieved to see that it was, at least, heading west. Now, all he had to worry about was getting off at the Tachikawa station which should be the next stop and, fortunately for Treasury Agent Simmons, it was. He was expecting Tachikawa to be a small hick town since it was 40 kilometers west of the central Tokyo metropolis, but it was not.

There was no break in the metropolis and Tachikawa looked a lot like Shinjuku which looked a lot like central Tokyo. He scrambled off the train following the example of other passengers. Japanese trains stay on schedule and do not wait for hesitant foreign passengers.

As promised, inspector Kuno was waiting on the platform. He smiled and congratulated Monty on making the 40-minute trip. "Hisashi, I am very glad to see you. Is Tachikawa really a suburb of Tokyo? It all looks like one giant city to me."

"Yes, the cities have merged, but to Japanese people Tokyo is *the city* because it is a very old and Tachikawa is a suburb because it began its history only in 1941 during the war years."

They got into the black Toyota police car and were driving south out of the station when Monty asked, "Where is your house from here, Hisashi?"

"Maybe 20 kilometers, I live on perimeter of Tachikawa. Perimeter is correct word, Monty?"

"Yes, perimeter works fine. This area we are going through looks a bit run down compared to other parts of the city I have seen."

"That is because it is red light district of Tachikawa. Perhaps I should make a brief stop here for you, Monty-san" replied the inspector trying to conceal a sly smile.

"Thank you, inspector but I think I can make it through the next few days. Maybe then." Both men laughed at this exchange. Monty saw a prominent sign that had the English name *San*

Bernardino, California on it and asked the policeman "What is that sign telling us, Hisashi?"

"It tells us that Tachikawa and San Bernardino are sister cities. These cities exchange students, gifts and cultural events. Look over there Monty, we pass bank famous for biggest robbery in history of Japan. Bad guys take 604 million yen in 70 bags of cash."

"Wow, that is a lot of money, did you catch the robbers?"

"Yes, we get money back and arrest six people, all Yakuza. You know about them Monty?"

"Oh yes, an international crime syndicate of bad asses, we have them committing crimes in the US as well. I have arrested a few of them myself."

"Excuse please, Monty, but what is 'bad asses'?"

"It is slang that means they are violent, desperate killers of the worst kind, Hisashi."

"Yes, this is true. They are worst element in Japan and seem to grow faster than weeds in garden."

At this point, inspector Kuno pulled up to his house, a relatively compact structure, featuring prominent vertical and horizontal wooden beams, a steeply sloping roof of light grey tiles and quite deep eaves. The entrance was elevated three steps above the foundation and featured a porch with two wooden folding-chairs overlooking a simple, but appealing, Zen garden. Most of these attributes were mirrored by neighboring houses which were more closely spaced than in most New England neighborhoods that

Monty was familiar with. Certainly, it was a far cry from the architectural style and open spaces of Llano, Texas. Here, one was impressed by simplicity, a sense of order and serenity, as opposed to uniformity. It was different from the spacious rambling homes and chaotic yards seen in many America cities.

At the door Kuno, kicked off his European style black shoes and donned a pair of flip flops, a move facilitated by his split-toed tabi socks. Monty tried to follow suit with one of several pairs of flip flops but was defeated by his American socks. Kuno watched with obvious amusement as Simmons was forced to remove his socks, place them in his pocket and then wiggle his bare feet into the sandals. Agent Simmons knew Japanese etiquette required taking off shoes before entering the house to protect the tatami mats covering the polished wooden floors. His tour book told him this much, but it did not mention tabi socks.

Inspector Kuno was rushed by two adolescent girls as he entered the house. He hugged them both and introduced them to Monty as Naoki, 14 years of age, and Natsumi, 10 years of age, and introduced Monty to his daughters in Japanese. He was not sure what Hisashi said to the girls but their giggling ceased immediately and they solemnly bowed to Monty. He returned their bows with equal solemnity and hoped he was on firm social ground. He wanted to look around at the interior furnishings but the inspector's brother, Katsu, was suddenly shaking his hand and saying "I hear you made the train ride from downtown, Monty. No major screw ups, I hope."

"No, not really Katsu but I was a little surprised when the train left Tokyo Station heading south instead of north."

"Don't worry about that Monty, nobody ever knows what direction the train leaves the station but they all go to the same place. How about a beer?"

"Sounds good, Katsu" replied Monty with a wide smile.

The inspector introduced his wife, Midori, who evidently did not speak English and Katsu's wife, Kamiko, who did. Bows all around and then the group went out to the backyard patio which overlooked another Zen garden featuring a miniature waterfall that emptied into a large glazed pot. Katsu served the men Asahi beers from a cooler distinguished by a Budweiser logo on its side; the ladies and children drank tea.

Three hibachis were blazing away with charcoal that was clearly charred wood fragments of irregular shape rather than the uniform briquettes familiar to Americans. Katsu was cutting the backbones out of three chickens with poultry shears and brushing them with red paste. "Do you grill in your back yard, Monty?"

"No, I don't have a back yard, Katsu but my geologist friend, Dr. Martin, does. He will ask me for details on what you are doing to those chickens, so tell me everything."

"Ok, first I *spatchcock* the birds and marinate them in a paste of soy sauce, brown sugar, and crushed garlic, ginger and red chilies. That just means I remove the spine so they lay out flat like a book so the whole chicken grills uniformly. They do it in Europe all the time but not much in the states. Then I put them on the hibachi at medium heat, so it's not much different than what Americans do, except your grills are much bigger. One thing I learned in America, Monty, is that Americans love big. When the chickens are nearly done, I will stack them in one of the hibachis, close the vent, and put the lid on to cut down the heat and keep them warm. At this point, Kamiko will start preparing fried rice in the kitchen."

Hisashi had listened to this discourse while holding three open beers. "I will drink these beers, myself, if you gentlemen wish to continue with the chicken seminar."

"No, I want to drink beer" said Monty "and I want to discuss where you think we are on our case. You know, I will have to leave Japan soon."

"Let us sit with beers and talk like policemen then, Monty. First, we have two murders and no suspects. Not so good, but we have connection between victims, Colombian platinum and Fugimora ship that carries platinum, but not Colombian platinum. This smells like rotten octopus to me. I think Fugimora ship finds Colombian platinum somewhere and smuggles it into Japan. What do you think Monty?"

"My thoughts, exactly, inspector. We need to know who is behind this Fugimora ship and get our hands on the samples collected by Japanese customs. This might not be easy since customs may not want to share with National Police."

Kuno smiled at this and said "You are right, but I will get their samples even if they do not wish to cooperate. I will ask Dr.

Nakamura of the Tokyo mint to analyze these samples and send results to Dr. Martin in Texas."

"Yes, that will save time and, who knows, maybe even someone's head. I am sure Dr. Martin will consider these samples essential to finding how this Colombian stuff got into the country." The two men finished their beers and walked over to the hibachis and watched Katsu turn over his *spatchcocked* chickens.

"What are you doing now, Katsu?" asked Monty, looking over his shoulder as the metallurgist began impaling vegetables marinated in some kind of brown sauce on long bamboo skewers.

"I am making vegetable kebabs; very traditional, you know. I spear chunks of eggplant, shiitake mushroom and zucchini squash in sequence and repeat till skewer is full and we will give them a quick grilling on the two open hibachis. By the time they are done, Kamiko will have the rice finished and we eat."

"Maybe you should tell me about the sauce you use, in case Martin asks."

"Yeah sure, Monty, it is just a very simple combination of sesame oil, soy sauce and rice vinegar spiced up with chili paste, chopped green onions, ginger and garlic. It's good for marinating anything, chicken, fish, shrimp, or veggies. We pour a little glaze of red pepper-red onion jelly, that Midori preserves every year, over the kebabs when we eat them. It is a super good combination."

The men continued to drink beer while the two ladies began setting the low table which clearly was designed to make the diners sit on the tatami mats. It would be interesting. Meanwhile, Miss Naoki, the 14-year-old, approached agent Simmons and boldly asked in passable English "Are you a policeman like my father?"

"Yes, I am, Naoki. I work for the US Treasury Department. Do you go to school?"

"Of course, all children go to school. You are the first westerner that I have ever met. I am not sure that I like you."

"Well, I am truly sorry if you don't like me, Naoki, because I have a great liking for you. I was just admiring the unusual socks you are wearing." The child had on enormous bulky white socks, fully 36 inches long, piled up in lumpy rings between her ankles and knees.

"Do you like them? They are called 'loose socks' and all the girls at school wear them."

"Yes, I like them very much, but I am wondering how you are able to keep such big socks up to your knees."

"Well, you must be a very bad policeman if you cannot figure that out. It should be obvious that they are held up by sock glue" replied the cheeky teen.

Monty was wishing this smart-ass brat would disappear. He drank a big slug of beer and walked over to see what was happening on the hibachi grills. Mrs. Kamiko Kuno was there, next to her husband, and was drinking a bottle of Asahi just like an American woman. He was glad to see that. Hisashi walked up at that moment and asked his sister-in-law if he could see her 50,000-yen tooth. Kamiko laughed and said "Feast your eyes on it, boys.

One false tooth and it is worth more than my parent's home." She opened her mouth wide and pointed to the lower rear molar on the left side. Hisashi and Monty both peered into her mouth and followed the finger to the implant.

"Looks like a normal molar tooth to me, I do not see any platinum in it at all" observed the inspector.

"No, I don't see anything metallic, either" Monty agreed.

"The platinum forms the core of the fake tooth and it is completely surrounded by dental porcelain" Katsu informed them. "It is supposed to look like a normal tooth."

"Well thank you, Kamiko-san, you have been a great help to our current investigation" quipped Hisashi with a grin.

"You are welcome, brother-in-law. Is there a reward for helping the National Police?" laughed Kamiko.

"Your reward is to know that you are protecting the security and honor of Japan" replied the inspector, drily, and this drew a laugh from the crowd.

The dinner was a great success and Katsu was praised by all the adults. The children ate in silence under the watchful eye of their father and were excused as soon as they had finished. Monty found eating on the floor, Indian-fashion, a little odd but quite pleasant in this friendly family group. The adults continued to drink beer throughout the meal which, possibly, contributed to Monty losing his flip flops under the table.

After the meal, the group adjourned back to the patio where coffee and tea were served by Midori. Monty asked Katsu if he felt up to answering some technical questions about platinum refinement. Katsu smiled and said, "What do you boys want to know about my business?"

"Well, first, I would like to ask if there is any chance of determining the point of origin of platinum after it is refined" inquired Simmons.

"Zero chance, Monty and that's because the original ratios of platinum group metals in the ore are eliminated by separating the elements through a series of complicated chemical procedures."

Inspector Kuno then asked, "Can you give us a short explanation of the processes involved with a minimum of science talk?"

"Ok, let's start at the beginning. Ores are mixtures of metallic minerals and the rock enclosing them. Most of the rock will be liberated from the valuable material by the process of crushing and milling. The milled waste rock is eliminated by some kind of concentration process which usually means flotation, if metal sulfides are present, or hydraulic methods, if they are absent. If it is a sulfide concentrate, it will be roasted to produce a matte which will then be leached of copper, nickel, iron, *et cetera* leaving the platinum metals behind. If it is not a sulfide concentrate it goes directly to the leaching process. Are you policemen still with me here?"

The two cops looked at each other and both said "Maybe" simultaneously.

"Well, at any rate, the next step is leaching with aqua regia, a powerful acid, which takes platinum and palladium into solution but leaves the other PGE metals in the residue. Both elements are precipitated from this solution as salts then converted back to the metallic state. The acid residue still contains all the other PGE, meaning iridium, osmium, rhenium and rhodium. They have to be individually taken into solution and converted back to metal. This is the classical extraction method. It's complicated, isn't it?" The policemen groaned.

"So, when you finally recover each of the six individual platinum group metals, you have the elements in the form of powdered metal, very ugly powdered metal. To convert them to the massive, bright, beautiful metals you see in bullion, these powders have to be melted and that is not easy at all. Platinum and palladium have melting points of 1772 and 1552 degrees Celsius respectively and can be melted in conventional induction furnaces. On the other hand, rhenium requires 1963 degrees, ruthenium 2250 degrees, iridium 2443 degrees, and osmium requires a whopping-ass 3027 degrees Celsius to melt. Temperatures this high require melting in an electron beam. So, how do you like metallurgy so far, guys?"

Monty said, "My head is spinning".

Hisashi said "I need another beer."

CHAPTER 24

Tobey Alive

Caribou Valley at 65.1° north latitude is barren, forestless, tundra country and no place to spend a night without an expensive goose-down mummy bag anytime, even in mid-July. Tobey knew he would die of exposure, if he did not bleed to death first, and if the sniper did not get him in his sights again. These were big ifs. As he painfully and slowly descended the eastern ridge enclosing Caribou Valley he realized he must get to his sleeping bag or it would all be over.

The dense mist that limited visibility to a few feet was in his favor, the fact that he had to trudge two miles across difficult open tundra back to his camp was not. If the weather cleared in the next two hours he was finished. Going through swampy knee-high tussocks in sock feet was no picnic, his feet were numbed by icy water, his shoulder throbbed, and he was acutely concerned about leaving a blood trail that the sniper, or worse yet, an actual grizzly could follow.

He got his bearings with his compass and headed south-southeast towards the junction of Gulch Creek and Salcha River which was a knee-deep creek here in its headwaters. Reuben could hear the rushing water of the Salcha through the dense foggy atmosphere and pushed on at a steady pace, pausing periodically to examine his back trail for drops of blood. He reached the Salcha and his camp after two hours of very tough downhill trudging for a man with a bullet hole in him.

The weather remained closed in, so the shooter, who would by then, be on the ridge above the shooting scene, examining the remains of the grizz picnic, could not see him. Absent a blood trail, no human could track him across the tundra. Those hated tussocks, such a bitch to walk on, retained human foot impressions less than 60 seconds before closing back to their original shape. He made the camp site and quickly stuffed his mummy bag into a small day pack along with dry socks, a woolen sock cap, and two cans of Chef Boyardee ravioli. With intense pain, he awkwardly managed to don the spare rubber knee boots he had set up on sticks to dry the day before. He disturbed the camp site as little as possible as he thought the dick-head sniper might have checked out the place before he went to work with his rifle. If the bastard was dumb enough, he would go for the faked grizzly scenario, but if he had any brains he would soon realize that a wounded man would be forced to return to the camp and would check for the missing sleeping bag.

Reuben wished he had a second mummy bag to leave behind in the tent but he didn't. Instead he rumpled up two heavy blankets that he used as a sleeping pad, tossed his heavy parka over them and threw his long johns into the mix. It might fool a dumb-shit, but he couldn't count on it.

Within five minutes, the wounded geologist was heading for hill 3744, one mile southeast of the air strip. He liked this hill because it had a good exposure of diopside-garnet-wollastonite skarn but he was not going there for mineral collecting today. He was going there because, from the summit, he would be able to watch the camp to see if the shooter made an appearance. If he had to run for it, he could contour around the hill to the south, parallel to Willow Creek, and reach the larger hill 4442. This hill was at the northern extremity of an elongate, northeast-trending ridge, from which he thought he could elude anybody.

The weather showed no signs of clearing as the Bushwalker president reached the summit of 3744. This was good as far as the sniper was concerned but not so good for a man with a gunshot wound who was wet and cold. Luckily the bandage had held and he had not lost any more blood as far as he could tell. The cold weather helped restrain the bleeding, he figured. He re-dressed the wound which was beginning to scab over and made adjustments to his sling. Then he took off the wet remnants of his clothes and socks and got into his mummy bag naked.

He wrapped his wet clothes and socks in the space blanket for a pillow, hoping they might not freeze when the temperature fell.

From a sitting position, he could watch the camp and the open approach to it from Caribou Valley when the mist cleared. Lying down he could not be seen by anyone from the north or west. He was warm now and used his trusty belt knife to open a can of Chef Boyardee's best. It was awkward with one hand but he managed without cutting himself. There was really no need to lose more blood.

Tobey looked at his watch. It had been a little more than four hours since he had been shot and the sun was showing signs of breaking through the mist. He realized that he was extremely lucky to be in the position he was in. He was warm, his belly seemed satisfied with cold ravioli professionally prepared by the Chef and there were at least three miles between him and the shit-head with a rifle. Of course, there was no question of building a fire which would have added to his comfort immeasurably. No fuel for one thing, but the smoke would certainly give the game away. The sky began to clear, which favored him now, rather than the sniper. He managed to stay on watch until about 6:30 p.m. before sleep overtook him. By 8:40 p.m. he was back on watch. At this latitude and time of the year there is no real darkness, only a sort of twilight; it is the land of the midnight sun after all.

Ryota Fugimora studied the site through his binoculars from a rocky ledge on the ridge about 100 yards away. There was no movement, but neither was there a body that he could see. Since everyone in bear country carried a gun he did not wish to approach the scene any closer. He watched patiently for an hour and then very carefully closed in to about 30 yards and studied the scene again. At this distance his binoculars revealed a chaotic display of scattered, bloody clothing, equipment and freshly overturned rocks. He could clearly make out the orange pack, a shining camera, and a holster that still contained a pistol. Holding his rifle at the ready, he slowly closed the distance to 10 yards.

There was no sign of life, but there was plenty of blood. It was everywhere, on the rocks, on the boots, on the ragged pieces of clothing but there was no Dr. Tobey. It occurred to the Japanese business man that this was exactly the scenario that one might expect if a grizzly had come onto the scene and ate up the body of his downed geologist. He could see a belt buckle and the remains of a belt some distance from it, a dispersed pair of distressed rubber boots, and the big rock hammer with teeth marks on the handle. As he studied the orange back pack he was gratified to see three bullet holes defining quite a nice tight pattern for 879 yards, especially considering the rather poor shooting conditions.

Fugimora rewarded himself with a candy bar as he continued to survey the scene of what were, evidently, two distinct crimes. "Poor Dr. Tobey" thought Fugimora with a vulpine smile "Shot by a bad man and then eaten up by a hungry, vicious bear, or, perhaps, even three bears". Ryota wondered if Dr. Dung-heap was alive when the bears got to him, he hoped so, but doubted it; he knew his first shot was a good, solid hit from the movement of the pack and the bullet pattern on this same pack suggested the second and third shots were simply over-kill. Too bad really; Ryota would have enjoyed thinking about poor Reuben-san being crushed alive under the slavering jaws and hideous yellow fangs of a ravenous, man-eating grizzly.

Fugimora wanted to collect a trophy for this kill and his preference would be Dr. Tobey's skull, but this particular object was nowhere to be seen. Evidently eaten, completely eaten. But he dared not approach the bloody scene any closer for the sake of a trophy. It would be most unwise to get blood on his boots and then have this same man-eater track and eat him as well.

Ryota shouldered his gear and made the ascent of the east wall of Caribou Valley and headed north along the ridge towards the rocks where he had stashed his pack. After carefully glassing all of the slopes leading down into Caribou Creek for bears, he lashed his rifle to the pack and began his descent keeping his eyes peeled for moving dots on the opposite slopes. The weathered had begun to clear and this was a signal to put his blue underpants on his head again.

Ryota walked steadily for three hours before he decided to stop for tea and a snack. While the water was heating, he was approached by two arctic rock ptarmigans. These ground birds were brown with white breasts and wings with a tiny bit of red over each eye. They resembled the grouse he had shot in Ireland and he figured they were good to eat. They were also extremely stupid birds and he easily killed them both with stones. He drank his tea through his underwear, a most distasteful and humiliating experience, and plucked his dinner. When finished, he put the birds in a plastic zip-lock bag, mounted up and continued his trek down to the junctions of Puzzle Gulch and Birch Creeks.

At this point, he was too tired to continue further without a meal and some rest. He gathered an armful of dry drift wood scattered around on the gravel bar between the creeks; by now he had enough experience to know that he was lucky to find any fuel at all in this arctic hell hole. But it would suffice to roast his birds on a green willow sapling. After eating his dinner, he happened to look at his watch; it was 1:30 a.m.! He cursed this cold, barren, unholy land where night and darkness did not exist. Ryota Fugimora was beginning to appreciate what the Yukon poet meant by the "Great Alone".

Tobey managed to keep watch through the cold hours of the evening but dozed off a second time, around 10:30 p.m. He awoke two hours later with an extremely painful throb in his shoulder. He changed his bandage again using the last of the gauze and cotton pads in his first-aid kit. The exit wound looked clean, no signs of infection and a lovely, crusty scab. He had no idea of the condition of the entrance wound on the back side of his shoulder. He watched the camp below him intently for anything that would suggest the presence of a human, but he saw nothing. He had two more days to wait for his scheduled pick up by the helicopter from Circle City. This thought led him to consider how the sniper had gotten his miserable ass to Caribou Valley.

Reuben was positive the shooter could not have flown by helicopter or fixed wing to any point remotely close to his Salcha camp. A man in this county can hear aircraft approaching from many miles away. So, the shooter must have flown into Fairbanks where he rented a vehicle and drove east on the Steese Highway. Alternatively, he might have chartered a float plane to drop him on some lake or perhaps even the Yukon River. But the latter option could not get him within reasonable walking distance of the Salcha camp. It followed that he must have driven to the villages of either Circle City or Circle Hot Springs. The latter would be closer if one were going to hoof it to Caribou Valley. It would be a damn tough hike even for a Navy Seal carrying the necessary camp gear and a sniper rifle.

From Circle Hot Springs, the sniper would have to hike due south to the confluence of Yukon Fork and the South Fork of Birch Creek and then continue south along the South Fork to its junction with Caribou Creek. A further seven-mile traverse southeast along Caribou Creek would get him to Caribou Valley. It could be done, but it was 30 or 35 miles through trackless tough country and the guy would have to know exactly where he was going. Of course, that would be the easiest part, since everyone in the bars of both Circle Hot Springs and Circle City would know that geologists routinely use the Salcha camp site because bush pilots can land fixed-wing aircraft there and deliver supplies from Fairbanks. These same people, however, would also take notice of a stranger asking questions about such things.

Tobey concluded that Circle Hot Springs must be where the fuck-head with the rifle left civilization and this would entail two days of hard hiking at least. That meant the shooter must make camp coming and going. He spent the next hour with his attention split between the camp below, the approach from Caribou Valley, and searching the northern horizon for smoke from a camp fire. There was nothing, nothing that is, until a few minutes past 1:30 in the morning, when he noticed a very faint wisp of smoke rising on the northern sky line. He slept better during the remaining hours of the morning and rose about 8 a.m. to make his descent down to his camp and wait for the helicopter. After a bit of rest and food, he thought he might even venture back to the site of the shooting to pick up his gear.

CHAPTER 25

The Grey Parrot

Doc Martin was on his porch drinking coffee, reading his paper and enjoying a brilliant magenta sunrise when the telephone rang at 6:30 a.m. Doc took a sip of coffee and said "Good morning" into the phone.

"It may be morning where you are, Doc, but it sure as hell isn't here in Tokyo" answered Monty Simmons.

"Well, well, if it isn't Simmons of US Treasury making the world safe for widows and orphans."

"Yes, it is me and I hope to see you at the Parrot tomorrow night about 6 p.m., give or take an hour or two. I'll call you again when I'm on the ground in Houston."

"Ok, it's a date. I presume you have plenty to tell me after three weeks of intensive detective work in Japanese bars and whore houses."

"That I do, and some questions as well. See you tomorrow night."

This was the second unexpected phone call in the last 12 hours. Last night, he talked with Reuben Tobey, chief geologist for Bushwalker Enterprises operating out of Anchorage, Alaska. Doc was finishing the final report on a project for him in east-central Alaska. Tobey had insisted on coming to Llano to receive it in person. This was a little odd but he mentioned that he also wanted to discuss another matter. Perhaps it was another consulting project. At any rate, he would be arriving the next afternoon by rental car from DFW Airport.

This was a teaching day for Doc, so, after he had drunk his second cup of coffee and swallowed a clove of pickled garlic, he grabbed a yellow pad. He made notes to remind him which specimens he would need for his lecture on pegmatite minerals. Longstreet hungrily eyed the yellow writing tablet Doc was holding; the General considered this item a very special delicacy.

When Doc walked into the Grey Parrot Bar that evening, Dr. Reuben Tobey was seated on Doc's stool at the end of the bar with a big mug of beer. He was in deep conversation with Rhoda, naturally. Martin and Tobey had known each other in grad school at New Mexico Tech a few decades back and their paths had occasionally crossed as each man trotted the globe in pursuit of fame and fortune in the precious metals business; Singapore, Johannesburg, Stockholm, Guadalajara among other places. These encounters virtually always ended in drinking all night but the last such night must have been at least six or eight years back. Tobey looked about the same, less hair and a bit greyer, perhaps, maybe

10 pounds heavier. Doc sat on the stool next to him and said in a voice loud enough for everyone in the bar to hear "I thought you were running from the IRS."

Tobey smiled back via the bar mirror and said "Yeah, they got all my money so the rich Texas consultant will have to pay my bar bill here."

Rhoda returned with a glass of red wine for Doc and playfully said "If this gentleman is a fugitive I am pretty sure we will have a Treasury agent here in a few minutes".

"Yeah, that's right, Rhoda, we will have to restrain him until Agent Simmons arrives."

"Keep the beer coming and I'll wait right here for him."

"So, old friend, what brings you to hot and dusty Llano? I can't believe that the chief geologist for Bushwalker has to fly from Anchorage for a report on skarn mineralogy" said Doc, taking a sip of his wine and giving Rhoda a wink.

"Yeah, I am the chief geologist but I am also the only geologist. Bushwalker is a one dog sled and I am the dog. But I recently got shot, up in the Salcha country, and I came down here to talk about it with you."

"Really! A jealous husband chased you all the way to the headwaters of the Salcha River to shoot you, and you want to talk with *me* about it?" Doc asked with a broad grin.

"Yeah, that's it. You want to see the bullet hole?" Tobey asked, flashing his eyebrows up and down in Groucho Marx fashion. He unbuttoned and removed his shirt for all to see and informed the patrons of the Grey Parrot "There on my back is the entrance wound through the left scapula, the exit wound is here in front on my left shoulder." Both wounds were about the size of a dime and still red where new flesh was forming.

"That is impressive, Tobey, but you are lucky hubby wasn't carrying a .44 magnum loaded with hollow points" volunteered Doc with mock sympathy.

"I was lucky all around, Dr. Martin. I'm just real damn lucky to be here drinking beer on your tab" responded the wounded geologist, putting his shirt back on.

At that moment, Agent Monty Simmons walked in wearing his cowboy get up. "Hey what's going on here, a male strip show?"

"Yeah, and you just missed the action, Monty" Rhoda quipped.

"Monty, meet Dr. Reuben Tobey, famous geologist from the land of the midnight sun. Reuben, meet Agent Monty Simmons, international crime crusader. Rhoda, give everyone in the house, except Nestor, a drink please" said Doc with another grin.

Luckily for Doc's bar tab, there were not that many patrons in the Parrot. The three men seated themselves at a table and took turns buying rounds for the house. It was good for Rhoda's business, as well as the other patrons, but not much in the way of crime fighting took place.

The conversation eventually rolled around to the attempt on Tobey's life in the middle of nowhere, a place where men do not belong. When he had finished his story, Monty asked if there were any clues to the identity of the sniper. "Yeah, the state police quizzed the people in Circle Hot Springs and found out that the only stranger to come in the place for weeks was a young Japanese guy with an Irish accent. He left a rental car there for four days and I think I know exactly who he is" Tobey replied, again flashing his eyebrows. "A young guy, by the name of Fugimori or Fugimora, or something like that, he is a big money man from Tokyo."

This name immediately captured the attention of Agent Simmons who was in the process of signaling Rhoda to serve them up again. "You know the guy's name, but the state police don't? Monty asked incredulously.

"That's right. How many young Japs with Irish accents would you expect to see in the back country of arctic Alaska? I did business with just such a guy a few weeks before I was bushwhacked, while I was on contract work for Goodnews Mining. This guy bought almost 18,000 ounces of platinum ore averaging 82 % platinum" announced Tobey arching his bushy brows again for emphasis.

"Well, Dr. Tobey, this is certainly a weird coincidence, because I just happen to be on the trail of a criminal ship carrying platinum ore from Goodnews Bay to Japan. The name of this ship is the *Aoki Maru*. It belongs to Fugimora Maritime Transport. Does this ring a bell?" queried the Treasury agent.

"That was the name of the ship I loaded my platinum on. It was a big sale, more than half the company's production for the year. Hard to forget a sale like that, the bosses were so happy that we all stayed drunk for a week."

"Could you translate 18,000 ounces to kilograms for me Reuben? Monty asked.

"18,000 troy ounces equate to approximately 550 kilograms" interjected Doc Martin, who was following the conversation with interest.

"Tobey, are you sure that the amount was 550 kilograms of ore? I ask because I have examined this ship's manifest which reported that only 100 kilograms were purchased from Goodnews Mining."

"I am damned sure, Monty; it was about six months of our dredge production. I recorded the weight of the loaded truck myself and sent the crated ore to the ship while I took the Jap dude out to the dredge on a tour. You know, we try to keep track of such trifles when 22 million bucks' worth of metal is going out the door."

"Look boys" interjected Doc "it seems that we are onto something important here. Let's get Nestor to feed us and continue this conversation at my place." All agreed, but Tobey insisted on buying another round while Nestor cooked up beef and greens on rice for the three professional gentlemen, each of whom now considered they had a pretty good reason to celebrate on this night. The dinner helped, but there was a further round of rounds which included toasts to both Rhoda and Nestor who had come out of the kitchen to watch the fun. Rhoda decided that Doc was in the best shape and that he should drive the merry band to the ranch. She insisted on the keys of the two rental cars.

During the drive to the ranch, Dr. Tobey opened the conversation with "Hey Monty, has Martin here ever told you about the time he got our asses arrested in Tlaque-Plaque?"

"No, I think I would remember a story involving the arrest of my consultant. What the hell is a Tlaque-Plaque, anyhow?

"It's not a thing, it's a place just outside of Guadalajara in Jalisco, Mexico and we had a chance meeting there in a bar called *El Gato Negro*." Doc Martin said nothing but began to smile as he recalled this particular adventure with his inebriated former school mate. "Yeah, Martin and I were working on unrelated jobs but just happened to choose the same bar on the same night. He had been to the Sunday bullfights in Guadalajara and I had been on a bus tour to the famous village of Tequila, some 60 or 70-kilometers northwest of the big city. I'm afraid I came back a little drunk from the Jose Cuervo distillery and I am quite certain Martin got drunk at the bullfight arena. Anyhow, I'm having a beer at the bar in *Gato Negro* and who should walk into the place but my old buddy from Socorro. Another example of great minds thinking alike, ain't that right Martin?"

Doc was concentrating on his driving but also laughing at the recollection of this drunken encounter with the irrepressible Tobey, who only became this loquacious when he was exceptionally drunk. Doc dutifully played his part by answering "Yeah that's right Tobey, we were definitely the two best-educated drunks in the *Gato Negro* that night. New Mexico Tech would have been real proud of us." This drew a laugh from both Monty and Tobey.

Tobey resumed with his story "Well, anyhow, we had a couple of beers at the bar and then went to a table and ordered some dinner. While we were eating, I made the fatal mistake of pulling out a bottle of Jose's finest from my day pack; damn thing cost me 60 bucks U.S. at the distillery, if you can believe it, but it was the finest blue agave on this planet. We started taking hits and by the time we finished dinner we were both completely in the bag."

Doc interjected with "I think Monty will believe it, at least he ought to, after seeing us tonight".

"So, after we were bitten by the blue agave snake, we hit every bar in Tlaque-Plaque. I don't remember much of that part but we ended up in a strip club and the eminent Dr. Martin, here, got us arrested by fingering one of the girls on the stage" continued Tobey. All three of the drunken amigos were laughing by this point.

Doc had to interject again with "God damn it Tobey! That was you who fingered the girl, not me".

Tobey wound the story down as Doc slowed and turned onto the dirt lane leading up to the ranch "So the next morning, we wake up in the damn Tlaque-Plaque jail with a mean headache and no one to make our bail. Finally, Martin here gets the idea to call his hotel in Guadalajara and ask the manager to get us out so he can pay his hotel bill and the guy actually does it; and, best of all, he adds our bail cost to Doc's bill. All I can say is that manager saved our asses. And the greatest thing about the whole damn story is that, since both of us work for ourselves, nobody could fire us." They pulled up to the ranch house laughing to the point of tears.

The boys had arrived at the ranch without incident or accident. But, when General Longstreet made his customary appearance, Dr. Tobey announced, "I am going to kick that goat's ass". Doc warned against this choice of action but Tobey shouted, "No worries mates, I know all there is to know about goats." Once out of the truck Tobey lunged in an attempt to grab the General's horns. Longstreet, on his part, had some experience with drunks and reacted by quickly pulling his horns back out of reach and then, with rear legs coiled, sprang forward into Tobey's extended body delivering a first-class butt to the geologist's forehead. This stunning blow was not fatal, but it did end the evening goat wrestling event. Doc and Monty supported the defeated geologist in an oscillatory group traverse to the house, during which Tobey moaned "Gawd damn it Purple, your fucking goat almost killed me."

Once the three celebrants succeeded in making their way into the house, Tobey was deposited on the couch with an icepack for the egg-size red knot already forming on his forehead. Meanwhile, Doc opened a bottle of wine and filled glasses for Monty and himself. "Well Monty, it seems like the information Tobey gave you about Goodnews Bay is some kind of Rosetta Stone in your investigation. Is it?"

"Yes, and I think this is where you can help me as well, Doc. Why would the Fugimora ship find it necessary to lie about ore purchased legally in Alaska?"

"I have an idea about that Monty but first tell me what else that ship's manifest told you."

"It said the ship left its home port of Yokosuka, Japan on May 22 and arrived at Goodnews Bay, Alaska on June 2. Then it goes on to Vancouver, British Columbia, arriving on June 4, where it picked up another 900 kilograms of platinum placer. After that it went on to Weno in the Federated States of Micronesia to off-load dental equipment on June 11, and finally it returned to Yokosuka on June 18."

Doc was silent a moment and then asked, "And did the manifest say where this 900-kilos of Canadian ore originated?"

"Yeah, the manifest listed the point of origin as a locality in British Columbia called Tulameen."

"Really?" laughed Doc "These platinum crooks are not as smart as they think they are, Monty. Would you be surprised to learn that Tulameen has not produced an ounce of platinum since 1932? No one would stockpile that amount of ore during the phenomenal price increases that platinum has seen in the last 90 years. Besides that, production for the entire history of operations in the Tulameen area is estimated at 20,000 ounces." He pulled out a pocket calculator and punched a few buttons. "20,000 ounces are equal to 622 kilograms, Monty. From the 1870's to the 1930's, Tulameen produced a little more than 620 kilos of platinum concentrate, so obviously, no one can buy 900 kilos of platinum in British Columbia. Not now, and not ever."

"You are saying they didn't buy any platinum ore in Vancouver?"

"I'm saying it is impossible to do so" Doc replied taking a sip of wine and looking straight into Monty's eyes.

It was Monty's turn to remain silent. Finally, he asked "Then what the hell are these ass holes up to? Why all this deception, why lie about ores that could be legally imported to Japan?"

"Monty, you are ignoring the fact that we have a supply of illegal platinum from Colombia to consider. My guess is that they mixed the Chocó stuff with ore from Goodnews Bay on the ship so they could import it as Tulameen ore. It is a damn good idea, because it avoids any claims by the Colombian government and doesn't raise any red flags with Japanese customs. You and Inspector Kuno have to figure that 900 kilos of mixed platinum got through Japanese customs plus another 100 kilos of legal ore. That is one hell of a lot of platinum, buddy. I can calculate its dollar value for you but it has to be in the neighborhood of 40 to 50 million bucks.

Monty was stunned by the dollar amount Doc quoted and took gulp of wine to digest this revelation. This amount of money could certainly get a few heads cut off and the Fugimora name was ass-deep in the whole thing.

"Would we, I mean you, Doc, be able to recognize this mixed ore if I can get an analysis of it? Japanese officials took samples of the Tulameen ore and the Goodnews Bay ore when the ship passed through customs."

"Sure, as long as the analysis is good, any sort of mixture will fall on a straight line in a simple two-component mixing diagram. Real Tulameen ore is so high in osmium it would plot well away from a line for any combination of Chocó and Goodnews Bay ores. You do know, I suppose, that you have to find this mixture before it goes to a refinery, don't you?"

"Yeah, I know, Doc. I didn't understand that mixing-line stuff but I can get an analysis of the Tulameen stuff from Kuno in Japan. He is supposed to get the customs samples analyzed by Dr. Nakamura, the big shot at the Tokyo mint, who first got us on the trail of the Chocó ore. Let's have another drink and go to bed."

From the couch, Dr. Tobey was heard mumbling "I'm going to shoot that fucking goat tomorrow."

CHAPTER 26

Three Skulls Not Four

Inspector Hisashi Kuno of the Japanese National Police sipped his tea and stared pensively at the screen of his lap top. He had needed his English-Japanese dictionary to translate several words in the e-mail message sent by Agent Monty Simmons from Texas. This message provided the link between the two vicious murders in Yokosuka, an attempted murder in Alaska and smuggled platinum from Chocó, Colombia. It was now clear that the manifest of the Fugimora ship *Aoki Maru* was fraudulent, implying involvement of the captain, a certain Satoshi Hiraki. It was not clear how this South American platinum got on that ship but it was quite clear how it got off.

The Tulameen mixing scheme was clever, clever enough at least to fool those dumb-asses in Japanese customs who permitted 900 kilograms of illegal platinum to get past them. The value of this platinum was so incredibly immense that it could justify a hundred murders. But where did it go when it left the ship in Yokosuka? More importantly, where is it at this moment?

He detailed one man to research Mr. Ryota Fugimora,

president of Fugimora Maritime, another to examine linkages between the various entities comprising Fugimora Enterprises and a third to investigate Captain Hiraki. Clearly, no time could be lost in confiscating this mixture before it was refined and became untraceable. But now, at least, he had the name of a solid suspect, Ryota Fugimora, and he would soon know all about him. It was imperative to get the sample of the mixed ore from customs, have it analyzed, and send the results to Dr. Martin in Texas. Without this, there would be no proof that mixing had even taken place. He sent e-mails to both his brother, Dr. Katsu Kuno, at the mint branch in Osaka and Dr. Riku Nakamura at the Tokyo mint branch instructing them to alert all refineries in the country to immediately report, to him personally, any platinum ore submitted from Tulameen, British Colombia.

Ten minutes later, Inspector Kuno's brother Katsu telephoned his personal number. "Hi brother, I just got your e-mail and wanted to tell you what I have done. First, all the mint branches are on the lookout for a large shipment of Tulameen ore. Second, I sent your message to the chief metallurgists at all the major private refineries in the country; this includes Asahi Pretec, Furuya Metal Company, Ishifuku Metal Industry, Matsuda Sangyo Company, Tanaka Kikinzoku Kogyo K.K., and the Tokuriki-Horten Company. These are the big outfits that work in platinum metal refinement and none of them have even heard of ore from Tulameen, British Colombia. So, I think it is impossible for your bad guys to get their ore processed by the private refineries. The mint branches are out of the question, of course. The only alternative is one of the small labs that serve the dental industry, and then, only with collaboration by their metallurgy staff."

"Thank you, Katsu, I am worried about these dental labs. I also think one of them could be involved."

"One more thing, big brother, I telephoned Dr. Martin in the states and he told me about his mixing theory and the size of the mixed ore shipment that slipped past our customs agents. 900 kilograms is a hell of a large job, even for major refineries. If a small dental lab is doing this work, they would probably be limited to 20-kilo runs, or less, by the size of their furnaces. Since the PGE separation process takes almost anyone at least a week, it would require something like 45 weeks to complete such a project. That should be enough time for a super cop, like my brother, to track them down."

"Yes, thank you again, Katsu. I appreciate your faith in me and the Japanese legal system. This time-information is useful. Now I must get back to my crime fighting. Goodbye Katsu."

Inspector Kuno closed his eyes and tried to picture the entire situation: the murders of the sailor and his wife, the ore mixing scheme, the failure of customs to prevent importation, the current location of some 50 million US dollars in illegal platinum. The Fugimora ship *Aoki Maru* was the nexus of all of it. He must get that damn sample from customs.

Kuno had begun two weeks earlier with a polite request to the assistant director of the Ministry of Finance and was assured of a quick response by the subordinate office of the Customs and Tariff Bureau. Their response was quick but in the form of a letter thanking him for his interest in the affairs of the CTB and nothing more. His next call was to the Chief of CTB who promised immediate action. That was a week ago, and there had been no further response.

Inspector Kuno could not be called an emotional man or one who was inordinately intolerant of government bureaucracy; after all, he was part of that bureaucracy. But he could get pissed, and now he was pissed, as he called the number of the Chief of CTB again. He told the Chief in his sternest tone "If that sample is not on my desk by noon today, I will come to your office and personally arrest and handcuff your fat ass in front of your workers." Miraculously, the sample was delivered by messenger at 11:15 a.m.

This sample, labeled "Japan Customs, Yokosuka, number 22134, consisted of a glass vial containing 250 grams of black sand. He wondered if it would be adequate for analysis by the mint scientists. He telephoned Dr. Riku Nakamura at the Tokyo mint and explained the situation.

"Yes, Inspector Kuno, I certainly understand why you need this sample analyzed. Your brother has explained the mixing scheme to me. I will analyze a few of the grains individually by electron microprobe which should be good enough to demonstrate that some grains are from Chocó and others are from Alaska. Then I will analyze the remaining sample for the entire platinum group of elements. Dr. Martin, in Texas, will need this bulk composition to work out the mixing ratio. It should take about a week. If you will get your sample to me today, I can start the sample preparation immediately. I know you will be concerned about security, so I will do all the work personally. No one but me will have access to the sample."

"Thank you very much, Dr. Nakamura. That will be most satisfactory. I will send a man to deliver the sample to you, personally, within the hour. Goodbye."

Miss Chika Oshiro was a good-looking young woman in the Japanese way with shoulder-length, raven-black hair and eyebrow-length bangs, perfect white teeth, and radiant smiles for everyone. She was a 20-year-old student in the Department of Materials Science and Technology of the Tokyo Science University-Kaguazaka Campus. Chika was studying to become a traditional metallurgist and was clearly a smart, thinking woman who enjoyed competing with the male students who dominated her field of study. These young men enjoyed the pleasure of her figure, especially her breasts, which were large for a Japanese woman. She had stimulating smiles for them every day, that is, every day except those upon which examinations were given. On these days, she presented them with the fierce visage of a pissed-off Samurai warrior.

Chika was not banking on a mythical future husband to take care of her. She had finished two years of her four-year course of study with excellent marks and had accepted a third-year internship at the Tokyo branch of the National Mint. These accomplishments were remarkable, of course, but not as remarkable as they might otherwise have been, since this internship was obtained through the influence of Fugimora Precious Metals. This same entity also paid her educational expenses through an endowed scholarship fund in the Materials Science Department at the university.

Her "grandfather" Aoki was a wealthy and influential personage and this was a very good thing for Miss Chika Oshiro. In fact, "grandfather" Aoki had given her his very personal phone number at his downtown headquarters with specific instructions to keep him informed about all mint activities involving work on platinum.

Her duties at the mint normally involved dealing with the public on behalf of the technical staff, answering telephone inquiries, logging jewelry items submitted for appraisal, and on occasions dealing with actual ore samples in rock or powdered form submitted by miners, both professional and amateur.

On this particular day, she logged in a sample of black sand that was extremely odd in that it was delivered by an armed policeman and was labeled as being from the Office of Japanese Customs in Yokosuka, number 22134. It was marked for the personal attention of Dr. Riku Nakamura, Chief Metallurgist. Naturally she promptly called Dr. Nakamura's laboratory and informed him of this arrival. He appeared at her desk almost immediately. This was unusual in itself, as the mint scientists did not usually take much interest in the samples passing through her hands. After personally taking charge of the black sand sample, Dr. Nakamura told her "No calls or visitors to my lab until further notice. I will be busy with this sample the rest of the day and throughout the night." This combination of oddities certainly struck the lovely Miss Chika Oshiro as something "grandfather" Aoki would want to know about.

Three human skulls gazed solemnly at Ryota Fugimora from their respective stations on his desk as he contemplated his next move. He could not avoid thinking it should be four skulls but for a damned grizzly bear who lunched on one of them. He had heard they were fearsome and ferocious beasts and now he had good reason to believe it. What a bloody mess the creature had made of the unfortunate Dr. Tobey, not a single bone or scrap of flesh remained un-eaten. He was very glad that he did not encounter one of these monsters at close quarters during his four-day adventure in the wilderness of Alaska. Viewing them at the distance of one mile was enough of a thrill for him.

Young Fugimora was concerned with the possibility that the customs authorities and police might not buy into the deception of the Tulameen platinum. In that case, they would not be long in tracking down the location of the Fugimora secure warehouse. He needed to move his treasure to a safe place, not connected to the Fugimora name, but where? He must call his father.

"Hello, my son" answered Dr. Aoki Fugimora, "I have been considering your problem and I think I have a good solution. I have contacted your mother, Lady Fumiko, in Kyoto and she has a large and very secure vault in which she keeps her art treasures. It can accommodate your goods and is in no way connected with our family name. I can send a truck from Tokyo with trusted guards to make the transfer within the hour, if you wish to pursue this plan."

"Yes father, this is an excellent idea. I will await the truck here at the warehouse."

"There is another thing you must know, Ryota. I have been informed that the police have delivered a sample of black sand from Yokosuka Customs to the Tokyo mint for analysis. Evidently, this is a very high priority sample, as their chief metallurgist, a certain Dr. Nakamura, will be working on it all night. I suspect this sample will be of some interest to you."

"Thank you, father, yes, this is of great importance to me as it means that I have unfinished business at the Tokyo mint. Then, I think I must disappear for a time."

"I have also given some thought to an escape plan for you, Ryota and have another suggestion for you to consider."

"Thank you, father. I am definitely in need of such a plan. I do not think Yokosuka will be a healthy place for me after tonight."

"Ryota, when your business at the mint is completed, telephone me. I have our company jet standing by and it can take you to our facility on Truk Atoll. You will be comfortable and safe there and can share in the riotous lifestyle of our dental staff. The authorities there are my close friends. Do not think of using, or even approaching, our ship *Aoki Maru.* It is surely under surveillance."

"Yes father, this is also a good plan. I will call you later tonight but it may be quite late."

"No matter my son, I am an old man and do not sleep well at night. I will make the arrangements and wait for your call."

While the young Fugimora waited for the truck from Tokyo, he spray-painted the crate containing the platinum hoard in green and re-labeled it "Archeological Artifacts". He then packed a small trunk with clothes, personal items, passport, and $50,000 in US currency. He did not forget to include his 200-year-old his Kris dagger but repressed the temptation to take the family sword and the three grinning skulls in front of him.

CHAPTER 27

Murder in the Mint

Dr. Riku Nakamura was bent over his research microscope in one of the laboratories of the Tokyo mint branch. In the intense beam of reflected light, he could see obvious see textural differences among the six grains in the polished section; grains 1, 2 and 3 differed significantly from grains 4, 5, and 6. He immediately recognized that he was looking at two different natural ferro platinum alloys which necessarily had to record two source areas. This sample had to record a mixture of Goodnews Bay and Chocó ores that Dr. Martin from the USA had suggested. He photographed each of the six grains in the polished section and sent the electronic images with notes for each to the lab desktop computer as well as his personal laptop. Then, he returned the polished section of mixed grains to the cabinet where he stored his working collection.

Nakamura placed the remaining black sand from Inspector Kuno's sample in a small crusher which reduced the grains to a fine powder and then ran the powder through a gravimetric separator. He then placed the dense fraction of the sample in an aqua regia bath under the chemical hood to separate platinum and palladium from the remaining platinum group elements. It was a few minutes before midnight when he reached the point at which platinum, iridium, osmium, palladium, rhenium and ruthenium were each in solution in individual beakers. Tomorrow, he would precipitate them as metallic powders, dry and weigh them. But now he was tired and needed sleep.

Dr. Riku Nakamura was totally oblivious to the sound of a stealthy tread on the polished concrete floor behind him. Ryota Fugimora looked down on the convulsing body of the Tokyo mint's senior metallurgist without remorse, without emotion, and so profoundly devoid of pity, that even Rodion Raskolnikov would have been envious. His father had informed him that his bag of black sand, stolen by Atkins, was now in the hands of the police and had been identified as Chocó ore by the man now lying motionless at his feet. He began searching the laboratory for the sample of mixed ore collected by Japanese customs but found nothing that he could recognize as his platinum ore.

Ryota was dazzled by the array of microscopes, bewildering scientific apparatus, endless cabinets of chemical reagents, and Frankenstein-looking glass tubes and pipes that reached almost to the ceiling. He saw the six critical beakers filled with liquids that Nakamura was working on. But the labels on these beakers, marked by the international symbols Pt, Pd, Ir, Os, Rh, and Ru, were quite meaningless to this venal young killer who had not troubled himself to study the periodic table of the elements in an elementary chemistry course. He wiped the blade of the 200-year-old Kris dagger with a paper towel and stuck this potentially incriminating evidence in the pocket of his black kung fu outfit. Then, he exited the lab and retraced his steps to the second story window in the rear of the building where he had entered the mint to avoid the security desk at the main entrance.

It required only moments to descend his knotted rope, disengage its hook from the sill of the window and find his small back pack. He exchanged his kung fu outfit for a jogging suit, donned his running shoes, and packed up his rope and knife behind the bushes concealing the foundation. It was 1:05 a.m.

The streets of downtown Tokyo are never deserted, even in the wee hours of morning. There were the indigent of course, who are forced to walk to stay warm, as well as very early and disgustingly energetic young joggers, night watchmen, drunken people still trying to find their cars, old men walking off their insomnia, people walking their dogs, and traffic related to a wide spectrum of nocturnal businesses. Ryota had no difficulty in blending into this assemblage of odd and varied characters. He jogged 20 blocks before hailing a cab to take him to the downtown train station where he had stored his baggage for the flight to Truk. From the station, he telephoned his father, wrote down instructions for finding the waiting company jet, and hailed a second taxi.

Inspector Kuno entered his office, as usual, at exactly 8 a.m. A grim-faced lieutenant awaited him and the inspector immediately knew that the news was not good. "What is it Lieutenant, what bad tidings do you bring to me?"

"It is the mint scientist, sir, Dr. Nakamura. He was found dead a few minutes ago, murdered in his laboratory."

Inspector Kuno was not given to the use of expletives in either Japanese or English and received this news stoically but the voice in his mind was screaming "Fuck-Fuck-Fuck" in both languages.

When he recovered his composure sufficiently, he ordered his forensic team to the scene and sat down at his desk to call his brother in Osaka. "Hello, Katsu, I need you to meet me at the Tokyo mint as soon as possible. Nakamura has been murdered while working on our mixed platinum sample. I am sending a police helicopter to pick you up at your house. Tell Kamiko-san you may have to spend a few days with me."

Dr. Katsu Kuno, who was given to the use of both American and Japanese obscenities, responded to the news with "Oh fuck, not Nakamura, no, no, Christ, it can't be true…o.k. brother I will be ready in five minutes."

Hisashi Kuno ordered a cup of tea and sat at his desk forcing this new catastrophe into the rigorous logic system of his policeman's mind: 1) obviously, Nakamura is dead because of the damn sample he gave him yesterday; 2) he needed his brother to assess the progress Nakamura had made in the analysis; and 3) the killer was well-informed about activities at the mint and this required an in-house spy.

Inspector Kuno thought he knew what he would find when he

arrived at the crime scene but, in this case, he was mistaken. Dr. Nakamura was certainly dead but his head and hands were intact. A very large pool of blood had congealed on the floor but did not record any footprints, only the grotesque convulsions of a dying man. The victim was wearing his white lab coat, now horribly stained with his own blood, rubber gloves and safety goggles that had become dislodged from his head. Death appeared to be the result of a single fatal stab wound piercing just below the left scapula and probably entering the heart chamber. There was no evidence of a struggle with the attacker. The inspector instructed the forensic team to touch nothing on the lab bench that Nakamura was working at, or any of the scientific equipment in the lab until his brother arrived.

Katsu Kuno and Nakamura were longtime friends, as well as brother metallurgists, and there was no reason for his brother to see his good friend in this condition. Kuno ordered the body removed and taken to the forensic pathology lab. As the body exited the lab, the inspector heard the sound of a landing police helicopter.

Dr. Katsu Kuno became quite pale at the sight of the blood pool and the ghastly outline of his friend's body. "God-damn-it Hisashi, you fucking-well better find the bastard that did this."

"Yes, Katsu, I will find him and he will pay for this and other crimes just as horrible. Right now, I need you to tell me where Nakamura was in the process of analyzing my sample. Where is the sample, what can my people touch and what must remain untouched?"

"Fuck, Hisashi, it is all so horrible, I can't even think."

"Yes, I know brother but you must try to calm yourself and do what you can do to help us find the man who killed your friend. Can you do this? Can you be the scientist you are, in spite of this shocking scene?"

"Yes, you are right, of course, Hisashi. All I can do for poor Riku is help you catch the rotten, sister-fucking piece of dog shit that killed him and desecrated his lab. Let me look at what he was doing on the bench. Oh, God Hisashi! I can't step in his blood, I just can't."

"Katsu, you must become calm. I will get the blood cleaned up while you sit in a chair outside the lab. I will call when I am ready for you. Katsu left unsteadily while the forensic crew went to work on the blood mess. Some 20 minutes later, Inspector Kuno gently summoned his brother back to Nakamura's work area.

"Ok brother, here is what I see. Riku had finished the extraction process and separated the individual platinum group elements into their various salt solutions. See those six beakers filled with liquids of different colors? Written on each is the chemical symbol for the six platinum group elements. The original sample was only 250 grams to begin with, so he would have had to dissolve all of it for the analysis unless he made a polished section of some of the grains before running them through a crusher. Let's take a look at his microscope. I see the dust cover is off and that means he used it recently. This scope has a camera linked to an electronic imaging device and any images he studied would be stored on this desktop computer. We can see them, if I can guess his password. Most of us use our favorite chemical element and Riku's favorite was osmium so I am going to try Os-3027. 3,027 degrees is the melting point of osmium on the Celsius scale, brother. Did you know that?" The computer turned on and soon Katsu was looking at the images of the six platinum grains that Nakamura recorded before his death. "I will make a copy of these images, but we need to find the polished section Riku was looking at. Dr. Martin will be interested in both."

After a few minutes of searching through cabinets, Katsu returned with a black plastic disk three centimeters in diameter and one-centimeter thick in which six grains of native platinum alloy gleamed from the mirror-like polished surface. This innocuous-looking plastic disk spelled death, not only for Dr. Nakamura, but also for the evil aspirations of the Fugimora clan. "Here it is brother."

"Thank you, Katsu, you have been very helpful. Now that the sample is gone, I suppose there is no hope of getting the information Dr. Martin needs."

"You are wrong about that Mr. Policeman. Tomorrow I will come to this lab and pick up where Riku left off and Martin will have everything he needs. Your killer is a major-league dunce and a total dumb ass. If he had he known jack-shit about chemistry, he would have simply emptied these beakers down the drain and you and Martin would have been screwed. Right now, brother, I want you to buy a bottle of scotch whiskey and take me to your house and get me drunk."

"Yes, Katsu, an excellent idea but I think two bottles are in order since I also feel the need to get drunk. I must have this lab secured first, however, and post guards. I think there is a person at this mint who is in league with our killer and I do not wish these six beakers of platinum elements to disappear. Also, I must have someone inform Dr. Nakamura's wife of the situation. You know you must call on her tomorrow Katsu."

"Yes brother, I know, let's make it three bottles of scotch."

The next morning, neither of the Kuno brothers felt their best, but each was quite anxious to get on with his respective job. Katsu was taken by squad car to the mint laboratory where a heavy police presence provided security for him to complete the work Dr. Nakamura had begun. Inspector Kuno went directly to the police pathology lab to get a first-hand report on the forensic details of the murder.

Dr. Daichi Usami, chief of the forensic pathology unit, was an older gentleman with graying hair, old fashioned rimless spectacles and a grim visage that was entirely suitable for a working pathologist. He conducted the inspector through the dreary, silent halls of the morgue to a windowless room where Nakamura's nude body lay on a cold stainless steel table under intensely bright surgical lights. The inevitable, and horrifying, identification tag was attached to his right great toe.

The pathologist consulted his notes and began explaining the details of the knife wound. "The weapon was an extremely sharp double-edged, tapered dagger that produced a five-centimeter laceration on the rear upper left side of the victim, just below the scapula, pierced the heart and made a two centimeter exit wound in the left chest. The blade length was therefore in excess of 35 centimeters. This blade created extraordinary tissue damage relative to wounds produced by ordinary blades which puzzled me because it was obvious that the blade was not serrated."

Inspector Kuno leaned over the body to examine the exit wound and then, with the assistance of Dr. Usami, rolled the body onto its right side and examined the entrance wound. "Is there anything else, Dr. Usami?"

"Yes, inspector, there is and I must say that it is a rather bizarre thing. Along the blade path I found a curious white substance with the properties of latex. Our chemists determined this substance to be sap from *Excoecaria agallocha,* one of about 40 species of the poison plant family, *Euphorbiaceae.* Our forensic botanist researched this plant and found that it is widespread in mangrove swamps along the coasts of the Malaysian islands. It has been used as a knife poison for centuries. This fact leads me to suggest that the dagger used in this murder was a Malaysian Kris or something very much like one."

"A Kris?" asked Kuno.

"Yes, one of those wicked-looking daggers with a wavy blade coated with a latex poison."

The inspector considered this for a moment and then asked, "Did our man die of the stab wound or the poison?"

"He died of acute exsanguination within a minute of heart penetration but, had he lived for five minutes, he would have died by the poison."

"Thank you, doctor, please send me a copy of your final report."

Hisashi Kuno looked at his watch, it was only 10:15 a.m. and he was still feeling the effects of a hangover but he was beginning to think about the unopened third bottle of scotch patiently biding in his liquor cabinet. He telephoned his brother at the mint lab for a progress report on the platinum analysis. Everything was reported to be proceeding smoothly and the analytical work would be completed by the end of the day. Inspector Kuno walked out of the pathology building and drove to his office where he expected a report on Fugimora Enterprises.

CHAPTER 28

Fugimora Precious Metals, Ltd.

Inspector Kuno examined the report on Fugimora Enterprises which encompassed four subsidiary entities: Fugimora Dental Associates, organized in 1946, Fugimora College of Dentistry, organized in 1949, Fugimora Precious Metals, organized in 1951, and Fugimora Maritime Transport, organized in 1979. All, were registered corporations and all were owned by the same three stock holders in exactly the same proportions, Dr. Aoki Fugimora 50%, Madame Fumiko Hatori 25%, and Mr. Ryota Fugimora 25%. It meant that these three individuals were quite wealthy but that was not a crime. These were the four spokes of the Fugimora wheel of fortune but the hub of this wheel, the Chuuk Free Dentistry Clinic, was missing from this report because it was a non-profit organization.

The inspector knew that the ship *Aoki Maru* was purchased in 1979 and was the sole boat owned by Fugimora Maritime and he was quite sure that it was deeply involved in a criminal enterprise. He also knew that the president of this shipping company had purchased 550 kilograms of platinum concentrate from the

Goodnews Mining Company but declared only 100 kilograms to Japanese customs. This man was also the prime suspect in a bizarre attempt to murder the geologist who delivered this concentrate to the *Aoki Maru*. The name of this man was Ryota Fugimora, minority owner in all of the companies of under the rubric of Fugimora Enterprises and the son of Aoki Fugimora.

Dr. Aoki Fugimora's wealth, reputation for philanthropy, and friends in high places made it difficult to obtain a warrant to search the premises of Fugimora Precious Metals. It had taken time, valuable time, to get this warrant but, now that he had it, Inspector Kuno was going to turn that building upside down in a search for the 1000 kilograms of ore imported by Fugimora Maritime and listed on the cargo manifest of the *Aoki Maru*. He had assembled a team of six detectives, a forensic accountant and his brother Katsu, a professional metallurgist, to help in this search.

The team arrived at the door of Fugimora Precious Metals in the Shibuya district of southwestern Tokyo via Expressway 3 at precisely 8:01 a.m. Inspector Kuno summoned the chief of the dental laboratory, an extractive metallurgist by the name of Mr. Yoshito Hasegawa. Prior checking on Mr. Hasegawa revealed that he held a Bachelor of Engineering degree in metallurgy from the Mining College of Akita University in northwestern Honshu; he had no police record and was hired by Fugimora Precious Metals six years earlier.

Following the rather curt introductions, at least by Japanese standards, the inspector immediately asked for records accounting for 1000 kilograms of platinum concentrate delivered to the lab from the port of Yokosuka on, or about, June 18.

"Yes, certainly, Inspector Kuno. I keep very strict account of what comes in and leaves this facility." He pulled out a notebook and began to recite. "First, 100 kilograms of concentrate from Goodnews Bay, Alaska: unprocessed and still in shipping container which you may inspect. Second, 900 kilograms of concentrate from Tulameen, British Colombia: nearly all processed into bars of fine platinum with total mass of 600 kilograms. The location of these 1-kilogram ingots is as follows: Fugimora vault in Bank of Tokyo, 400 ingots; Fugimora Dental Associates, 50 ingots; Fugimora Dental College, 50 ingots; Chuuk Free Dental Clinic in the Federated States of Micronesia, 50 ingots; and 50 ingots still in house. In addition, we have a little more than 100 kilograms of platinum in metallic powder form, yet to be cast. Beyond this, we have about 100 kilograms of other platinum group elements, also in powder form, and about 75 kilograms of dross which will ultimately be sold to base metal dealers. Would you care to examine this material inspector?"

"Yes, I would like to see everything you have that is related to the Tulameen shipment. In addition, I wish my police accountant to examine all documents and licenses related to the dispersal of the refined platinum to the various destinations you cited."

As Hasegawa reeled off the numbers, Dr. Katsu Kuno added them on his pocket calculator: a total of 700-kilos of pure platinum from 900-kilos of concentrate equates with a platinum grade of about 78 weight % in the concentrate. Actually, a little higher, say about 80 % when recovery losses of 2 to 3 % are taken into account, so 700 kilos of fine platinum was about right.

Mr. Hasegawa conducted the police entourage to a barred vault room where 50 1-kilogram platinum ingots were stored. After donning white gloves, Inspector Kuno was invited to pick up one of the bars dramatically displayed on black velvet under bright lighting. They were exceptionally heavy for their size and with the staged lighting, the lustrous white metal seemed to emit a supernatural radiance. They were stamped with the English words *Fugimora Precious Metals, 1-kilogram fine platinum, 999.0.* The bars were individually and consecutively numbered and imprinted with the crossed samurai swords logo of Fugimora Enterprises.

As the company metallurgist began leading the group out of the vault, the inspector whispered in English to his brother "furnace capacity". Katsu understood immediately what his brother wanted. The group filed into the main laboratory room where men and machines were at work crushing, grinding, polishing, melting, and casting. Hasegawa named the machines as they were passed and explained what they did. From this room, they entered another filled with glassware, tubes, funnels, beakers, flasks and jars of chemical reagents beyond description. Hasegawa explained the various setups of chemical apparatus as the group wove their way between them.

Eventually they were led to a series of five white plastic buckets conspicuously labeled "Tulameen". These contained very fine black powders in varying amounts and were said to represent the platinum group metals, exclusive of platinum itself, with an aggregate mass of about 100 kilograms. Similar buckets marked "Tulameen" were said to contain 100 kilos of pure platinum in powered form.

Inspector Kuno was well aware that his surprise police visit had evolved into a dog-and-pony industrial tour by the adroit and articulate Mr. Hasegawa. Obviously, this visit came as no surprise to him. Kuno had to admit that this Fugimora organization was good, damn good. Below the surface, this place reeked of lies and criminality but he needed evidence, real physical evidence to make any kind of a move. That was the trouble with police work, criminals take weeks, months, even years to cultivate their schemes; cops have only hours to react to them. Still, he was satisfied with what he learned at Fugimora Precious Metals.

Mr. Hasegawa asked the inspector "Is there anything further that I can show the police or is there any additional paperwork you need?"

"No, thank you, Mr. Hasegawa, I have seen enough for today. I thank you for your courteous responses to my questions. No doubt we shall see each other again." This veiled threat made no visible impression on the imperturbable Mr. Hasegawa.

Inspector Kuno was silent as he drove east along Expressway 3, back toward the central district of Tokyo. Katsu knew that his brother was in deep thought and observed silence as well. After about 15 minutes, the policeman spoke. "Katsu, did you know that everything we heard today was a despicable lie?"

"Yes, brother, I did. There is no way in hell that this lab could have processed 900 kilos of ore in the time they claim. It is exactly as I told you Hisashi, they can do no more than about 20 kilos a week, so it is all a big fat lie."

"But you must admit, Katsu, they were very good lies. There are no weaknesses in the story and there is nothing that I can do to prove otherwise. The prime minister himself could not get a look into the Fugimora vault in the Bank of Tokyo to see if 400 bars of platinum are really there. I know the platinum we saw today could be from anywhere. I suppose it is an easy thing to substitute the Fugimora logo for whatever was originally stamped on the ingots."

"Yes, it is, Hisashi. It is illegal, of course, but still an easy thing."

"I suppose the numbers Hasegawa gave us regarding the amounts processed were reasonable as well."

"Very reasonable indeed, brother, Mr. Hasegawa was well prepared to meet the police today. It was an impressive show."

"Yes, it was, indeed, an impressive show, Katsu. These Fugimora criminals are smart, very smart and were very well prepared for our visit. But we know they are lying and therefore guilty of evil deeds and this is an advantage to us. I presume the 900 kilograms of so-called Tulameen ore has not even arrived at this Fugimora lab and is hidden somewhere. How large would this mass be, Katsu? Would it be difficult to hide?"

Katsu retrieved his pocket calculator for the second time this day and began pushing buttons. "With a density of 21 grams per cubic centimeter, the volume is going to be surprisingly small, brother." Katsu pushed a few more buttons and then said "The volume of 900 kilos of pure platinum with a density of 21 grams per cubic centimeter is 0.043 cubic meters', brother. Since the ore is in granular form and not pure platinum the actual volume will exceed this but not by much, say to about 0.050 cubic meters. Think of it as a cubic box with an edge of 37-centimeters, or about the size of four cases of canned beer. This means it can be hidden anywhere that would be safe to hide 44 million US dollars but, that cannot be just anywhere, can it, brother?"

"No, Katsu, one does not hide $44 million US just anywhere. It must be an extremely secure place but, ultimately, it must end up in the furnace at Fugimora Precious Metals. I must have the place watched."

CHAPTER 29

Science at Work

Doc Martin received the news of Nakamura's death and the analysis of mixed "Tulameen ore" completed by Dr. Katsu Kuno via email. The polished section containing six ore grains prepared by Nakamura arrived by special messenger from the Japanese consulate-general in Houston three days later. Martin sat at his reflected light microscope examining this section and referring to notes Nakamura had made before his death. These notes were handwritten in Japanese with translations into English by Katsu Kuno.

At a separate table in Martin's lab, agent Monty Simmons struggled with a pile of Japanese receipts that he could not read using a calculator that would not add correctly or convert yen to dollars. He was preparing his monthly expense report and having some difficulty with the justification of a $3478 first class, roundtrip ticket to Tokyo. It had seemed so perfectly logical at the time.

After about an hour of intense examination, Martin called agent Simmons over to his table and asked him to look at the computer screen. It showed six images stacked in two columns of three. "Dr. Nakamura has given us a pretty complete report on this polished section with quantitative measurements of reflectivity at four wavelengths, chromaticity calculations and Vickers hardness. I have verified his measurements and they are all very good. The three images you see on the left side of the screen are nuggets from Goodnews Bay, those on the right are from Chocó, Columbia. Nakamura must have known even before he made the polished section that he was dealing with a binary mixture because he mounted the section with the grains from the two localities in separate groups. In the GNB images, you see the dominant whitish grey phase is platinum-iron alloy enclosing lots of exsolved irregular blebs of osmiridium which is an iridium-osmium alloy. It is tough to see, perhaps, but the reflectance or brightness of the osmiridium is slightly higher than in the platinum-dominant host phase, about 71% compared with about 64%. But look at the little diamond-shaped indentations that Nakamura made in the two minerals, Monty. In the platinum-rich host phase they are about three times larger than in the small inclusions of the iridium-osmium phase. These indentations measure the hardness of the two phases: the platinum-rich phase with the large indentations is much softer than the osmiridium phase with the smaller indentations; about 375 and 975 respectively on the Vickers hardness scale. In the Chocó images, on the right-hand side, we see that the platinum-iron alloy lacks the exsolved blebs of osmiridium. No doubt about it, Nakamura was a damn good microscopist."

"I can see the grains on the left and right but they look the same to me" observed Monty "and I can see the diamond impressions are different sizes. So, what does it tell us, Doc?"

"It tells us, Mr. Treasury agent, that material from Goodnews Bay was mixed with Chocó ore aboard the *Aoki Maru* before the ore was sampled by customs in Yokosuka. And by the way, they do not look alike at all, Monty. Now, look here in this part of one of the GNB images, there is a tiny, grey, pyritohedral inclusion of laurite-erlichmanite inside a platinum-iron nugget; this is a super-hard and very rare osmium-ruthenium sulfide mineral. I wonder if Nakamura saw this; his notes don't mention it."

"I guess Kuno and I have been assuming that the mixing took place on the ship after the sailor stole some of it, but how in hell did the Colombian stuff get on the *Aoki Maru* in the first-place, Doc?" asked Simmons.

"That's easy, Monty. The ship stopped in Weno to off-load dental equipment. Weno is the main city on Chuuk Island in the Caroline Archipelago. That threw me for a while until I looked at an older map of the south Pacific. That island was formerly known as Truk Island, Truk Atoll or Truk Lagoon. Does that ring any bells, Monty?" asked Doc with a grin.

"No, not really, should it?"

"Yes, it should. Truk Lagoon was *the* major forward base of the Imperial Japanese Navy before and during WWII, buddy. The Japanese were very hard up for platinum, so what would be more logical than smuggling a load of platinum out of Colombia, transporting it to Truk, by submarine almost certainly, for later shipment to Japan. Only, Truk was cut off from Japan in 1944 and then over run by US forces in 1945. So, someone found it and stashed it and there it remained until June of this year. I'd be hunting for an 80-year-old veteran of the Imperial Navy by the name of Fugimora if I were a treasury agent."

"Damn it, Doc, I believe you have got it. It is all so simple and logical; I should have thought of it myself. I must get word to Kuno."

"Before you do that let's figure out exactly how much Colombian ore was mixed with Alaskan ore."

"We can do that?"

"Sure, we can. I have the analysis of the mixture made by Nakamura and Katsu Kuno. It will just take a few minutes to calculate some mixing scenarios. It almost has to be a 1:1 mixture since they declared 900 kilos to customs as being from Tulameen but let's make sure before you contact Inspector Kuno." Doc spent about 30 minutes doing calculations and entering numbers onto an a chart which looked like the following:

	GNB	Chocó	Tulameen	1:1 mix	2:1 mix	3:1 mix
Pt	73.56	87.47	74.06	80.51	78.15	77.04
Ir	13.16	1.57	1.17	7.37	9.34	10.26
Os	2.56	0.58	9.63	1.57	1.91	2.07
Ru	0.25	0.02		0.14	0.17	0.19
Rh	1.21	1.93	2.64	1.57	1.45	1.39
Pd	0.26	0.73	0.19	0.50	0.42	0.38
Fe	8.50	7.16	8.82	7.83	8.06	8.17
Cu	0.40	0.54	3.48	0.47	0.45	0.44
Ni	0.09			0.04	0.13	0.07
Co	0.01					
Total	100.00	100.00	99.99	100.00	100.00	100.01
Pt/Pt+Ir+Os	.82	.98	.87	.90	.87	.86
Ir	13.16	1.57	1.17	7.37	9.34	10.26
Os	2.56	0.58	9.63	1.57	1.91	2.07
Ru+Rh	1.46	1.95	2.64	1.71	1.62	1.58
Total	17.18	4.10	13.44	10.65	12.87	13.91
% Ir	76.6%	38.3%	8.7%	69.2%	72.60%	73.80%
% Os	14.9%	14.2%	71.7%	14.7%	14.80%	14.90%
% Ru+Rh	8.5%	47.6%	19.6%	16.1%	12.60%	11.40%
Total	100.0%	100.0%	100.0%	100.00%	100.00%	100.10%

"Now, Monty we can see the whole damn scheme on one sheet of paper. This ought to appeal to your background in economics and accounting."

"I don't have a background in accounting, Doc. If I did, I'd be working for the IRS."

"Ok, Monty, no accounting but the numbers you are looking at represent something like 40 million bucks, a fair part of which ought to go back to the government of Colombia. The first three columns are average analyses of the ores from Goodnews Bay, Choco and Tulameen that I pulled from the literature. The last three columns are hypothetical mixtures that I have calculated for different ratios of GNB to Chocó ores. I will make up a graph to illustrate this later, but I see a close match-up between the analysis that got Nakamura killed and the calculated 1:1 mixture column on the spreadsheet. Now, just look at the row showing the ratio of platinum to platinum plus osmium plus iridium. This ratio is a pretty reliable finger print for platinum deposits and the Chocó ore ratio of 0.98 stands out like a diamond in a goat's ass. Our bad guys were smart enough to know this and that is what forced them to mix it with something to lower this ratio. That something was ore from Goodnews Bay which has a ratio of only 0.82. Nakamura's analysis shows this ratio to be 0.907 and that is exactly what we see in the 1:1 mixture that I calculated. It is exactly half way between the Chocó and GNB values. So, what do you think now, Mr. Treasury agent?"

Monty stared at the numbers which were, in fact, meaningless to him and mumbled "Gee, I don't know what to think, Doc."

"Damn it man! It means the bad guys mixed equal parts of concentrate from Goodnews Bay and Chocó and called it Tulameen ore when it went through customs. Clearly, the mass of Chocó ore unaccounted for amounts to about 450 kilograms. Incidentally, you can also see from the spreadsheet that the 1:1 mixture is not even close to the composition of the ore that was actually produced from Tulameen. Tulameen ores are super-high in osmium; damn near 10 weight %. Anyone who knows shit about platinum deposits, would spot real Tulameen stuff right away by its high osmium signature."

"Yeah, sure they would. So, Doc, you are telling me that Kuno has to find 900 kilos of mixed platinum placer and 100 additional kilos of unadulterated Goodnews Bay black sand? Well, at least, we know it has to be in Japan. That is something, I guess. It's just too bad it wasn't caught at the dock when it came into the country. But I suppose all black sands look alike to customs inspectors and treasury agents. I'm going to suggest that Kuno arrest the captain of the ship as well as anybody connected with it by the name Fugimora."

"Monty, I'm going to get us a bottle of wine. We have something to celebrate, I think. I suggest you figure out what you need to tell Kuno and send him an email straightaway."

CHAPTER 30

Return to Truk Lagoon

It was raining in the Chuuk Islands as the Fugimora Enterprises jet set down on the lone international runway of Weno Island. Ryota Fugimora was aware, from his reading, that this airfield, on the northwest corner of the 7.3 square mile, triangular island was originally built by the Japanese Imperial Navy with Korean labor in the 1930's. The flight on the twin-engine Learjet 28 had taken exactly 7.5 hours to cover the 3044-mile distance from Tokyo to Weno. This included one half hour on the ground in Naha, Okinawa and another half hour in Agano, Guam for refueling. The two Fugimora pilots had accommodated their boss's son most handsomely with an excellent steak and a bottle of 15-year old single malt scotch as soon as he boarded the plane at 2:30 a.m. Ryota enjoyed this steak, drank four double scotches, loaded his money belt with $50,000 in US cash and fell asleep. He awakened just as the plane began its descent for the landing field in Weno.

It took only moments for the young business man to clear

FSM customs, thanks to his diplomatic passport and the Fugimora name. One of the pretty dental assistants met him at the gate and drove him to the Chuuk Free Dentistry Clinic where a party was in progress celebrating "Respect for the Aged Day" on the Japanese holiday calendar.

Since his last visit, the dentists and their lovely assistants had initiated the happy custom of celebrating all Chuuk State holidays, all Japanese holidays, all staff birthdays as well as the more important US holidays. This laudable respect for multiculturalism had the effect of presenting frequent opportunities for parties and maintained the retail liquor supplies on Chuuk Island within seemly bounds.

The six dentists, their six assistants and a few Japanese-speaking office personnel were lined up and presented formal bows in unison as Mr. Fugimora entered the lobby of the dental facility. "Please people, return to your merry-making. I shall join you, myself, presently" said Ryota with a broad smile and a papal wave of his hand. "Now would you kindly show me to a room where I may stow my trunk, Miss?"

The dental assistant who had driven him from the airport looked perplexed for a moment, then took him to a room designed to accommodate patients from distant islands who were obliged to stay overnight for treatment. This room was equipped with six beds, each with its own set of drawers, night stand and reading lamp. The fact that no islander ever chose to stay overnight at the clinic did not mean that these beds saw no use. In fact, all were in a state of disorder suggesting quite recent use. Fugimora had to smile as he noted a lacy bra peeking out amidst the rumpled sheets of one of these beds. "Thank you, Miss, I can handle things from here. Please rejoin the others in celebration of Respect for the Aged Day. I shall join you there soon." He placed his trunk under the least rumpled of the beds and hung his coat on the bed post to mark it off limits to the dentists and their lovely assistants for the remainder of the party.

The next morning Ryota was up early and commissioned a food-cart man that he found on the street to serve tea, cold tomato juice, fried kelp and squid as breakfast to the celebrants at the dental clinic. It was a work day for them and the islanders were already lining up in front of the clinic. During the next three-hours he busied himself with hiring a plumber, electrician, carpenter and six laborers who were instructed to appear with their tools in carts at the dental clinic at 12 noon.

Mr. Fugimora led his crew of workers down a series of hallways leading away from the main lobby and offices where most clinic activities took place and into a distant portion of the structure. He stopped, finally, and with a piece of blue carpenter's chalk drew a large rectangle on the coral wall of the passage. "Cut through the wall here. Behind it you will find a door leading to a large room that served as a laboratory for Imperial Navy dentists. You are going to renovate this room, so I can live in it."

Within 30 minutes the false wall was knocked down, the old lab door opened, and the crew was inside the lab which had served as Dr. Aoki Fugimora's war time refuge and platinum depository. Ryota Fugimora led the group around the lab explaining what to remove, what was to remain, and where the shower, toilet, bedroom and office were to be located. Electrical and water supplies could be tapped in the hallway and the electrician immediately went to work rigging temporary lights and power cords to operate the power tools of the other workers. The carpenter and plumber sketched their plans while laborers ripped out storage racks and two of the massive laboratory tables in the rear of the room.

That evening, after the workers were gone, Ryota returned to the construction site. A gap in the rear wall of the lab marked the location of the hidden vault built by 3-1-27 some 50 years before. The vault interior remained as he had left it a few weeks earlier, of course, the skull-less skeleton of 3-1-27 patiently bided within. The bad smell was, however, nearly dissipated. He sprayed the interior with a bleach compound and a flowery cover scent and then busied himself with coral blocks and mortar to seal the breach made by his deceased Filipino sailors.

The next week was chaotic with construction supplies coming in, debris going out, and workers scrambling on scaffolds throughout the lab. A false ceiling was constructed to conceal new wiring and plumbing, modern light fixtures were hung, and carpet was installed over the concrete floor. A new, very solid entrance door with an electric buzzer and peephole was hung. Finally, the painters were called and two days later new furniture was installed.

The dental staff of the Free Clinic were amazed to discover the existence of this spacious room and that much of its standing laboratory equipment, though in need of cleaning and of ancient vintage by their reckoning, were still serviceable. More importantly, the dentists and their assistants were agreed that completion of the "Fugimora Room" called for a party and Ryota agreed to host it to christen his new home.

The Fugimora Room celebration happened to coincide with Tree Planting Day on the neighboring island of Yap but, since none of the dentists or their assistants had ever been to Yap, it was anticipated that the clinic party committee would approve this change in their holiday schedule.

Inspector Kuno had no trouble obtaining a complete dossier on Dr. Aoki Fugimora, the well-known dentist, wealthy businessman, and philanthropist. This dossier contained Fugimora's military records indicating that he served as *Kaig Daii* in the Imperial Navy's Dental Service and was stationed on Truk Aoll from January 1942 until repatriation in September 1945. It was now quite clear that Dr. Martin's theory of how the platinum, smuggled from Chocó, Colombia, hidden on Chuuk Island for 50 odd years, and then, finally, smuggled into Yokosuka, Japan was correct. Dr. Fugimora was obviously both clever and exceedingly patient; but this rich old bastard was going down, Inspector Hisashi Kuno would make sure of that.

The murders were another thing, however. Two grotesque beheadings in Yokosuka and an attempted murder in the wilds of

Alaska were not the work of a wealthy septuagenarian dentist. They were the work of a young man trained in martial arts and this man was Ryota Fugimora. Kuno had contacted immigration authorities of the Federated States of Micronesia and they verified the fact that the young Fugimora had recently arrived on Chuuk Island by a private air carrier owned by Fugimora Enterprises and was in residence at the Chuuk Free Dentistry Clinic, a subordinate non-profit entity of Fugimora Enterprises.

Inspector Kuno decided it would be necessary for himself and US treasury agent, Monty Simmons, to go to Chuuk Island and arrest Mr. Ryota Fugimora. To do this they would need the cooperation of the Australian Federal Police who held legal jurisdiction over this region of the South Pacific. He telephoned the Federal Police in Canberra and discussed the matter with the Assistant Commissioner in command of the International Deployment Group which included the Pacific Island Police.

The commissioner agreed to provide Agent Patrick McVey, the AFP-liaison with PTCCC (Pacific Transnational Crime Coordination Centre) headquartered in Apia, Samoa. McVey would have full authority to make arrests anywhere in the Federated States of Micronesia of individuals named in Japanese and US arrest warrants. There would be no extradition problems for a Japanese citizen and the Federated States of Micronesia National Police in Palikir on Pohnpei Island would be notified only after the arrest was made.

The inspector asked his secretary to begin making travel

arrangements for him from Tokyo to Weno. This flight required an overnight layover on the island of Guam as did all flights bound for Truk from Japan or the US. Kuno telephoned Simmons who was still in residence at the Martin ranch in Texas and presented his plan. They agreed to meet up at the Mariott Guam Hotel near the airport. They could have dinner together and discuss how to handle the arrest of the younger Fugimora. Agent McVey would meet their flight from Guam at the Weno airport.

Agent Simmons called his boss in Washington and brought him up to date on the investigation and the fact that another international flight would be necessary. His boss approved the trip and told Monty that he would handle notification of the State Department and would personally alert Susan Cox, the US Ambassador to FSM, who could be helpful if there were complications.

Monty called a federal travel agent in D.C. who made reservations for the Mariott Guam and a Continental flight leaving Houston, Texas at 10:45 a.m. This flight boasted a stop in LA, an 11-hour layover in romantic Guam, and a promised arrival 31 hours and 51 minutes later on Truk at 10:40 a.m.; all this, for the nominal cost of $3561 to US tax payers.

Following the house-warming celebration for the Fugimora Room, an outstanding success in the view of the dentists and their assistants, and the two days required to restore order to the room, Ryota Fugimora settled into a routine. He made his morning tea in a new microwave, took exercise in the form of martial arts routines, and shaved and showered in his new bathroom. Then he walked to the commercial part of Weno to have a meal, after which, he visited a bookstore and the library. Young Fugimora was a voracious and serious reader with a taste for technical subjects as well as English and Irish history and literature.

The offerings of the Weno library and bookstore in these subject areas would be classed as dismal at best but, fortunately, the employees at both facilities were friendly and gladly ordered the books that he wanted. He liked to spend an hour or two in a remote corner of the library reading his current book. After a midday meal, he went to the Smiling Shark Dive Shop where he took lessons in scuba diving. He thought he might do a photo essay study of the historic Japanese naval ships resting on the bottom of Truk Lagoon.

In the late afternoon, he returned to the dental clinic to have tea, meditate, and read until the clinic closed for the day at 5:00 p.m. He always invited the dentists and their assistants to join him for dinner at a local restaurant and most accepted. Afterwards, he returned to the clinic alone, made tea and read for an hour or two and went to bed at an early hour. Ryota found a Zen-like solace in sleeping in this very dark stone room without windows.

These activities soon became a pleasant ritual for the young business man. He was acutely aware that the eyes of the Japanese National Police were searching for him and he avoided all contacts with the outside world, no emails to his father, no telephone calls, no credit cards and no contact with his company Fugimora

Maritime Transport. He knew his father would send word when it was safe to return to Japan. Meanwhile, his supply of US currency would be quite adequate to meet his simple needs.

One night, at a late hour, Ryota was awakened by muffled sounds coming from within his newly refurbished quarters. He arose with the Kris dagger that was kept on his nightstand and stealthily patrolled the black interior of the lab but the sounds were not repeated. He finally turned on the lights and made a careful inspection of the entire room. The door was securely bolted and barred from the inside; no one could possibly have entered and this was quite disquieting to a man wanted by the police. Finding nothing to justify alarm, he put his teapot in the microwave, brewed tea and took up his book dealing with diving theory and technique. An hour passed before he became drowsy so, he turned off the lights for the second time and fell back to sleep. His watch read 2:15 a.m.

Another hour passed and the muffled sounds were repeated. This time Ryota remained motionless in the bed, gripping the Kris, and trying to locate the source of the sound. He was sure it was coming from the vault he had sealed on the first day of construction, the same vault that confined the desiccated, but still articulated, remains of 3-1-27.

Agent Patrick McVey, of the Australian Federal Police, nervously paced the floor of the waiting room in the tiny air terminal of Weno on Chuuk Island. He was used to working on cases involving fishing disputes, poaching and friction between national, state and local police officials, but this case was different. It was a real, honest-to-God international crime, with a criminal wanted on murder charges in two countries; it was a policeman's dream coming true.

McVey looked at his watch for the hundredth time, it was 10:50 a.m. and the Guam plane was ten minutes late and nowhere in sight. It was also starting to rain. He hated rain, which was ironic, because his entire professional life had been spent in the tropics where it rained damn near every day. He preferred Australia's hot dry interior where rain is a welcome rarity, a place where he spent his boyhood on his father's cattle station.

Inspector Kuno and Special Agent Simons stepped off the plane and scurried toward the terminal through a warm tropical downpour. It was raining when they left Guam too. They were dripping wet by the time the Continental attendant handed each of them a fresh warm towel. Heat and humidity inside the small open-air terminal made the two policemen gasp for air in the wake of the relative comfort of their air-conditioned plane cabin. The lawmen dried themselves as best they could and threw their towels into a bin as a big, smiling Irishman, with a pronounced Aussie accent, stepped up to them and said, "Hallo gents, I'm Pat McVey from AFP and I have orders to take you anywhere you want to go on this island."

The three men introduced themselves and shook hands. McVey was a big man with an exceptionally firm grip. "Sorry about this nasty rain, mates. I have a rented motorcar standing by, but first let's pop over to customs and get your bags cleared. Have those passports handy mates, you'll need to show them to the inspector" shouted McVey over the clatter of rain on the sheet metal roof above.

Once in the car with their bags, Agent McVey asked to see the warrants the foreign policemen had in their possession. "Just a formality, gents" said McVey "but being policemen yourselves, you know I have to go by the book. Everything is in order with the warrants which tell me you are charging a Mr. Ryota Fugimora of Tokyo, Japan with murder. Now what about your side arms? In your bags, I suspect, just fetch them out so I can write down their identification numbers and you will be legal to shoot any desperate criminals we encounter."

Simmons and Kuno dug their guns out of their bags and handed them over to the Aussie who copied the serial numbers into his notebook and returned the weapons. "Better load up straight away, gents. Chuuk is a very small place so there is no telling when, or where, we might encounter this Fugimora fellow" advised McVey. "So, what will it be, gents, a hotel first or a go for the bad guy?"

Ryota removed one of the eye-level blocks sealing the former platinum vault and peered into the black interior with a flashlight. He was prepared to find a burrowing rodent of some kind but there was nothing, nothing alive that is. The still articulated, but headless, skeleton of 3-1-27 was there, of course, but had not been disturbed since his last visit. He saw nothing that would explain the eerie sounds that interrupted his sleep.

Young Fugimora did not sleep well on this night. He heard sounds, muffled and otherwise, he even imagined a voice, distant and indistinct. He rose from his bed in the early morning hours and approached the vault with flashlight in one hand and his Kris in the other. Under the beam of his light, he minutely examined every inch of the vault interior; no rodents, no insects, no bats, nothing but dry bones. He began to wonder about his sanity. Then a voice, distinct and near, said in broken Japanese "Fugimora does not sleep well tonight, why is that?"

The startled Ryota instinctively recoiled away from the opening and, in so-doing, dropped his flashlight into the dark vault where it came to rest illuminating the skeleton of 3-1-27. "Who speaks?" he managed to get out through trembling lips. "Who is in this room with me? Show yourself and prepare to die!" he shrieked while slicing the air wildly with the 200-year-old Kris dagger.

"I am here, but I am no one, and can die but once. You have nothing to fear from innocent vapors. Approach and speak to me."

Fugimora had vaulted at least two meters from the opening the instant he heard the voice. Now, cautiously, he crept forward towards it again. "Your Japanese is rotten, Spirit. Do you speak another language?"

"Would English suit thee better master Fugimora? I am afraid mine is rather antiquated" replied the Spirit, this time in English.

"Yes, I can understand your English better than your Japanese.

What is your native language?"

"Korean, but I have not had opportunity to speak it in decades."

After some thought, Fugimora asked "You seem to know me, ghost, but who are you?"

"Call me the Spirit of these fleshless bones condemned to spend eternity in this stygian crypt. I am aware that thou art the shameless malt-worm who stole my skull away. Have thou come to return it?"

"It is true, Spirit. Your skull resides on my desk in Yokosuka, but in a place of honor, I assure you. I suppose you were murdered by my father. Is that true Spirit?"

"Aye, and murder most foul; most foul, strange and unnatural it was."

Ryota knew this was true from what his father had told him. Since he did not believe in spirits, or ghosts of any kind, he was quite amazed to find himself feeling a weird kinship with this strange and ghostly entity. He no longer feared it. "Spirit, I would like to know what it is like to be in your situation."

"By situation, I suppose thou mean to be headless, dead and remain entombed for eternity?"

"Yes Spirit, to be headless and dead. What is death? I must know."

"I am forbidden to tell these secrets, the lightest word of which would harrow your soul and freeze your young blood. However, I am permitted to share details of the godless crime committed by that mewling, canker-blossom you call father. That is, of course, if you wish to hear of it." Fugimora nodded his assent and the Spirit recounted the details that resulted in his decapitation.

"I am truly sorry for you, Spirit. I think my father acted from necessity but still it is a cruel and ghastly thing for your part. I am sure you cannot forgive it. Is there anything I can do for you to make your condition better? Could I set you free from this crypt and guide you to the outside world?"

"Surely ye mock me, young gudgeon. Thy avaricious, sewer-drinking parent lifted my head after rendering me drunk. I may not leave this spot until the foul crimes against me are burnt and purged away."

"Ok, Spirit, then could you hand me my flashlight please?"

"Again, ye mock me, master Fugimora. Certain it is that my lack of materiality renders such a task impossible. Perhaps, if thou obtain a stiff piece of wire of sufficient length, thou might fetch it out thyself. Alternatively, ye might consider removing additional blocks from the wall to lay hands upon it more directly. As you should know, there is no danger in entering my crypt. Did you know, master Fugimora, that I hewed these blocks by hand, each and every one?"

"And a handsome job of masonry work it is, Spirit. Are you, I mean, were you, a mason by trade when you were alive?"

"I was trained in a Korean university to be a civil engineer. A profession I followed until your Japanese vermin invaded my

289

country. I learned the trade of masonry as slave laborer on this abominable island under the heel of maggot-eating, fen-sucking bastards of the Japanese Imperial Navy."

"I cannot blame you for your bitterness Spirit, and I take no offense. May I ask why your English has such a Shakespearian flair?"

"It is simple enough, young chickadee. I taught myself English and the only books in that language accessible to me were a set of Shakespeare's plays. I think you must agree that my English would be infinitely more tedious if those volumes had been by Fennimore Cooper. Now away, young fish and back to thy nest. I will not disturb thy sleep further. Mayhap we talk in morrow's night, if ye will it."

This was the beginning of what might be classified as a quixotic relationship between the skeleton in the vault and young Ryota Fugimora, murderer, smuggler and platinum magnate.

McVey pulled the rented black sedan up in front of the Chuuk Free Clinic and the three policemen checked their weapons and jacked shells into the firing chambers. Each making sure they had a loaded backup clip ready for action. They entered through the front door and approached an island lady at the front desk. McVey spoke first "We are from the federal police, madam, and it is our understanding that a Mr. Ryota Fugimora has taken up residence in this building. Would you guide us to his room please?"

The woman appeared confused and picked up the telephone saying, "I must call one of the dentists."

"No calls madam, just take us to Mr. Fugimora, now please" said McVey sternly.

The woman rose from her chair and said in a shaky voice "Yes, yes sir, please follow me. It is quite some distance from here I am afraid." They walked down a lengthy concrete hallway with four pairs of heels creating a considerable clacking echo as they progressed. After several turns, and five minutes of brisk walking, the woman halted at a wooden door with no name or number on it. "This is his room, sir. May I leave now?"

"Yes, of course, madam. Do you know if Mr. Fugimora is in at the moment?" asked McVey, again in his stern voice.

"I think he must be, as I have not seen him leave or enter the clinic during the past two days. I hope he is not sick in there."

"Thank you, madam, you may leave now" Kuno said politely. The island woman clattered down the hall at top speed and was quickly out of sight and sound. The policemen looked at each other grimly and drew their weapons.

Inspector Kuno rang the buzzer with the barrel of his pistol and shouted, "Federal Police, Mr. Fugimora, open your door!" No answer, and no sound, came from within. Kuno, knocking loudly with the butt of his gun, this time, repeated the command to open in Japanese. The policemen looked at each other. In a subdued voice Kuno said to his associates "This door is extremely solid, I do not think we can break it down, even with three men."

McVey smiled broadly at this and said, "No worries, mates, I have a half kilo of C4 in my pocket; enough to blow that damn door to the next island." He removed the wrapping from a small parcel revealing a cake of plastic explosive about the size of a soap bar. He tore away two pieces and rolled them into two finger-sized cigars and stuck them against the external parts of the hinges. Thin electrical wires were inserted into each piece of C4 and attached to a miniature detonating device. McVey motioned Simmons and Kuno back from the doorway and set off the charges.

The resulting explosion produced a colossally deafening noise and shock wave that refracted down the hall and throughout the entire clinic for a considerable period of time. When, at last, the smoke and dust cleared sufficiently, the policemen pointed their flashlight beams and weapons into the gloomy interior which was now partially illuminated by a horizontal shaft of light from the hallway.

Airborne debris floated in the dim light, like a swarm of ten thousand drunken mosquitoes. There was no sign of the heavy door, it was simply gone. Agent Simmons found a switch and turned on the interior lights. The three lawmen proceeded cautiously into the former dental lab with pistols at the ready.

Every inch of the former lab was carefully examined but revealed no sign of Ryota Fugimora. The bed had been slept in, a cold half-empty pot of tea sat on a small table next to a dirty cup and a book dealing with scuba diving. The policemen exchanged silent looks of frustration. Agent Simmons volunteered an American oath "God damn it, where the hell is that creepy bastard?"

After a sustained silence, Inspector Kuno said he was going make another search of the room and left the depressed group. About 15 minutes later he summoned the Aussie and the American to the rear of the former dental lab. "Look gentlemen" he said, with a smile of satisfaction on his face. "Just look at the wall here. This is fresh mortar, not yet completely dry, and it has been squeezed out between these blocks from the backside of the wall."

"Well, feed me a crock turd and call me Murphy" volunteered McVey in his quaint Aussie accent. Simmons pulled out a small pocket knife and dug into one of the ridges of mortar and rubbed the material between his thumb and forefinger. "Damn, if you're not right, Hisashi, this mortar was applied hours ago. What the hell does it mean?"

Kuno was thoughtful for a moment and then said in a low voice "It means that our fugitive recently sealed this wall from the back side. There is either an escape tunnel on the other side or a room where he waits until we give up the search. He made a mistake by locking the door from the inside. I suggest that we get some tools and break through this wall."

McVey left the lab in search of tools and returned 30 minutes later with a sledge hammer, a pickaxe, a mason's hammer and a chisel. McVey slammed the big sledge into a central block in the wall. It shattered and a burst of coral rock chunks splattered in all directions. He took up the mason's hammer and began to enlarge the hole. "You gents keep your guns trained on this hole, just in case we have a really pissed off Jap on the other side. Umm, sorry

Inspector Kuno, I didn't mean that the way it sounded."

"I am not offended, Agent McVey. If Fugimora is in there, he most certainly will be pissed to be discovered. Can you shine your light through the hole yet?"

"I can, but I am wary of putting me face in front of that hole. Now, I wish I had a tear gas canister at hand" McVey replied.

"Yes, we understand. Let us remove another block, it can be done without placing your body in front of the hole" suggested Kuno. McVey wound up and easily shattered another coral block below the first. The policemen put their ears close to the opening and listened intently for the sounds of breathing. There were no sounds, no sounds at all, coming from beyond the breached wall. A third and fourth block were removed in similar fashion making the opening wide enough to allow the policemen to direct the beams of their flashlights diagonally into the space behind the wall without standing directly in front of the enlarged opening.

Inspector Kuno shouted "There, I see a body now and it is in a prone position. I think he is dead."

Agent McVey leaned into the opening with pistol and light trained on the prone figure. "Yeah, he looks dead, alright. I am disappointed that we won't get to arrest anyone. Let's get more of these blocks out of the way so we can get him out of there."

McVey picked up the sledge again and attacked the wall. Kuno and Simmons moved the dislodged fragments of coral and cleared a path into the chamber. They each grabbed a foot of the dead man and dragged him into the light of the room while McVey held his pistol trained on the emerging body. They could now see the dry white bones of 3-1-27 glistening in the recesses of the vault. The body was that of Ryota Fugimora and he was obviously quite dead and the cause of his death was equally obvious. A 200-year-old Javanese poisoned Kris dagger was lodged to the hilt in his heart.

CHAPTER 31

Despedida

The nightmare flight from Weno via Guam and Los Angeles to Houston crossed God-only-knows-how-many time zones and placed Monty Simmons in Texas the day before he left the Pacific island. This was followed by a three-hour sojourn in a rental car, so Agent Simmons was in a bad state when he finally arrived at the Martin ranch in Llano, Texas at 7:00 a.m. Naturally, General Longstreet greeted his favorite visitor in his customary manner and Doc had to send the goat to his pen so Monty could get out of the car.

"Jesus, Monty, you look like shit" declared Doc.

"You would too, Doc, if you had just made the flight from hell. God, I hope you have some coffee. What day is it here?" queried the haggard federal agent.

"Don't worry about all that, you'll just confuse yourself" Doc said with a grin. "What is important, is that I know what day it is. You just sit down and I'll bring some coffee. You can unwind and then try for some sleep. I'm planning a party to celebrate the successful completion of our little project."

"Oh God, I hope it's not for tonight. I don't think I can party any time soon."

"No, not tonight buddy, but tomorrow night we party. You'll be ok by then, I promise. Done it many times myself" Doc said laughing outright at his exhausted friend.

The men drank coffee and watched the orange Texas sun climb above the eastern horizon. Monty broke the silence saying "I see that damn goat of yours is still in good health. I thought Dr. Toby was going to shoot him."

"Toby gets a little crazy when he's drunk but he and Longstreet kissed and made up the next day. He had a hell of a knot on his head, but nobody got shot."

"How's everyone at the Parrot?" asked Monty.

"They are fine and they all want to see you and hear about your adventures in paradise. I haven't told them anything yet but they saw a TV news report dealing with beheadings and 45 million bucks worth of WWII platinum smuggled into Japan. They know that we are involved, and you will have to tell the story, or we might be lynched. Worse yet, we might be barred from the Grey Parrot. Rhoda has been on my ass ever since she saw that broadcast. They all think you are a hero and want to know how many criminals you shot."

"Christ, Doc, they are going to be disappointed because I didn't shoot anybody. Kuno did the real detective work and arrested all the bad guys who were still on their feet. And, hell, you did the science stuff that allowed Kuno to figure out the whole damn scam. I was really just an observer."

"Now, now, Monty you mustn't be so modest. They think you are a police action hero and protesting will just encourage them. Texans don't change their minds about their heroes, buddy. Not ever."

"Alright, Doc, I'm a goddamned hero. Give me another cup of coffee and send me to bed" Monty said with a look of disgust.

Doc Martin conducted Monty to the guest room and then went out to the rental car and retrieved his suitcase from the trunk. He spotted the cowboy boots, hat, jeans and western shirt in a paper shopping bag and carried both back to the bedroom. Treasury Agent Simmons was sound asleep.

Doc was not teaching this day and directed his thoughts to what he would serve at the party he was planning for Simmons. He drove over to Dona Modesta's place to discuss the matter with her. He found her gathering eggs in her hen house. *"Oi, Dona Modesta, como vai?"*

"Tudo bem senhor Professor, e voce?" she replied to his greeting.

"O mesmo, senhora. I come to discuss the menu for a party, tomorrow night, in honor of our heroic federal agent."

Modesta had a bucket of eggs in her hand and continued plucking eggs from the nest boxes. "Ah, yes, I see. I suppose he arrived this morning about seven. I saw a strange car driving past our gate at that time. Do you have something in mind *senhor* Doc?"

"Yes, I think the party must be a *despedida para Senhor* Monty. I know about this from my time in Brazil but am not sure what they do on such occasions in Portugal."

"Hmmm, yes, a *despedida*, a farewell party; that is an excellent idea. Often in Portugal a *despedida* involves *cabrito assado,* but maybe they do not eat goat meat in Washington DC."

"I am sure you are right about that, Modesta but I'm guessing they do on Truk Atoll. Spit-roasted goat it will be, Modesta. What shall I serve with it? What do they do in Portugal?"

Modesta thought for a second and then said "Salad and bread, of course, and usually beans, rice and roasted potatoes with mint leaves. I will make these for *Senhor* Monty's *despedida*; I think you will be too busy attending to the goat."

"That sounds great, Modesta. But I can make the rice. I have a special type of rice, *arroz bomba,* from Valencia, Spain" declared Martin with mock enthusiasm.

"I think you say this to give me the piss, Professor Martin. You know very well how it is with the Spanish and the Portuguese. I will make rice from the valley of *Rio Mondego* in Portugal that my mother sends to me. No arguments from evil professors!"

Doc anticipated this reaction from his fiery Portuguese neighbor since, in fact, he had no rice from Valencia, Spain. He loved to make her swear in English because she did it reluctantly and badly and he enjoyed her expressions when her temper was up. "Ok, Modesta, you can make the rice. Now, what about a goat? I think we will need one of about 15 kilos."

"I will send Felice over with one in the morning, but it will not be a Spanish goat, nor a goat that has heard even a single word of Spanish!"

"*Obrigado, Dona Modesta,* I will see you and the family about four o'clock tomorrow afternoon. I plan to get you drunk" teased Doc. He heard an egg splatter against the door of the hen house as he walked away.

Martin then drove into Llano and stopped at the grocery to buy orange juice, mango juice and a jar of mango spears. His next stop was the Grey Parrot where he exchanged the usual greetings with Nestor who was fishing for catfish in a very hot deep fryer filled with bubbling peanut oil. Rhoda sat down next to Doc and immediately started to pump him for information about the criminals involved in the 45-million-dollar platinum heist.

"Rhoda, you are going to hear all the details from Agent Monty himself tomorrow night. He got into town this morning, directly from Truk Lagoon."

"Well, did he shoot anybody? Did he find the platinum? Are the bad guys in jail? Rhoda asked with machine-gun rapidity.

"Damn, Rhoda, I don't know squat about any these things. Monty had a cup of coffee and went to bed and will probably sleep into tomorrow. We will all find out together at the farewell party I'm throwing for him tomorrow night. You and Nestor should come about four o'clock. That's when the goat goes on the fire."

Rhoda pouted a little but recovered enough to ask, "What can I bring?"

"Maybe some of that fine port you have, if you haven't drunk all of it."

"Purple Martin, you are a rat!" she said with a hint of a smile on her face and a near fatal dose of X-radiation from those impossible grey eyes.

Simmons rose the next morning to the sound of Doc's automatic coffee machine beginning its grind cycle at precisely 6:00 a.m. He dressed in his western garb and was waiting for Doc when he stepped out on the porch to greet the sunrise. Monty could see Longstreet in the faint horizontal shafts of pink sunlight on his return from the paved road with the paper between his teeth. He greeted his host with "Good morning, Doc, is the coffee ready?"

"It will be in just a few minutes. How do you feel this morning, Mr. Federal Agent?"

"Excellent, it's remarkable what 24 hours of sleep can do for a person."

"Well, those long flights are murder on anybody. Ah, here is the General with the paper" said Doc, removing the plastic wrapped bundle from the goat's mouth. "Why don't you read the crime report for Llano while I get the coffee?" Martin went into the kitchen and returned with two steaming mugs of black coffee.

"What is on the schedule for today Doc? You know I have to leave for DC tomorrow."

"I figured that, Monty and that's why I planned our get-together for this afternoon. I'm going to roast a goat in your honor, Monty. I hope you like goat, do you?"

"Well, before spending time on Chuuk and Guam I would have said no but, in fact, the islanders eat it all the time, that and fish, and I find I like it quite well. I don't think I could kill one, with the notable exception of General Longstreet here" Monty said, directing an evil eye toward that harmless, fun-loving creature.

"Yeah, I couldn't do it myself, either, but my neighbor Felice can, and he will be bringing one by sometime this morning."

"You know, Doc, speaking of food, I wrote down some recipes for you that I got from Katsu Kuno. He made a fine dinner of grilled chicken and veggie kebabs when I visited the inspector at his home in Tachikawa City."

"Thanks buddy, I'm interested in outdoor cooking recipes, particularly foreign ones. I suppose you know that when a man invites a foreigner, meaning you, Monty, to his house, it means he really likes you."

"I know that, Doc. I really like Hisashi and he is one of the best policemen I have ever seen in action and so was that big Irish Aussie, Pat McVey."

"This is the first I've heard of McVey, maybe you can tell me about his role in this case." Monty related the details of meeting McVey on Truk and their attempt to arrest Ryota Fugimora. Doc laughed wildly at the part where McVey pulled C4 out of his trousers.

"I can see why you like this guy, Monty. He's up for

anything. Most of the Aussie geologists I've met are the same way. I'll get some more coffee for us and then why don't you tell me how Kuno rounded up the rest of the evil-doers and the platinum."

"Well, it was just like you said. Dr. Aoki Fugimora was an Imperial Navy dentist stationed on Truk during the war. Somehow, he got his hands on 450-kilos of platinum concentrate from Chocó, Colombia, but we still don't know how. The Japanese were marooned there until repatriation in 1945. He couldn't take the platinum with him, so he hid it behind a false wall in the rear of the dental lab.

This vault also contained the headless skeleton of a Korean slave laborer whose identity has yet to be determined. We found a brass dog tag with the number of 3-1-27 on it; maybe records can be found to correlate this number to a real person but it is a long shot. This Korean was beheaded by samurai sword. Does that sound familiar? Kuno found an antique samurai sword, an old skull, and two new ones belonging to the Atkins couple at Ryota Fugimora's hideout in Yokosuka. We figure the old skull belonged to this 3-1-27 guy but why it ended up in Yokosuka, Japan is anyone's guess. Anyhow, we found the son, Ryota Fugimora, in this vault, dead with a dagger in his heart; a dagger, they tell me, that was coated in some jungle plant poison. He used this same dagger to kill Nakamura in Tokyo. We think he killed himself after sealing up this vault from the back side. It was positively the weirdest thing I've ever seen, Doc."

"It sounds like a variation on Poe's story about the Cask of

Amontillado" interjected the geologist.

"Sorry, I'm not much of horror story fan, Doc, but I can tell you we would never have discovered this bastard, but for the sharp eyes and mind of Inspector Kuno. Then, after Hisashi gets back to Japan, he goes to arrest the father, Aoki Fugimora, and the old bird keels over and dies of a heart attack when Kuno tells him his son was found dead, lying on top of the skeleton of 3-1-27 in his old vault on Truk."

"Rather ironic that, don't you think Monty?" observed Martin.

"Plenty of irony throughout this whole damned affair, is what I think, Doc. Well, to finish the story, Kuno figures out where the platinum is from the fact that all the Fugimora companies are owned by the same three shareholders: Aoki Fugimora, Ryota Fugimora and Fumiko Hatori who turns out to be the mother of Ryota and a wealthy woman in her own right. Kuno paid her a visit at her home in Kyota. Of course, she was shocked by the death of her son, but not to the point of dying over it. She revealed that her son had stored what she called 'his inheritance' in a safe storage facility she maintains for her art treasures. When Kuno searched the place, he found a green crate labeled 'Archeological Artifacts' and guess what was in it, Doc? … 900-kilos of platinum concentrate. Kuno is not charging the lady, so she will be the sole owner of whatever is left of Fugimora Enterprises."

"Kuno found a fifty-fifty mixture, I presume" observed Doc, drily."

"Exactly as you predicted Doc, fifty percent from Colombia

and fifty percent from Goodnews Bay."

"And I suppose Kuno is arranging for Colombia to get its share of this treasure back."

"Right, it will take some time to go through all the channels and red tape, but they are going to get the market value of their damn platinum back. The Bank of Colombia is happy as a pig in shit because of the gigantic increase in platinum prices during the last 50 years."

"I think you are picking up some Tejano-isms, Monty, and I'm pretty sure that one came from Rhoda."

"She has a colorful western vocabulary, Doc. I hope she is coming tonight."

"She said she wouldn't miss it for all the sheep shit in Shiloh, Monty."

"Well that is almost the entire story except for the arrest of the captain of the ship used to smuggle the platinum into Yokosuka. Captain Satoshi Hiraki is charged with smuggling and making a fraudulent manifest and he gave up young Fugimora for two additional murders on the ship. It appears our guy used two Filipino sailors to get the stash out of the dental lab and onto the ship and then killed them. And that, my geologist friend, is where our first victim, the headless American sailor comes in. He worked on that ship and evidently witnessed these murders and managed to get his hands on a bag of the Colombian platinum before it was mixed with the Alaskan ore. Evidently, this sailor, one Donald Atkins, doctored his platinum with graphite before he smuggled it off the ship to get past customs. His payoff was to have Ryota behead both him and his wife. I saw the scene of the wife's murder and it was gruesome in the extreme."

"Quite a story you have there, Monty, how many murders were there in all? I lost track."

"We attribute five killings to the son and one to the dad, six in all, at this point. But there is one more thing you should know, Doc. Kuno arrested a college girl who worked at the Tokyo mint. Her name is Chika Oshiro and she turns out to be the daughter of Captain Hiraki. She kept old Fugimora informed of any platinum activity at the mint and he informed his son. That is how our friend, Dr. Nakamura, got stabbed to death and the jo-san lady got beheaded."

"Christ, Monty, I feel like a drink but it's too early. I'm pretty sure we'll be drinking tonight."

At that moment, the neighbor, Felice Gomez da Silva, drove up to the house. He carried the cabrito into the kitchen over his shoulder and greeted the two men as he removed the butcher paper wrapping. "I think this will do for tonight, Doc. I weighed him and he dressed out at 18 kilos, a little bigger than you asked for, but as close as I could come."

"That is just fine, Felice. Thanks a lot for doing this on short notice. What do I owe you?

"Nothing, Doc, we will call it a breeding fee for General Longstreet's service. Every doe he screwed is with twins."

"Ok, Felice, would you take this box of egg cartons and jars to

Modesta please?" He slipped a twenty between two of the jars. It was always this way with Felice. He would never take money from Martin, but his wife was more practical about such things. He picked up the box without looking at it, shook hands with Monty and Doc and climbed into his truck.

"Anything else you need, Doc? I'm going into town later today and would be glad to pick up something for you."

"Thank you, Felice, it would save me a trip if you could bring back a hundred pounds of block ice."

"Sure, no problem, Doc, are you sure you have enough beer?"

"I'm stocked up on beer and wine both, Felice. We don't want to run low on the essentials."

After Felice left, Doc began gathering the herbs and spices he needed for the dry rub on the goat: garlic cloves, coriander, cumin, kosher salt, black and red pepper. He placed these items in his mortar, ground them and mixed the combination into a paste with olive oil. Next, he brushed the paste all over the cabrito, inside and out, replaced the paper wrapping around the goat and crammed it back into his fridge. Monty watched in fascination, cooking was a black art to him.

Doc poured orange juice and mango juice in a 2:1 ratio in a saucepan and brought it to a gentle boil while stirring. When the volume had reduced by half he added chopped garlic, chopped mango spears, salt, red pepper, a dollop of black cane molasses, and the juice of a lime; then he turned the heat off and stirred until the sauce was mixed.

"Well, Monty the inside work is done. Let's have a drink. It's nearly one o'clock, so I think we'll be ok. The folks will be coming around four so I don't think we can get into too much trouble." He opened two bottles of cold Shiner Bock and led the way to the granite courtyard.

The men sipped their beers and stared at Enchanted Rock for several minutes without talking. Martin finally broke the silence with "One thing about this case that still puzzles me Monty and that is why the old navy dentist took so long before trying to claim his treasure. Do you know?"

Monty looked at Doc with a smile and said "Gee, Doc, I'm surprised to hear that anything puzzles a famous science guy like you."

"I don't understand people as well as I understand rocks, Monty, and criminals I don't understand at all."

"Kuno and I have discussed this topic at length, Doc, and we have come up with a list of reasons that probably convinced old man Fugimora to leave the platinum on Truk for so long. The first, is that Truk was part of a UN mandate to the USA from 1947 to 1979 and Fugimora probably figured he could not get access to the old Imperial Navy dental facility. Even if he got access, he must have realized he could not get it refined in Japan without the Colombian government finding out and claiming it. That is where the mixing scheme and the *Aoki Maru* come in. You know better than anyone, Doc, that it takes a lot of money to buy 550 kilos of platinum ore these days, not to mention the cost of an ocean-going ship to haul it. It took the old bastard years to accumulate the wealth he needed to carry this scheme off. Then it was necessary to gain influence over government officials once the FSM became independent. That was the purpose of his Chuuk Free Dentistry Clinic and its location. Sound reasonable, Doc?"

"It does, Agent Monty, very reasonable indeed, how about another beer?" Doc got up and returned with the beers and then placed bag of charcoal on the grill and lit it. "We want to let this burn down quite a bit before we put Mr. Cabrito on the spit."

Felice drove in as they were finishing their second beer and backed his truck up to the granite enclosure and the three men transferred the ice to the infamous stock tank. "Got time for a beer with us, Felice?" Doc asked.

"I will make time *Senhor* Doc" said Felice and helped himself to a cold Shiner. "When will you put the meat on?" Felice asked examining the hot coals.

"By the time these coals die down it should be close to two o'clock. If I put it on then, it should be ready by six at the latest. I don't want my guests to be too drunk before I serve the chow. Is Modesta still angry with me about the Spanish rice?"

"No Doc, she realized later that you were just teasing her and we both know how she likes to be teased" Felice responded with a wide grin.

Doc asked Felice to help him truss the cabrito. Monty watched as the two men removed the paper wrapping and laid the goat on its back on one of the picnic tables. Felice pressed the front legs into the chest cavity then Doc pressed the hind legs over the front legs and held them while Felice tied them in place with wire. Next the spit rod was inserted through the cavity and secured to the carcass with lock-on tines. Together, they lifted the rod into place above the grill. A geared-down electric motor was attached to the spit rod, plugged in, and Mr. Cabrito began rotating above the coals at 20 revolutions per minute.

All three of these gentlemen agreed that this culinary feat called for another beer. They sipped this beer staring silently and hypnotically at the rotating beast. At length, Doc said "We can't forget to baste this guy every 30 minutes." He went into the kitchen and returned with a long-handled brush, his mango sauce, and a meat thermometer.

Nestor drove into the yard about 3 p.m. and joined the boys drinking beer and watching the revolving goat. His arrival reminded Felice that he should go home to load up the kids and items his wife was bringing. Felice reluctantly yielded his chair to Nestor who detoured past the stock tank to bring his friends another round and to point out that the goat needed basting.

Doc went to the kitchen to make more mango sauce while Monty and Nestor discussed the comparative ballistics of the large, slow, rifle projectiles of yesteryear versus smaller caliber, faster, flatter-shooting bullets favored in the modern era. When Doc returned, their conversation had evolved to prospects for next years' deer season, the hunting skills of the Ryder brothers, and a few high school football stories involving their old buddy, Red

Ryder, the boys' dad.

An hour slipped by, but the goat got its basting at 30 minute intervals. A cloud of dust announced the arrival of Rhoda in her red VW beetle and the Gomez da Silva family. These events sparked Longstreet into action. On this occasion, the general was rewarded with a bundle of raw collard greens, a goat favorite since biblical times. Rhoda had prepared a large pot of southern style collard greens for the goat roast. The men got off their butts and hastened to carry in the dinner items and participate in *abraços* with the Portuguese family. For Agent Simmons, this marked a recently acquired cultural awareness that pleased Doc Martin.

After greetings and handshakes, the crowd settled down with their chosen drinks in their favorite chairs, or on benches, and called for Monty to begin the saga of the 45-million-dollar platinum caper. He told the story more or less chronologically with emphasis on police methodology and forensic detail. He was interrupted many times for more details on the murders and especially the death of Ryota Fugimora. Was his death a suicide? Did he go crazy in the vault? In true police fashion the federal agent refused to speculate where evidence was lacking. This, of course, only fueled more intense questions requiring even greater degrees of speculation. Doc had to jump like a fart in a skillet to keep his guests glasses full throughout the narration.

The story that Simmons related to Doc in a span of 15 minutes required an hour and a half before this audience. Monty, as it turned out, was something of a raconteur with a generous slice of ham added.   By the end of Monty's account, the entire audience, with the exception of the Gomez da Silva children and General Longstreet, naturally, were both happy and drunk.

General Longstreet followed these proceedings in mute disgust.   He did not like parties that involved this much drinking and loud talk and he most certainly did not approve of goat roasts.

The End

THE AUTHOR

Dr. Lowell was born and raised on a small dairy farm outside of Modesto, California. He attended high school in Glendora, California and San Jose State University where he received a B.S. degree in Geology. His passion for minerals led him to the New Mexico Institute of Mining and Technology where he received a PhD degree in Geology three years later.

A long academic career followed at Southeast Missouri State, a two-year posting at a Brazilian university, and eight years at University of Texas-Arlington. During this period, Dr. Lowell published 104 scientific works, consulted for mineral industry, presented research at conferences all over the world and lived in both Brazil and Portugal.

Since retirement, Dr. Lowell has occupied himself writing short fiction and has six stand-alone works in publication and a collection of nine stories in a publication (Full Moon Publishing). His stories are often set in Alaska, Portugal or Brazil and involve odd characters, geology and, sometimes, talking animals! He reads widely and is especially fond of 19th century classics; his favorite novels include *Don Quixote, Les Miserables, and My Ántonia.* Dr. Lowell and his wife Vicki live in Arlington, Texas; their adult children live nearby.